GUMPTION & GUMSHOES

ALEX KIDWELL

Dreamspinner Press

Published by
Dreamspinner Press
5032 Capital Circle SW
Ste 2, PMB# 279
Tallahassee, FL 32305-7886
USA
http://www.dreamspinnerpress.com/

Cover Art by Robin Saxon
http://www.saxonandkidwell.com

ISBN: 978-1-62798-086-9
Digital ISBN: 978-1-62798-087-6

Printed in the United States of America
First Edition
August 2013

A THOUSAND thanks to Jenny, for her inspiration. I hope August steals your heart the way he stole mine.

And, always, to my glorious Robin. Our love is a friendship caught fire, my darling.

CHAPTER ONE

AUGUST

It wasn't dark out. It wasn't stormy. The sun was doing that spitting thing through thin bands of fluffy clouds, peeking out in flashes not long enough to warrant a good mood, not short enough to evoke anything but boredom. In stories, the weather always mirrors the drama of the moment—epic storms, brilliant sunshine, deluges of rain or fat, fluffy snow. Here, though, in my small town, it was generally just this. Somewhere between a musical and a tragedy.

Kind of like my life.

"Auggie, you have those reports done? I'm getting my ass chewed out here."

My boss waddled past, his suspenders straining over his stomach. Between his permanently rosy cheeks and ever-present scowl, I often wondered if the reason I'd never gotten the Super Spy Kit for Christmas when I was eight was because Mr. Olson had eaten Santa. If the jolly guy came with a side of ranch, I was pretty sure he would.

"Yeah, Mr. Olson, I'm just about done." I refocused on the screen, striking the keyboard with a bit more force, as if the clatter would convince everyone I was very serious about data entry.

"I'd hate to have to talk to you about your quotas again, Auggie." Olson wheezed when he said anything more than a single syllable. "So let's try to keep up the pace, hm?"

Yeah. My life was just freaking awesome.

The drone of typing washed over me and I tried to focus. Two more hours and I had six more reports to enter. Unless, of course, I wanted to sit in Olson's cramped, overheated office, staring at his bobblehead collection of the stars of *Happy Days*.

I typed faster.

The office was hot, the clack of keys around me some soothing, rhythmic lullaby, and as the time passed, I found myself fighting the urge to just put my head down and give up. My stack of work was dwindling, but slowly. All I had to do was keep focused for a little while longer.

I couldn't help it, though. Even as I tried to keep working, going through the reports, my mind wandered, away from the boring deluge of information I didn't really understand. It was so easy to let my thoughts drift, to paint myself as a hero rather than an underpaid cubicle dweller. Instead of some guy sitting at a computer, I was a private eye, sitting in my office, waiting for my next case. Some tall drink of water, legs all the way down to the floor, all pouty lips and trouble. He'd walk in and I'd just know I was in for it. But I'd take the case, because—

"August."

Jerking so hard I nearly fell out of the chair, my knee knocking painfully against my desk, I swore to God my heart had just stopped. The pencil I'd been gnawing on nearly got bitten in half. "Holy crap." Gasping, I looked up to find Olson standing there, scowling. "Uh. Hi?"

"Jesus Christ, Mendez, I've been saying your name for five minutes." He shoved his thick fingers through his salt-and-pepper—heavy on the salt—hair. "Everyone else has gone home. You have a fit or something?"

"No, sorry. Just… I guess I got distracted."

Olson rolled his eyes exaggeratedly. "Great. I've got corporate riding my ass about numbers, and August Mendez is over here in la-la land."

August Adahy Mendez, that was me. Screwup, serial daydreamer, lover of fast food and chocolate pie. And now the one getting a lecture by my really obnoxious boss and trying damn hard not to make it obvious that I wanted to be anywhere but there. Fifteen minutes later and I was bolting for the door, struggling to shove my arms into my jacket, tripping over my own feet while I made it out of the building. Olson and his number obsession were forgotten as soon as I slipped into my old VW Beetle, peeling blue paint and crackling cloth seats fitting me like a glove.

After a quick adjustment to the rearview mirror, I shoved my shaggy dark hair out of my eyes, checked to make sure no one was watching, and turned the crackling radio on high. Blasting out music I could sing along with, I powered out of the parking lot and onto the highway. A sense of freedom surged through me, that euphoric realization that I was staring at a whole weekend of nothing but cheese curls and old movies, pants optional. Maybe I'd do a marathon of my favorite flicks—the classic black-and-white fifties detective stories, all the gumshoes and femmes fatales I could handle.

Sometimes being single sucked. This was not one of those times.

By the time I'd turned onto my street, heading toward my slightly sketchy but still this side of crack-house apartment, I'd shaken off the depressing doldrums of work and gotten myself into the proper mood for being utterly lazy. It took work to be as slothful as I was planning on being.

First order of business was to lose the pants. Boxers only on weekends; it was practically the eleventh commandment. And because of the said singleness, I didn't have to worry when my stomach poked out too much, or that my legs were too knobby, or that my round face matched roundness elsewhere. I was alone with my studio apartment, my wide-screen TV, and a huge collection of movies. No one was fat in the privacy of their own home, after all.

"Reheated pizza or mac and cheese?" I contemplated the dinner situation, rifling through my fridge for options. "Decisions, decisions."

Mac and cheese won out, simply because, on further recollection, I couldn't decide if I'd originally ordered the pizza this Tuesday or last Tuesday. Absently chewing on the end of a wooden spoon as I waited for water to boil, I zoned out, pretty damn content.

Until my phone rang.

Flailing, I nearly upended the whole stupid pan of hot water. The shrill buzz of the phone had sent my heart racing; I skidded across the tiny kitchen floor to my table to go digging through old newspapers and stacks of books to find the receiver. Which had apparently been hiding under an entire pile of comic books.

Every surface of my tiny apartment was covered in books or magazines, newspapers usually hanging around for a good month or so before I bundled them up for recycling. I felt comforted by the cozy surroundings, and for a kid who'd grown up lonely and chubby, books were a great substitute for friends. Right now, though, I was cursing them as I realized my one kitchen chair had been commandeered for last weekend's garage sale finds. Instead I trailed out to the couch and plopped down on the worn fabric as I answered the phone. "Hello?"

"Auggie?" It was my mom, her voice wavering.

I immediately sat up straight, dread circling a cold trail around my spine. "What's wrong?"

She sighed, and I could picture the exact face she'd be wearing at the moment, her softly graying hair in a long braid down her back, her face crinkled in distress. "It's your grandfather. He passed away last night. I'm so sorry, hon, we just got back from the funeral home."

My family was close. Not because we all liked one another, not because we were the Waltons or the Brady Bunch or because we ran a secret underground criminal cartel. We were close because we had to be. For a lot of little reasons—and one really big one—we lived near each other, we kept tabs on each other, and we barely let a week go by without checking in with everyone. I'd just spoken to Pop Pop a few days ago. And now he was gone.

People on my dad's side of the family, with the Mendez bloodline, we didn't seem to have the long lives of my mom's side. My Grams had been gone at seventy-five, Pop Pop had been eighty. Meanwhile, my other set of grandparents were still out golfing, and my great-grandparents had both hit ninety-eight before they'd passed. Maybe it had something to do with the Mendez family's particular gift, maybe it was all the deep-fried tortillas and pork my Grams had insisted on feeding everyone she got her hands on. In any case, my first thought was that Pop Pop was too young. Eighty was nothing, really, was it? Maybe it only felt that way to people left behind. All at once, I could do nothing but mentally list all the things I'd never gotten around to doing with him, all the things I'd never found enough time to say or ask or talk about.

"Auggie?" My mom sounded worried.

I scrubbed the tears from my cheeks and I nodded, sucking in a quick breath. "I'm still here. Uh. How's Dad?"

There was a rustle of noise, faint voices I couldn't quite hear—my mom had put her hand over the phone, I realized. And then my dad's voice, cracking all around the edges, like I couldn't find enough duct tape in the world to shore him back up. "Hey, guy," Dad said, and I heard the traces of crying he was struggling to hide.

"Dad." Christ. What did you even say in situations like this? I felt the *missing* of Pop Pop like an ache, but Dad sounded like he was barely holding it together. "I'm so sorry." Lame. So lame. But I couldn't think of anything else.

"Yeah." Dad took a shaky breath in. "Look, uh, some of the family, they're coming here tonight. The funeral is going to be Sunday. That okay?"

"Sure." I was already trying to decide if I had enough in my bank account for gas. My parents lived an hour away, in the same suburban home I'd grown up in. Their neighborhood had shady trees and quiet streets, and my aunt lived two blocks over. "Yeah, I'll be there tonight."

"Okay." Dad exhaled, and I almost could hear his shoulders slumping. "Okay, good. We'll see you later."

"Bye, Dad."

In something like a daze, I walked around, turning off the stove before I went to pack, shoving hoodies and jeans and clean boxers into a duffel bag. Crap. What was I supposed to wear to a funeral? For a long time, far too long, I stared at my closet and hated everything I owned. Stupid, it was all so *stupid*. What was I, a kid? Who wore fucking hoodies and T-shirts with starships on them when they were thirty? Nothing in there was good enough to say good-bye to Pop Pop in, and I felt the tears start up again as I cursed my worn jeans and faded khakis. I owned a single pair of old black dress pants; they were too snug, but they'd have to do. I found one of the few button-down shirts that weren't left over from two sizes ago, the deep charcoal-gray the closest I could get to black. My dad would have a tie I could borrow, I hoped. Someday I'd be a grown-up. Someday I'd have a wardrobe that didn't consist mostly of polos and khakis for work and six different sci-fi-related T-shirts.

Maybe if I wore my fedora? I tried it on, scrubbing a hand across my reddened eyes and trying to look presentable. One glance in the mirror was all I needed. With a muttered oath, I tore the hat off my head; no matter how slick Cary Grant had been in one of those, I was definitely not him. I just looked like a tool.

I always said I'd look better in black and white. Too bad my life was lived in garish color, pointing out every flaw and roll. I was too short, too fat, and spent way too much of my time inside my own head. No wonder I dressed like a fifteen-year-old. What was the point of dressing up someone no one was going to waste time on anyway?

"And the drama queen of the year award goes to…." I sighed at my reflection, pulling a face. Okay. So I didn't have a nice suit. Pop Pop was gone and I was going there for my family, not for a fashion show. I just wanted to look respectful. Carefully, I laid out the gray shirt and the black slacks, then folded them and put them gently into the duffel bag. I found the nicest shoes I had, the ones that pinched my feet, and added them as well before zipping up my luggage and grabbing my coat.

All thoughts of freedom or a weekend of laziness and cheese curls were forgotten. When the radio in my car blurted out some cheery pop hit, I switched it off roughly, glowering like the DJs of the world had conspired to play something completely inappropriate. The hour passed quickly, my drive uneventful. I didn't even run out of gas. I'd fiddled with a pencil, one of the pack I kept in my glove box, gnawing on it to calm my nerves.

I had friends who thought the habit was weird or gross. In school I'd claimed it helped me think; in truth, it was a necessary thing that had become a self-soothing ritual. Turned some of us into raging oral fetishists, but what could you do? My aunt preferred to chew on these awesome applewood sticks she got from the local farmers' market, but my budget wouldn't allow for the splurge. Maybe someday. I did steal a handful every time I was at her house though.

By the time I turned into my parents' driveway, I'd managed to pull myself back from a full-on panic to something more subdued. I wasn't the only one there, judging by the cars packed onto the sides of the street, the driveway, even one big pickup truck in the yard. My uncle Max's, I thought. We were a herd, all of us, and when something happened we all came out in droves. There were about thirty of us living close by—I was the farthest one out, the family rebel, which was both hilarious and kind of sad—and over the next few days, I was sure every one of them would be showing up. Aunts and uncles, cousins, great-whatevers, once and twice removed, we'd all pile in together in an exhausted heap of family support and bury Pop Pop; we'd grieve together and share stories, and life would go on. It was how we worked. We were all bound by blood or marriage, after all, and we all kept the secret. It was what held us close.

"Auggie!" My mom engulfed me in a hug the moment I walked through the door. She was shorter than me, her plump arms squeezing me tight, her head the perfect height to press against my shoulder. "Was the drive all right? Come in, come in, we're just getting supper around."

I nodded hello to the family gathered around the table, to the press of people in the kitchen. Every surface was covered in food being chopped or cooked or mixed. My dad was there, with his sister and brother, seated at the table by the window and drinking coffee. There were no less than five plates of cake, brownies, and cookies, all spread around for people to snack on as they talked and worked.

My aunt called me over, and I was soon pressed in with them. My dad pulled me into a tight hug. We talked about Pop Pop, and my dad wiped tears away, but we laughed too. We always laughed. Dinner was a massive spread, all of us crowded around my parents' huge table, knees knocking together.

We used food as the platform for everything: for the reason to gather, for the underpinnings to every meeting. If we were together as a family, we were eating. Even now, grieving, sad, we ate.

And even now, grieving, sad, my mother and my aunt clucked over my weight. "You should do something about that, Auggie," my mom said, sad behind her own chubby cheeks. "You could be so handsome."

"You *are* so handsome," my aunt joined in.

"Of course he is," my mom agreed, smiling at me. And I couldn't be mad, because she gave me another hug and kissed my cheek. "But think of how much better you'd feel if you just lost a few pounds."

The conversation was held, as always, over plates of food, over pasta and roasts and baked goods passed hand to hand. Food was our comfort. Always. It just was the enemy all at the same time.

I slept that night in my old bedroom, the single bed uncomfortable, the pillow too thin. Staring up at the ceiling, arms behind my head, I listened to the house. The quiet murmur of voices, the settling of the walls, the gentle clink of plates being washed up. And then silence as everyone left or found a bed. When I finally found sleep, it was restless and light; the morning woke me up like a damned bell ringing, the sunlight cracking across my eyelids and forcing me out of bed.

The day passed in a blur. Maybe I didn't want to focus on it. I just knew that we ate more, we had more family come in, and by the time evening came, I knew I'd both gained ten pounds and was exhausted. I was up in my old room, laying out my clothes for the morning when my mom poked her head in, carrying a blue tie.

"Your dad asked me to bring this to you. Do you need to iron anything, honey?"

I shook out my pants, crinkling my nose. "Maybe." I could pretty much see a road map in the wrinkles. "Yeah," I sighed. "Everything still in the same spot?"

She nodded and patted my shoulder; I set up the board and plugged in the iron while she fussed with the comforter on the bed. "How are you doing, Auggie?"

Ah. The same conversation we had every time I came over. "Fine, Mom." I spread the shirt out on the board and started pressing out the creases. "Work is fine. My apartment is not suddenly overrun with crack dealers. I haven't lost weight. And no"—I shot her a look, cutting off her next question—"I'm not dating anyone."

She bit her lip, attempting to look chagrined, but I wasn't fooled. "You know," she went on in that oh-so-casual tone mothers everywhere got when talking about their kids' love lives, "I know this nice young man who works at the library."

"Thanks, Mom." I bit back a laugh. It was either that or cry. Every time I came home, it was the same. No matter how many times I told my mom I was all right, that I could handle my own dating life, there was always *a nice young man* she knew. Heaven only knew if said nice man was gay or single or interested in overweight, awkward nerds. It was embarrassing on so many different levels. "But I don't need any help. I'm doing just fine." I wasn't. It'd been six months since I last even tried to ask anyone out. But I hadn't crossed over into scary, loner, cat-owner hoarder yet, so I figured I'd get there someday. Hopefully without my mommy setting me up with random people she encountered.

Mom tutted over me, but she smiled, patting my cheek. "Well. If you change your mind."

"Sure," I agreed. Problem was, I just kind of *sucked* at the relationship thing. In theory, sure, it all sounded great. But my family had this huge secret, and I was a terrible liar. All I wanted was to be able to be myself—wasn't that pretty typical? Every freaking romantic comedy was based around that. But because of what we were, it wasn't possible. I didn't want to meet some nice guy who I'd have to pretend around until we either broke up or, even worse, we decided to make a commitment. Because that was when you told them, and I wasn't sure I could look someone in the eyes who thought they knew me and tell them the truth.

We were skinwalkers. Shifters. Whatever it was called now. Part of some ancient bloodline that meant we could change when we wanted to. And no one could know, because as fun as it was to be a freak, we knew people would go full-on *E.T.* on us if they ever discovered what we could do. Human beings, no matter what century or country, weren't very tolerant of things they couldn't explain. That was the first rule of being a Chincha.

The second rule was that the herd was everything. And now we were going to bury one of our own.

THE service was nice. My pants were snug enough to make a band around my stomach that hurt, my shoes were pinching my little toe, and I really didn't care. Because we were all sitting together in a church, and Pop Pop was gone.

He had been cremated, like all of us would be. After the funeral, we all went to the woods and spread Pop Pop's ashes, my dad silently weeping while we stood and said our final good-byes.

We sat and ate lunch together before, slowly, the family began to leave. In twos and threes, in groups and singly, we all went back to our lives. Sadder, yes, and missing Pop Pop, but the herd had come together to support each other through it. I was one of the last to go, one of my second cousins, Hermes, stopping me as I was loading my bag in the trunk.

"Hey, August. I, uh, I don't know if your dad told you, but my dad's firm is the executor of the will. So can I set a time to talk to you this week? Maybe get lunch?"

I rubbed a hand through my hair, frowning. "Will?"

"Yeah. I haven't gone over everything yet, but I know you're mentioned, so I figured I'd set up an appointment now."

Pop Pop had a will? Which, yeah, I guessed made sense. He owned his house, his car, probably some savings—grown-up stuff that meant he would have had to think about what would happen to them when he was gone. Unlike me, who would only have to worry about who would clean out my fridge before the milk started to smell too bad. "Sure, yeah. How about Tuesday?"

"Fantastic." Hermes clasped me on the shoulder. "Text me where we can meet, okay? I've got to run. See you Tuesday."

"Yeah, uh, sure. Bye, Hermes."

I watched as he took off, fiddling a pencil out of my pocket and gnawing on it as I thought. Why would I be mentioned in Pop Pop's will?

MONROE'S Cafe was my favorite lunchtime spot. Cheap food, good service, and no one judged me if I got a milkshake with my meal instead of water. Which was pretty much all the time, because who didn't want ice cream in the middle of the day? It spoke to my inner eight-year-old, who had always wanted dessert before dinner. I had arranged to meet Hermes there on my lunch break; two days of wondering what was going on had not helped my nerves any. I was sitting, waiting for him, fiddling with the straw in my chocolate shake.

"You know, that much sugar is only going to make you crash later." Hermes was tall and thin, willowy like his mom. He was one of us, but whereas when I shifted the chubby-cheeked theme was carried over, Hermes was confident and graceful in either form. We shared the same dusky skin, the same dark hair and eyes, but the resemblance stopped there.

I smirked slightly. "Clearly you haven't heard about my afternoon M&M fix. Perks me right up."

Hermes sat opposite me in the booth and ordered a black coffee when the waitress came over. "You know, eating like that is going to give you diabetes." He tugged off his scarf as he looked around. "Nice. I haven't been to this side of town before."

"It's close to work," I agreed with a shrug. I ignored the other comment. I was used to it. It was how my family cared—they fussed over my food choices. "You hungry? They have really good burgers."

"No, thanks, I have to get back. I just wanted to touch base with you." He pulled a folder out of his briefcase, smiling briefly at the waitress as she brought his drink. "Okay. So, apparently Charles had quite a few more assets than anyone realized."

Charles—Pop Pop—had been a simple guy. He'd been a plumber, like my dad, like my uncle, like his father had been. His house had been modest, his car had been ten years old, and he had a penchant for old sweaters and thrift stores. I didn't even know if he'd known what *assets* were, really. "Uh." I poked at a fry, eyes going up to Hermes and then back down again, forehead wrinkling in confusion. I ventured a guess. "He had another car?"

Hermes chuckled, then took a sip of coffee. "Not quite." He slid a piece of paper over to me. It was a bunch of legal jargon, and my eyes glazed over as I tried to read it.

Except. What was that number? I jabbed the line on the page; I could feel my eyes widen as my gaze went up to find Hermes smiling at me. "That…. What…."

"That is what Charles left you in his will," Hermes said gently. "Fifty thousand dollars."

Holy shit.

"Pop Pop didn't have fifty thousand dollars," I protested weakly.

"No," Hermes agreed. "He had five million. You're just one of the beneficiaries. Most of the herd got something, and there's a trust fund set up for all the minors...." Hermes rubbed a hand across his face, shaking his head. "He took care of us. Just like always."

Five. Million. Dollars.

How was that even possible? How did Pop Pop have *five million dollars*? He could have traveled, he could have done anything he wanted to do. But he'd kept it from us. And he'd... done just what Hermes had said. He'd taken care of us. He was still taking care of us.

"Yeah," I whispered, stunned, sitting back in the booth. I picked up the paper and read it again. Fifty thousand dollars.

"There's a note for you," Hermes pointed out. "Just here." He pointed farther down the sheet.

For my boy. Dream big, August, and find your own path.

Holy shit.

MY *PATH* wasn't a dead-end job that I hated. I was damn sure of that. By the time I'd picked my jaw up off the floor and seen Hermes off, I had formulated a plan. A very small plan, yes, but a plan. For today, I was going to quit my job. My inheritance wasn't enough to live like Bruce Wayne forever, no, but it was enough to keep me going while I figured out what I wanted to do with my life.

"August." Olson was glowering at me when I made my way back to the office. I felt dazed, like my feet hadn't once hit the ground, like I was pushing my way through fog. Pop Pop was gone and I was semirich, and I felt like a shitheel for being either happy or sad. If I wallowed, wasn't I disrespecting this incredible gift? If I was happy, wasn't I forgetting why I had it? So I trembled between the two, sitting at my desk and staring at the computer for several long minutes.

Dimly, I became aware of Olson saying my name, volume increasing, wheezing between every syllable. Spittle had gathered in the corners of his lips, white and gooey, and I raised my eyes to stare at him. He was lecturing me, impotent rage at my lack of response causing him to hop slightly after every word.

"I quit." I said the words in almost a whisper, like they were a talisman I held out. He didn't stop, though, so I repeated them, louder, more firm. "I quit, Olson."

He spluttered to a halt. "What?"

"I said you can take this job and shove it." I stood, grabbing my coffee mug, my stash of pencils. "I quit."

Olson kept his beady eyes on me, staring agape as I brushed past him and headed for the door. Free.

Thanks, Pop Pop.

CHAPTER
TWO

SAM

Most days, Sam found, it wasn't worth getting out of bed. Just flat-out was not worth the time or bother. And really, what was so great about the outside world? People were dicks, by and large, and dealing with them only put him in an increasingly foul temper.

All of this held doubly true on rent day.

Rent day was like a holiday designed by a masochist. Owning a building had sounded like a great idea before he'd actually, well, *owned the damn building.* Before, it'd just been a job where he would be his own boss, set his own rules, where he could insulate himself from the dickbags of the world. Do some repairs when they were called for, change light bulbs, paint once a year—the whole thing had been perfect. But that was before he'd known about *rent day.*

Sam slammed his fist on the door, barking out three quick beats. "Mrs. Pritchett, it's Sam Ewing. It's the sixth, Mrs. Pritchett, I'm sorry, but I need to collect the rent. Lights don't go on by themselves, you know?" Yeah, this was exactly what he wanted his life to be. Harassing little old ladies for the rent to their offices. At least it wasn't apartments. If he had to throw someone out of their home he was pretty sure he'd just give up completely.

Mrs. Pritchett owned a little hair-and-nail salon on the first floor. It was good for business, nice storefront, drove foot traffic. People liked to rent in a building that had all that shit. Four floors, seventeen tenants, and him living in the walk-out basement he'd converted. It wasn't a bad gig, really. Except for today. Today he had to be up at seven to try to catch people before they opened for business, knock on doors, and be the bad guy.

He wasn't the fucking bad guy. He was just the guy who wanted to get paid.

Sighing, he fished out one of the Rent Due notices from his pocket and stuck it to the door. Someone was bound to see it when they came to open up, and if he didn't hear from Mrs. Pritchett by noon he'd have to come back. Silently, Sam begged her to call. He hated coming back in front of customers; it was just... awkward.

Next stop was the fourth floor. Room 403 was the smallest office space he had; he almost hadn't bothered renting it at all. It was barely big enough for a desk, some bookshelves, and a coffee maker. But every so often a fledgling business liked to get a cheap storefront to start, and it wasn't hard to keep up with the maintenance on it. So Sam rented it for a song, made the lease six months instead of twelve, and kept it pretty well occupied. He hadn't had much cause to come up there, really, rent day or no.

At least, not until five months ago.

Five months ago he'd gone against his gut and signed a lease with some chubby, wide-eyed kid in a damn fedora. Something told him that he'd be trouble, but Sam was a sucker for brown eyes, and he'd been cute, in a roly-poly kind of way. Aw, hell, in *any* way, though Sam was trying real hard to not think about it. At first, it'd been fine. Rent had been paid on time, guy had been quiet, no worries. For the first month.

"Mr. Mendez, it's Sam Ewing." Sam frowned at the door, repressing the urge to sigh heavily. He could hear the squeak of a chair, the distinct noise of someone stumbling, a muffled curse. "Mr. Mendez, it's the sixth."

There was another curse and a heavy crash. The brass sign on the door proclaiming *August Mendez, Private Detective* reflected Sam's face back to him, the eye roll of disbelief echoed there. Finally, though, cautious footsteps approached the door and August opened it, peering through. Sam was struck again by how attractive the guy was, dusky skin and dark, wavy hair framing a round face that seemed to broadcast every emotion. Not that he was there to flirt. Not that Sam *flirted* anymore.

"Uh. Hey, Sam," August said, giving Sam his best innocent smile.

"Mr. Mendez," Sam sighed.

He was interrupted by, "I told you, you can call me August. Or Auggie, whichever. You probably wouldn't be the *Auggie* type, though, you know? Not that there's a type. Or that that's a bad thing! Just, you're all stern and you'd probably look weird calling me by the nickname I got as a baby when you're just, you know." August trailed off, smile faltering, a miserable expression taking its place.

"Not a baby?" Sam suggested, expression still firm even as the corners of his lips twitched slightly.

"Exactly." August nodded before he seemed to hear what Sam had said. Horrified, he quickly amended, "No! I mean yes, you are definitely a man. An old man. Not that you're old!" Letting out an explosive breath, August sagged against the doorframe in surrender. "I'll have the cash for you this afternoon?"

"Thank you, August." Sam turned, hiding his smile and heading toward the elevator. Well, that had been slightly better than expected.

AUGUST

Fifty thousand dollars, by the way, sounded like it would last for freaking ever. It sounded like I could retire early, buy an island, all of that, at least to the guy who had fifteen bucks in his savings account on payday. Fun fact—fifty thousand dollars was actually not that much. Especially not if you didn't buy that island and instead decided, like a schmuck, to pay taxes and open a business.

So that was why I was currently hiding in my office from Sam, the landlord. Here was the thing—Sam had dark hair fading to light gray at the temples, gray stubble, a body that was seriously built for sin or bench-pressing large things, and brilliant blue eyes that scared the ever-living crap out of me. I turned into a babbling puddle of Jell-O around him. Never mind that I was late with rent. Again. Sam probably worked out and lifted things and he was older—not gross older, but like George-Clooney-hot older—and I was intimidated. Because I had a spot on my shirt that was either from tacos last night or ramen noodles the night before. Because I was overweight and wore stupid hats in no way ironically. Even if I hadn't owed Sam a dime, I still would have been a mess.

Opening my own detective agency had been *such* a great idea when my bank account had showed more zeroes. But it was okay. If I did my laundry in the sink—again—and ate peanut butter and jelly for the rest of the week, I'd make it. Because I had a job. A real detective job. And it was going to go so much better than the last ones.

It turned out that being a private detective was not as easy as the movies made it seem. Buying a trench coat and fedora and developing a crippling addiction to coffee—two creams, five sugars—had not instantly made me Philip Marlowe. My first case had been a cheating husband. All I'd had to do was follow the guy for a few nights, snap some pictures, and present the wife with confirmation that her spouse was, in fact, banging the babysitter. Two hundred dollars had been mine.

Yeah, I hadn't been too smart about pricing.

Of course, I'd gotten *caught* by the husband and he'd tried to break my camera. I'd gotten away with a sprained ankle and a cracked lens, which was a total win in my book. In any case, most of my jobs tended to be along those lines. Follow someone, watch someone, take pictures of someone; not the glamorous life I'd been envisioning. No murderers or big-city corruption, just a bunch of guys who couldn't keep it in their pants. And a couple of women too. Infidelity was not gender-constrained.

But this time, I had a big job. Not a couple hundred bucks either; if I did this right, it'd be enough for next month's rent all by itself. All I had to do was figure out who was stealing out of the register at the dry cleaners across the street. The manager for the shop, Mr. Petros, had hired me to investigate. I even had a plan. I'd taken a few pictures around there today, pretending to be bird-watching, and tonight I'd sit in my car outside and see who closed up.

It was going to be fine. And the next time I saw Sam Ewing, maybe I wouldn't act like a total idiot.

Fishing the last couple of dollars I needed from under Cocky, the ceramic rooster on my desk—my good-luck charm and rainy-day funds keeper—I smoothed out the bills and neatly tucked them into an envelope.

For Sam I scrawled on the front. After a moment's consideration, I added, *You're really not old.*

There.

After slipping it under his door, I escaped the building and got lost in the crush of people on the sidewalk. Crowds like this weren't really my thing; I dug in my pocket to find a pencil, feeling some of that tension ease when I was able to gnaw it between my teeth. Shoving a hand through my hair, I plunged into the flow of pedestrians, winding my way to the corner and then across the street.

Sally's Family Dry Cleaners was this neat little shop tucked between a bakery and a print shop. Guess which one caught my wandering eye? It was only a few minutes, after all, and I would totally start the peanut butter diet tomorrow. Today? There were fresh red velvet doughnuts with cream cheese frosting. Not even Sam Spade could have passed that up.

So I was licking frosting from my fingers and tucking a paper sack with one—okay *two*—more of those delicious baked goods into my messenger bag when I saw him. A big guy, sides of his head shaved tight, piercings, a nose that veered to one side like it'd been knocked off and jammed back in place haphazardly. He was manning the counter at Sally's, looking surly and like he might live up a beanstalk or something. Seriously, the guy was huge. He scowled at me as I came in the door and I froze, staring, nose twitching as I tried not to just bolt.

"You want something?" he grunted in my general direction. *Jake* his name badge declared him. Jake didn't look friendly. Or much like he wanted me to be, you know, *alive*.

"Um, sorry, I was looking for Mr. Petros?" Christ, my voice cracked like a freaking choirboy's. I didn't have a problem with big burly men with piercings, really. Some of my favorite pornos featured that very thing. But Jake didn't look like he wanted to deliver a package or have a conversation or anything. He looked like he wanted me to scuttle away and hide. Scary was not sexy, and my instincts were telling me to move right along.

"He ain't here." Jake looked me up and down, practically radiating bored annoyance. "What do you want? Get frosting on your shirt?"

Why yes, I probably had. Not that it was any concern of his. "He was going to leave me something," I mumbled, shoulders rounding forward. I found staring down at my feet a much better use of my time. "I'm, uh, I'm August? He said he'd leave it at the front counter if he was going to be out. If you see it. You know, if it's not too much trouble. It shouldn't be heavy. Not that that would matter, because I bet you could lift really big things, but—" Oh God, I was going to die of fatal mouth-flapping syndrome.

I could practically hear him rolling his eyes, but a manila envelope landed on the counter with a slap. "Here. Anything else for you, Pillsbury?"

Ha-ha. That was hilarious. I was laughing so hard, really, on the inside. Where it counted. "Nope," I managed, snatching the package up and all but tripping over my feet in the effort to bolt for the door. "Have a nice day."

Escaping, I darted across the street and back up to my office. I was breathing hard, cheeks flushed, cursing stairs and *Jake* and my bone-deep aversion to gym class. He'd startled me, he'd shaken me, and now my heart was hammering so loudly I expected the lawyer who shared an office wall with me to come in and file a noise complaint.

I wanted to shift. I didn't often, because seriously, what would be the point? None of us did. Personally, I was just really hooked on the opposable thumbs thing that I had as a human. But right then, I wanted to be smaller. I wanted to hide. Instead, though, I concentrated on deep breaths; with shaky fingers I grabbed a pencil and gnawed fiercely on the wood until I felt the panic ease.

Right. Okay. Everything was going perfect.

Sliding behind my desk, I sagged back in the chair and stared at the ceiling for a moment. Gathering my thoughts, as it were. The fake-leather chair squeaked under me as I pushed off with my toe to gently twist back and forth. My office was cluttered, the bathroom in the corner barely more than a closet, but I loved it. Hell, I'd better love it— if things didn't pick up, I'd be living in it. My apartment was a one bedroom two blocks over, cramped and tiny and with zero water pressure, but rent was a lot higher downtown than it'd ever been in my old neighborhood. Worth it though. I woke up in the morning and walked to my own detective agency. What could be better than that?

Picking up the envelope, I dumped the contents out onto my desk. As I'd requested, he'd given me last week's surveillance camera tape. I'd already been over this with Mr. Petros and apparently nothing showed up on the tape. It was only after the weekly count was done that the stealing was apparent. Still, maybe I would see something he hadn't. I was a detective, after all.

Also included was a sheet listing all the employees' schedules. The family that actually owned Sally's had franchised three years ago, opening two more locations and hiring Mr. Petros to manage their downtown store. Petros was in charge of all the daily operations, including the employees here. Scanning the list, my heart sank. Crap. Jake's name was listed as closing every night but one. Someone else was always there with him though; Mr. Petros had said he didn't like to make anyone stay by themselves after dark. So maybe it was just a coincidence. Just because he was big and surly and looked like he tore people like me apart for fun didn't mean he was a criminal.

Crap.

Sighing, I flipped open my laptop. Background check time. I went to a search engine and typed in the first employee's name. Two hundred forty seven thousand, six hundred and eleven matches. Yeah. Now would be a good time to figure out how to use that background checking software I'd bought.

Double crap. How did people on TV do this so fast? There was no peppy inspirational music montage to accompany my searching. Just scrolling through possible matches, searching for relevant information, sight going bleary from staring at the screen. Rubbing my eyes, I reached into my desk drawer for my trusty stash of peanut butter M&Ms. This was clearly time for a sugar high.

SAM

The worst part about living in the basement—lousy television reception. All Sam wanted to do was sit in peace and quiet and watch the damn game. Maybe crack open a cold beer, poke at the leftover pizza sitting in the fridge—a nice, simple afternoon. But his television was insisting on only showing him static, no matter how hard he banged on the side or what impossible angles he shoved the antenna into.

He really should upgrade. "Every damn time," he muttered, yanking the antenna wires, trying to stretch them over to the far window. "Every goddamn time the Steelers are on, you go on the fritz. Fucking TV." The television was older than dirt, but it'd been his before the divorce, and Sam had stubbornly clung to it. Every few months he thought about breaking down and getting cable, but it seemed ridiculous to pay that much when all he really wanted was the evening news and the occasional football game.

Finally, he manipulated the antenna just so before duct taping it to the side of the windowsill, and the game blurred into focus. Triumphant, Sam slouched down into his chair, taking a long-deserved pull of beer and generally feeling pretty damn content.

Until there was a knock at his door.

At first Sam just scowled in the door's direction. The television could certainly be heard out in the hallway, but he didn't care that the uninvited visitor would know he was in. In fact, he hoped they realized that not only was he *there*, but he was purposely not answering the door.

Another knock. "Not here," Sam barked, resolutely sagging farther down in his chair, arms folded. On the TV, Johnson, the Steelers' quarterback, was getting ready to make a pass. Sam's attention was jerked away, though, by a third knock, this one more timid than the last.

"Oh for fuck's sake." Shoving himself out of the chair, he set his beer down with more force than necessary. "Yeah, yeah, keep your pants on." Tugging open the door, Sam's scowl only faltered slightly when he found August Mendez in the hallway.

"Sorry," August apologized, shoulders in his usual hunch forward, as though he thought he could curl up like a pill bug and disappear. "I, um." He stuttered to a halt and wordlessly held out a battered white paper bag. "Do you like doughnuts?"

Blinking, Sam stared for a beat, confused. "You came down here to ask me that?"

"No," August admitted. "I just had this for a snack later and I thought I could bribe you with one? Uh." He peered around Sam, apparently catching sight of the television in the background. "Sorry to interrupt your game." August offered Sam a hopeful little grin, those deep brown eyes lighting up in a way that made it almost impossible for Sam to keep the irritated frown on his face. Something about the guy got under Sam's skin; instead of barking an annoyed question, he just tilted his head, inviting August in.

"So, are we winning?" August asked brightly, ducking past Sam into the room where he then stood awkwardly, fidgeting with his shirtsleeves. Everything Sam had ever seen August wear was oversized, as if August were desperately trying to hide in fabric. It was a damn shame, Sam thought.

"Depends on who you root for." Sam grabbed another beer for August. "You a Steelers fan?"

There was a long pause, a myriad of possible answers passing across August's expression. In the end, though, he sagged slightly, wincing. "I have no idea. To be honest, the only time I watch sports is when there's the possibility of nacho cheese."

Snorting a laugh, Sam just offered August the beer. "No cheese, but I've got beer and leftover pizza." Why the hell was he trying to get August to stick around? Watching the game *alone* was fully half the point of watching the damn game. But here he was, fussing with the pillows on his fucking couch, offering August the best spot to sit.

"Sure." August kept cutting him little looks, disbelief clearly written on his face. "I never turn down pizza." He forced a little laugh, patting his stomach. "Obviously." There was a smile on his face, slightly forced around the edges—August making a joke before Sam could. Pointing out what August thought was the elephant in the room before Sam did.

Sam just took a long swig of beer. "Never saw a problem with someone who likes to eat." He shrugged. Sprawling back on the couch, legs akimbo, Sam rested his beer on one knee. For a few moments he just watched the game, thumb absently picking at the bottle label. August was sitting with his still unopened beer, frowning faintly, as though he'd been expecting the whole conversation to play out differently.

As the game progressed, though, as Sam watched August out of the corner of his eye, August started to relax. His shoulders ticked back, out of that awkward hunch, and he slowly sank back into the couch. There was the noise of action on the TV, a whistle blown, commentary, and the roar of the crowd, but Sam was finding it hard to pay attention. Again and again, his gaze was pulled over to August. When the guy didn't think anyone was looking at him he lost that painful effort to disappear. There was something *about* August. Some intangible thing that forced Sam to pay attention. It'd been a long-ass time since Sam had felt anything like that. Maybe that was why he'd shanghaied the guy in here to watch a game.

There was the rustle of a bag, and August held out a doughnut to Sam with a smile. Sam hadn't noticed how much August had seemed ready to jump out of his skin around Sam until right then; for the first time, he seemed slightly confident. "Probably doesn't go with beer," August offered sheepishly. "But it's red velvet, and I actually put in my will that I'm going to be buried in a vat of that frosting."

Sam felt his lips twitch upward into a smile. "A warrior's burial," he intoned. Taking the doughnut, he raised it in cheers, putting his beer aside in favor of the pastry.

"Damn straight," August replied, a twinkle in his eyes. He tapped his doughnut lightly against Sam's and took a bite, tongue darting out to clean frosting from his mouth.

Sam wasn't really a *sweets* person, per se, but he tried a taste. His eyebrows winged up in surprise. "That's really good. You make these?"

"Oh hell, no," August laughed. "I can barely work my microwave. I got them at Sweeties Bakery, across the street." August dragged a finger through the frosting on his doughnut, before bringing it up to his lips and licking it off. Sam was surprised at the sudden surge of heat that shot straight through his gut at the sight. Damn it, he was not going to get a *crush* on the guy who wore fedoras and thought he was a damn detective.

August might not be Kyle, might actually be the opposite of everything he'd been, but Sam had learned his lesson about falling for incompatible men. He wasn't even going to let himself go there.

"Huh." Sam took another bite. "Not bad."

"They have killer éclairs too." August grinned at him, and Sam's stomach did a sharp flip.

Goddamn it.

"You come down here for something?" he all but growled, setting the doughnut down in favor of grabbing his beer again. "Other than to talk baked goods?"

As if sensing the shift in Sam's mood, August's shoulders got that damn rounded hunch again, the bright smile fading from his face completely. "Yeah. Sorry, I, um. I was hoping to bribe you into giving me a hand? The light's out in my office and I know that you don't normally make that a priority...." The words faded into August's wince, and he lowered his eyes to his hands, which were twisting together. "I'm just working a case, so."

Sam refused to feel like a shitheel about the way the tentative confidence had gotten squashed. August—*Mr. Mendez*—was a tenant. Tenants did not get invited in to watch games.

"That's my job," Sam grunted, standing and flipping off the television. He didn't have a clue what was going on there anyway. He'd completely lost track of the flow of the game. Good thing the news had recaps. "Don't need to play nice with me to get me to do my job." After toeing on his boots, he shrugged a faded flannel shirt on over the T-shirt he'd been wearing, and nodded toward the door. "Come on, I'll take care of it now."

"Yeah, sure, great." August was nodding, smiling, but it wasn't the same. 'Course it wasn't. Whatever flicker of *something else* there'd been before was just stupid; Sam didn't *want* it to be the same. He wanted it to be like it was when he collected rent. He was the landlord; he stomped around and fixed shit and collected money and that was all. End of story.

August watched while Sam locked his apartment door, and trailed after him as Sam headed to the large storage closet down the hall. When Sam glanced back, he saw the guy was chewing fiercely on a pencil, clutching it like a smoker grabbing their first cigarette of the day. Once Sam hefted the ladder up on one shoulder and grabbed a box of bulbs, they took a silent ride in the elevator up to the fourth floor.

Sidelong glances revealed that August kept shifting back and forth, foot to foot, opening and closing his mouth as though he were trying to think of something to say. The expression on Sam's face, however, was apparently enough to end any attempts at conversation. August led the way to his office. After unlocking the door, he stepped back for Sam to head inside.

The place was a mess. Somehow August had crammed a couch and coffee table in there along with his desk and a few chairs, Sam assumed for clients. Books were shoved into bookshelves and littered nearly every flat surface. There was a ceramic rooster on the desk, posters from black-and-white detective movies on every wall, and a whole shelf of pictures. Sam paused to glance at them; August was in most, smiling, arms around what Sam had to assume were family members. He looked happy. But in every one, Sam could see how August tried to avoid being directly in front, hiding behind what Sam guessed was his mom—they had the same smile—or placing himself in the very back of a group shot. Sam wondered about that.

Not that he cared. He was just here to put in a goddamn light bulb.

The tiny corner bathroom had the door open, the only light in the room coming from the vanity inside. Sam grunted, getting the ladder set up and hitching himself up the steps to reach the overhead light. The top floor had high ceilings, and Sam regretted not putting in the standard fluorescent lights. He just hated how the damn things reminded him of a decade spent in an office, crammed into suits and working every day in a cubicle, listening to the hum of the lights. So he'd done softer bulbs, more traditional light fixtures, but that just meant he changed the bulbs twice as often. That's what he got for being sentimental.

Kyle had liked them.

Kyle could go fuck himself.

"You should get a lamp," he informed August while he worked. "If you had a lamp you wouldn't have to tromp all the way to the basement in order to keep working."

"I thought about it—" August started, but Sam just kept grumbling.

"I mean, who doesn't have a lamp? It's an office. Get a desk lamp. They're better for your eyes, anyway."

There was a pause as Sam finished screwing in the bulbs and stomped his way down the ladder. "I'm sorry," August said as Sam reached the bottom. "I didn't mean to bother you. I mean, it's Friday afternoon, it's almost dinnertime, I'm surprised you were even in."

Sam cut him a glance, lips twisted downward, eyebrow hitching.

Immediately, August flushed and started to do the thing where he rocked side to side, a nervous habit Sam had noticed seemed to get worse the longer August had to talk to him. "Not that it's weird you're home! Or that you shouldn't be. I mean, being single isn't a big deal. I'm single!"

Sam's eyebrows almost touched his hairline; he just stood, staring at August, wordless.

"Oh, God, not that you're single. Or that I think about you being single! And you definitely don't care about *me* being single." August was in high-speed babbling mode now, practically wringing his hands. "I mean, you're straight. Which, hey, is great! I mean, not that you *shouldn't* be straight. Or single. Or at home. All of those are...." He gulped in a miserable breath, finally ending with an awkward "Great."

For a few more beats, Sam just stared at him. He honestly wasn't sure, most days, what to do with August when he got going like that. On the one hand, it was slightly amusing to see how big of a hole he'd verbally dig. But a lot of times he said things, things Sam wasn't sure he should pay attention to or if when August got nervous his brain just strung nouns and verbs together in some vain effort to make his body run out of oxygen so it'd stop.

"Am I straight?" Sam wound up replying, giving August an inscrutable look.

And then he left, ladder over one shoulder, leaving August alone in his newly lighted office.

If he had any luck, he'd catch a replay of the game and his beer would still be cold.

CHAPTER
THREE

AUGUST

Really, honestly, it'd been *super* important for me to get the lights going again. I was working a case. I wanted to do a stakeout tonight to see who did the final closing before the weekly deposit was counted. These were legitimate reasons to need the overhead light working. Hell, I'd even brought my treasured doughnuts as a bribe. None of that should have blown up in my face.

And yet. There I was, sitting at my desk, staring at the file I'd compiled for this job, and all I could think about was Sam.

The guy terrified me. He was big, with broad shoulders that stretched his damn T-shirt and forced all sorts of thoughts in my brain. He had a gruff voice that seemed to be honey over gravel, and yeah, I was intimidated. Until that evening, I didn't think I'd ever seen him smile. But before I'd known it I was in his apartment, sitting next to him on the couch, and he'd gone from the totally scary landlord to… *Sam.*

If my life depended on it, I'd never be able to say a single thing that had gone on in that game. But I could have described, now, in absolute detail the way Sam's fingers had played with the label on his beer bottle, how his jaw was underscored with dark stubble edging toward gray, mirroring the faint hint of silver at his temples. All because the guy had smiled, and it'd seemed like he'd become a whole *person*, just with that, rather than the closed-off, grumpy guy who I tried to hide from.

And his parting shot had left me feeling…. Something.

Something that was not about people stealing money from a dry cleaner's and therefore was irrelevant, *self.* Jesus, I had to focus a little better. I was not going to sit here and get distracted by shiny things. That was so stereotypical I could not handle it.

In any case, turning Sam from a scary-hot to a crush-hot classification was not worth the effort. It was nice to have my fantasies neatly categorized, sure, but somehow I thought wasting time crushing on Sam was about as worthwhile as contemplating if I could eat as many candy bars as I wanted on the moon due to the difference in gravity. I could think about it, sure, but probably NASA wasn't going to call.

So I'd just work. Because that was what I was supposed to be doing.

Flipping through the schedule again, I rested my head on one hand, absently tapping a pencil against the desk with the other. There was a pattern here; I knew it. There had to be. If all those years of reading mysteries had taught me anything, it was that there was *always* a pattern. There was always something there, if you looked.

My giant buddy Jake had closed nearly every night, except for Wednesday. There was a Tina on the schedule who had closed Monday, Wednesday, and Friday, and a Marjorie who had closed the rest of the nights. It had to be one of those three, right? Mr. Petros wouldn't have hired me if it was him, because he wouldn't want any more scrutiny. So my three suspects were right there.

"Is it terrible that I just want it to be Igor the Horrible?" I muttered to Cocky, his ceramic rooster head overseeing the investigation majestically. "I probably can't just decide he's guilty because he was a jerk, huh?"

Cocky didn't answer. That was okay. He didn't need to point out the obvious.

Fine, so I'd do the whole stakeout thing and see what happened. I was close; I knew it.

After I locked up, I tugged on a black sweatshirt and headed down to my car. On the way out the main entrance I passed the stairway leading down to the basement. I could see a faint light; obviously Sam was still up and around. For a moment I had an incredibly stupid urge to go down there. What would I even say? "Hi, I'm back to spaz all over you some more, hope you weren't busy being gorgeous and normal."

Yeah, pass.

It was dark outside, starting to spit rain. The cars sloshed through the streets, lights reflecting in puddles like melted crayons. Sighing, I tugged on my fedora and power-walked the two blocks to my car. The spot I'd managed to find that morning wasn't the greatest. And now I was blocked in by an oversized truck and a stupid sporty car that looked like a penis replacement. Fan-friggin-tastic.

Two inches forward. Stop. Reverse three inches. Stop. Crank the wheel left. Forward two inches. Over and over again, while I muttered curses and tried to remember how much my insurance deductible was. Finally I eked out of the spot, pulling out onto the main road and making my way back toward the dry cleaners.

By then I was later than I'd wanted to be, and I barely got parked in a good spot out front when the outside lights were turned off. I could see Jake and a woman who must be Tina moving around inside the shop, doing their closing duties, I imagined. The car engine pinged softly as it cooled, the rain spattered the windshield, and I slouched down in my seat, watching.

Just like a real detective.

Sometimes my life got cool all at once.

And sometimes it was forty-five minutes of sitting in my car, staring at two people mopping a floor. No one was twirling a mustache or tying anyone to train tracks. No obvious signs of chicanery. Just two employees trying to close up shop after a long day.

Damn.

Just when I was about to call it a night, there was a flare of light from the alley beside the dry cleaners. I caught sight of Tina taking out two large trash bags to toss them into the bins. When she walked back inside, though, I could still see the faint outline of the door; she hadn't closed it properly behind her. On purpose? Or maybe the stolen money was leaving with the garbage.

Either way, I knew I had to get in that alley. I could see Tina and Jake turning off lights, moving toward the exit. I took my chance to duck out of my car, cursing quietly when it dinged at me for leaving the keys in the ignition. I darted into the alley, my eyes taking far too long to adjust to the dark. Tripping over my feet, I almost slammed my head into a wall, barely getting my hand up in time to save my nose. There was a flare of pain on my palm, and I hissed in a breath, looking down to barely make out the shimmer of blood. I'd scraped the skin off. Fantastic.

Shaking the sleeve of my hoodie down to cover it, I kept going. I wanted to take a look in those trash bags. The dumpster was sitting open, and I grabbed the closest garbage sack. There was the distinct sour scent of rotting things all mixed together with the pervasive piss smell all alleys seemed to have. Choking a little, eyes watering, I hauled the bag out and ripped it open. It was a lot of paper, huge clumps of lint like basketball-sized tumbleweeds, and I dragged it a little closer to the seam of light creeping out from the ajar door.

I dug through the garbage. There seemed to be a lot of receipts, huge handfuls of them, like they'd been ripped from a book and stuffed in here. I frowned, uncrumpling one, tipping it toward the light so I could read it better. It was just tallying up an order, although I had a momentary thought that it seemed like Petros was charging an awful lot for laundry.

"Hey!" The sharp voice broke my concentration, and I dropped the receipts I was holding, scrambling back. Jake was in the doorway, scowling at me. "What the fuck are you doing?"

Shit, shit, *shit*. I shoved myself away, stumbling as I struggled to my feet. I saw Jake's big, meaty hand reaching out for my hoodie. Christ, if that guy caught me, I was mush.

So I took off running. I didn't *run* a lot. Or ever. But now the not-so-jolly giant was chasing me, so it seemed like a *really* good time to start. Heaving in panicked breaths, my sneakers skidding on the wet pavement, I darted out across the street. Horns blared but I didn't dare stop. I could hear him on my heels, cursing, the sound of his footsteps pounding behind me.

I was going to die. Holy fuck, that giant-ass man was going to kill me.

And that was when I realized I didn't have my keys. I couldn't get into the building.

Fuck.

Changing direction at the last second, I dodged into the alley that ran alongside my building. If I could double around, maybe get lost in the foot traffic the next street over, I could shake him. My heartbeat was throbbing in my ears, a stabbing pain in my side with every heaving breath I took. The fear slamming through me with every step, though, kept me desperately throwing myself forward.

The alley wasn't very long. There were dumpsters and closed doors that I staggered my way past, no help in sight. It was pitch-black; I didn't see the fence until I slammed into it full force. "No, no, no," I muttered, frantically grabbing at the chain link, pulling it like I was suddenly going to Hulk out and be able to yank it out of my way.

I was trapped.

There were seconds until Jake came around the corner. There was no way I could face him like I was. So I did the only thing I could think of.

I changed.

It started as an itch in my nose, a prickle along my skin. The world got very big very quickly as I shrank down, the ground rushing up to meet me. The night world flared to life, scents and sounds filling my senses. And then I wasn't human anymore. My nose twitched, ears pricking at the sound of footsteps. Two sets. I could smell one sweaty human; he stank like cigarettes and jerky. Jake appeared at the end of the alley, searching for me. But there was another man there, the tang of soap and beer, but more importantly behind him was an open doorway.

I zoomed off, nails skidding on the cement, hurtling myself toward the escape. There was the thunder of boots in my way, and I squeaked aloud in terror as I tried to correct course. Before I was stepped on, though, a hand reached down, wrapping around me. There wasn't time for me to react before I was pushed gently into a huge pocket and left there to tremble. I had no fucking clue what had just happened.

Well, I did. I was a chinchilla in someone's pocket.

Fuck.

SAM

There was a chinchilla in his pocket. He thought it was a chinchilla, anyway. Maybe a really fat hamster? A small rodent of some kind, anyway, and it was in his pocket. Which, sure, would be weird enough. Except it wasn't really *just* a chinchilla.

He'd stepped outside to take out the trash. Rain was just barely coming down, misting the streets into a shimmering pool of reflected streetlights, and the glow from the hallway behind him had lit the alley up just enough to see August Mendez change. He'd actually shrunk down and *changed* into a little fluffy ball of possible chinchilla. And then some huge guy had come running down the alley, obviously looking for someone, and August—the chinchilla—had bolted toward Sam in an effort to get away. So Sam had scooped the little guy up and dumped him into the front pocket of his hoodie.

It'd seemed like such a good idea at the time.

"Can I help you with something?" A thread of steel wound its way through Sam's voice as he watched the big guy search through the alley.

"Mind your own business, old man" was the retort, and Sam had to restrain himself from rolling his eyes. The other man looked like some haphazard mishmash of body parts—too long arms, huge shoulders, a flat head, and a nose that was off enough to make his face look doughy. Whoever he was, Sam took an instant dislike. Maybe because he'd chased August into a blind alley. Maybe because he was currently digging through their dumpster, strewing garbage everywhere.

"I kind of think this is my business, bud," Sam all but growled. "That's my shit you're throwing everywhere. This is my property. So why don't you get on home before I start getting aggravated?"

"I'm looking for some punk-ass fatty who was poking his nose in where it don't belong." At least the guy had stopped throwing trash bags everywhere. "You see him?"

The chinchilla in his pocket shivered, and Sam nearly winced at the feel of claws digging into his stomach. Goddamn, someone needed a manicure. Crossing his arms across his chest, giving the man a long glare, Sam watched all that bravado whither a bit. "Does it look like anyone is hiding here?" he bit out. "Now fuck off. And clean up that mess."

He stayed long enough to see the man, grumbling, start heaving the strewn trash bags back into the dumpster. Sam slammed the door behind him and stomped back to his basement apartment, muttering under his breath the whole while. Once inside he locked the door behind him. Going to the high, small windows, Sam tugged all the shades closed. Just in case.

Finally, taking a deep breath, he pulled out August—the *chinchilla*—and put him carefully on the kitchen table. For a long moment, they just stared at each other, Sam shakily taking a seat and resting his chin on his arms to bring him eye level. The chinchilla was frozen, dark eyes looking back at him, and Sam almost began to think he'd imagined the whole thing. People couldn't turn into animals—that was just a fact.

So that meant he just had some random rodent on his kitchen table. Which was, weirdly, the best possible scenario. Huffing out a helpless little laugh, Sam rubbed his hand across his face. Maybe he'd had more beers than he'd thought.

"What the hell am I going to do with you now?" he wondered.

As if in response, the chinchilla backed up before waddling its way to the edge of the table and regarding the drop down cautiously. Baffled, Sam followed it, holding out his hands for the chinchilla to scoot itself into. He lowered the little guy down onto the floor, marveling at how soft its fur was. For a few moments he just stroked the chinchilla's back, smiling slightly at the way the animal butted up into his fingers. Well, at least it was a cute rodent.

Sitting back on his heels, Sam watched the chinchilla scurry off into the corner. Maybe it was looking for some food? "I'm not sure what you eat," Sam started with another quiet breath of a laugh, "but I bet—"

The chinchilla was getting bigger. Rapidly. It doubled its size before Sam had even realized what was happening; it continued to grow as Sam scrambled backward, falling onto his ass and pressing his back into the far wall. Eyes huge, Sam stared, watching as stubby limbs stretched to arms and legs, as the long nose faded back and ears slid down to the sides of the chinchilla's head. The fur receded back, leaving just a mop of deep brown hair above the same dark, intelligent eyes that had just been staring him down on the kitchen table.

August. Who had just been a chinchilla.

"What the fucking fuck?" Sam's vocabulary seemed to have dissipated into a puddle of curse words and random fragments of thought. "You—"

"Um. Hi?"

"What the *fucking fuck*?" Sam's heels dug into the floor as he shoved himself back even farther, holding out one arm as if to keep August on his side of the apartment.

August, for his part, kept very still, holding up his hands in surrender. "It's okay," he assured Sam, looking fucking ridiculous in his stupid sweatshirt and with those wide, earnest eyes under that damn unruly mop of hair, as though everything were normal. Everything was *not* goddamn *normal*.

"It's not *okay*, you were just…. And then you…. What the *fuck*?"

August winced a little. "Okay, um, I get that. Seeing that for the first time is probably a bit… strange, if you're not prepared."

"Uh, yeah," Sam shot back, pointing a shaking finger at him. "Yeah, just a little *strange*. You're a goddamn…. But how is that…."

"I'm a shifter. Or a skinwalker, I guess, but that's kind of an old-school term. We don't really use that anymore." August made a small step toward him. Sam jerked upright, all but shoving himself back farther against the wall. "Sorry." August immediately stopped. "Look, I'm really sorry. I didn't mean for you to see that. Um." He shifted a bit, foot to foot, worrying his lower lip. "Do you want some tea?"

Tea? Fuck that. "Whiskey," Sam muttered, rubbing his hand across his mouth. "Cupboard by the fridge." He couldn't stop *staring* at August, watching every movement as if he were trying to catch the tell. To see the thing that made him not human. But August was the same as ever, fumbling with the glass, giving Sam that big, sweet smile that seemed to make it impossible for Sam to stay *too* aloof, no matter how much he wanted to.

"Here." August pressed the glass into Sam's hands. Sam really didn't *want* to flinch away, he didn't, but the memory of the claws against his stomach flashed through his mind. How could that be the same thing as August? How the fuck was he supposed to reconcile the two? One had been a little fluffy *rodent*, for fuck's sake.

He tossed back the whiskey. As the alcohol hit his throat, Sam hissed in a breath between his teeth at the burn. Okay. Right. Clearly he needed to wrap his brain around this sooner rather than later. Giving August a sideways look, Sam stalked over to the bottle and poured himself another glass. "Sit." He gestured to the kitchen table. August did so.

Sam followed, grabbing the bottle of whiskey and setting it down between them. "Okay," he muttered, voice caught in gravel, low and unsure. "Why don't you start at the beginning?"

August folded his hands, obviously searching for a good way to explain things. Which, Sam guessed, probably was hard to do. How *did* you explain your ability to turn into a small, chubby little rodent to the average person?

"So, um, I don't suppose you've heard of the Chincha people?" August asked, hopeful look fading when Sam shook his head. "Okay, uh, so we'll start there. The Chinchas were a people group in the Andes Mountains. They're who the chinchilla is named after because, as outsiders said, they wore the chinchilla skins as cloaks and stuff. They were, um, conquered by the Incas, and the bloodline was diluted and dispersed." August nervously ran a hand through his hair. "Except the Chinchas didn't just wear the chinchilla fur. They could turn into them. That's, uh, kind of why we shift with clothing. It was part of the ritual. They'd put on their skins and... well." August waggled his fingers at himself vaguely. "Poof."

A light dawned, slowly. "Like the Native Americans," Sam realized. "Wearing bear skin or wolf pelt or whatever and turning into them. But those are just stories."

August's shoulders lifted in a quick shrug. "Not so much stories. I mean, not every douchebag with a tiger-skin rug can shift or anything. I've heard of some descendants of the shamans who used to go bear or wolf or whatever, but I've never met one. But, yeah, same thing. Becoming one with the spirit of the animals until you kind of... *are* the animal."

"And so you're one of the Chinchas?" Sam's eyebrows were beetled together as he struggled to understand.

"Like, a thousand times removed, but yeah. There's about thirty in my herd, around twenty family members who have the bloodline. It apparently doesn't take much in order to be able to shift." August had pulled a well-gnawed pencil out of his pocket and was nibbling it as he talked. "We, um, don't tell anyone. For obvious, anti-dissection reasons. When one of the herd meets someone, a nonshifter, they want to be with, we, uh, we usually wait until after they're married or whatever to tell them."

Blinking, Sam sat back, scrubbing both hands through his hair. "That's kind of a shit thing to do."

August grimaced slightly, but he nodded. "Yeah. I mean, I get why. If this got out, can you imagine? Look how you reacted and you're all Mr. Unflappable. Let some jackass see it, or worse, someone who wants to take us apart to see how we work? We'd all be in danger. Not just my herd, but *all* of us."

Sam hadn't known August all that long. And yeah, something about the guy was intriguing, but mostly Sam had been able to ignore that, because August was a tenant. He was a young guy who didn't know what the fuck he wanted or what he was doing; never mind that he was attractive and sweet and open—though apparently he could keep a hell of a secret—he just wasn't going to be worth the heartache that would inevitably follow. No one was.

But there was something in his eyes now. Some strength in his expression Sam hadn't seen until then. It made Sam pay just a little bit more attention, despite the way August was almost always hiding behind stupid hats or clothes or too much babble. Right then, Sam was looking just at *him*, and August met his gaze steadily. He didn't back away.

Taking a slow breath, Sam forced himself to look down, breaking the connection. "Still a shit thing to do to someone you care about," he mumbled, fingers wrapping tightly around his glass. He wanted another drink, but this was trippy enough sober.

"Yeah." August slumped down in his seat, tugging absently at the strings to his sweatshirt hood. "I think maybe that's why I can't get a date. I mean, I *date*. Sometimes. I have dated. I'm not, like, a eunuch or anything."

Sam's lips, despite himself, were threatening a smile at August's babbling.

"But, like, long-term dating and I are nonsimpatico. At all. Which, I mean, I'm mostly okay with. Kind of okay with." August was plucking at the seams of his jeans, rocking back and forth slightly as he went on. "Not really okay with at all, actually, but it's not *all* bad. I mean, I get to sit at home and play video games in my boxers! That's a, um, a plus. Also I get to pick the movies all the time, so there's another good point. But I've had sex before!"

Perhaps he should have tried harder to hold it back. But Sam snorted a laugh at that, ducking his head to hide his grin.

August faltered a little, hunching in on himself, voice trailing off as he looked for all the world like he wanted to hide. "As difficult as that is to believe."

Rolling his eyes, Sam went to the kitchen to find another glass. He poured a good shot of whiskey and handed it over to August, eyebrows tipping upward until August reluctantly took it. "I don't doubt you have," he said lowly.

August choked just as much on that as on the alcohol. "Um. Really? 'Cause most people don't like to think about it at all." He wiped his mouth with one sleeve, grimacing. "Wow, um. That's really strong."

About to make a retort involving tiny paper umbrellas and fruit on plastic spears, Sam paused. August had shaken his sleeve up around his wrist and Sam caught sight of the telltale rust-red color that could only be dried blood. Frowning in concern, he reached out to grasp August's arm, drawing him in. He held August's hand carefully between his own while he examined the palm, grunting his disapproval when he found gravel and dirt ground into the wound.

"You should have said you were hurt." He scowled, leading August to his bathroom. Sam had him take a seat on the edge of the tub. "This'll get infected."

Ignoring how he was far too concerned over a skinned palm, Sam ran a washcloth under warm water. Lips set tightly, Sam found his first-aid kit and a towel and carefully set out both as if preparing for something vastly more serious than a scrape. He settled himself beside August before resting August's hand palm up on his knee. Sam took hold of August's wrist firmly, fingers curling to rest against warm skin. He could feel August's pulse under his touch.

"I forgot about it," August admitted sheepishly. "I, uh, I almost fell when I was going into the alley, and it was either my hand or my face."

"This is going to sting." Sam dumped disinfectant onto the wound, holding August's hand still when he tried to jerk away in pain.

"Holy motherfucker," August hissed, stamping his foot a few times and clenching his jaw. "Jesus, what the hell?"

Sam gave him a bland look. "I said it'd sting."

"That was like the fire of a thousand suns, you jerk." August frowned down at his hand, watching as Sam very carefully began to clean it out. "Um. Thanks, though." August's fingers curled slightly, just barely touching Sam's hand as Sam gently brushed the washrag over the wound.

A tight lump got caught somewhere in Sam's chest; he cleared his throat, frown deepening, as he shoved that flicker of warmth away. "Yeah, well, I just don't want to hear you bitching when it gets gangrene and falls off."

Sam made the mistake of glancing up. Instead of looking down at his hand, August was watching him, gaze seemingly caught on the study of Sam's face. Everything went still. Sam's eyes met August's dark ones, and like a magnet on a string, he was pulled in. He could feel the rush of his pulse, the sharp tug of longing that drew him closer. August's lips were parted slightly. All at once, Sam was desperate to know how they tasted. If they were as soft as they looked, if they'd yield under his or if August would show that hidden strength again. If they'd fit together in a flash of heat.

"Sam," August murmured, barely more than an exhale. There was surprise in his expression, yes, probably mirrored in Sam's own. But his eyes had darkened further, gold flecks so easy to see now that Sam was so close, and he'd tilted his face up to meet Sam's.

Christ, he wanted August. It hit him, that realization, after all those months of pretending he didn't. August's free hand had come up to rest on Sam's chest, and all it'd take was one more inch, one more press forward. They were sharing air now, their twin exhales caught in the space between them. Their lips hovered, ghosting the promise of kisses, of an embrace Sam was desperate for.

One that would end the same way they all did. He'd been here before with a gorgeous boy, with the *possibilities* that so easily turned to ash. Sam's expression shuttered off, and he drew back, turning away to get the gauze from the first-aid kit.

"You should keep this dry," he muttered. Out of the corner of his eye he could see August sitting there still, looking stunned, before he drew back into his usual huddle. Sam felt a pang of guilt. Jesus fuck, he was a bastard.

But it was better that August should hate him now. Better for both of them if they didn't pretend the deck wasn't stacked. He was old and worn out; August should go make his mistakes with someone who at least could pretend life wasn't total shit.

"Yeah, um. Thanks." August awkwardly tugged his sleeve back down, covering his hand. "Sorry."

If he were a nice guy, he'd explain. He'd tell August all about Kyle and the shitstorm that had been his marriage. He'd show him the pictures of the dog he didn't have anymore, the house he couldn't go to, the half of his life he'd lost in a messy, protracted divorce. Instead, though, Sam just shrugged and cleaned up the mess, throwing the towel and the washrag in the laundry, ignoring the way August's face fell as he brushed over the whole thing with a scowl.

He wasn't a nice guy. Sooner August knew that the better off he'd be.

"So, what was that chucklefuck chasing you for, anyway?" Heading out into the kitchen, Sam relished the space, now, between him and August. Grabbing the coffeepot, Sam moved on to the sink to slosh water around in it, rinsing it out and refilling the maker. Coffee was a good "I'm not going to maul you like I increasingly want to" drink. Much better than more alcohol. "Didn't seem like your type."

August snorted, settling himself onto the couch. Sam could feel his eyes on his back, burning him straight through to the skin. He ignored it, though, refusing to give in and turn around. Just because he had some stupid, pointless crush did not mean he had to acknowledge that. He wasn't some damn teenager.

"I was, um, going through his trash." August's voice had trailed upward at the end of the sentence, making it into an almost question. "It's for a case I'm working on."

Honestly, Sam might like the way August looked—even under the far too baggy clothes and the ridiculous hat—and parts of him might melt at the way the guy smiled, but he didn't really get the *private detective* thing. Maybe because the last detective Sam had known hadn't had any of August's softness, any of his sincerity. Though he had fooled himself for a long-ass time thinking there was something real underneath all of the lies.

Then again, August had been keeping a pretty damn big secret himself, and Sam hadn't had a clue. So maybe the problem wasn't with the men who caught his attention. Maybe it was he who was fucked up.

"You in any kind of trouble?" he asked, watching the coffeepot gurgle and hiss, spitting out the first stream of fragrant brew. "He didn't look too happy with you."

"Yeah, um, I think I'm going to keep a low profile. I mean, I've got to figure this case out, but I'll just… I don't know." August shifted, wringing his hands together. "Have to do it without him seeing me."

It was clear August was worried about it. Sam wasn't too pleased himself with the idea of August getting close to the meathead. But it wasn't his place to say word one. He just nodded and poured the damn coffee.

"So this chinchilla thing." Sam tried for casual, but how casual could a guy be, asking something like that? "I mean, how do you live with it?"

The question gave August pause. He nodded at Sam in thanks when Sam handed him a mug of coffee, wrapping his fingers around the warmth. They sat on opposite sides of the couch, August mulling his answer over, Sam savoring the bracing caffeine. And it was awkward, because neither one seemed to know what to say, because the few feet between them felt like a chasm, but at the same time Sam was amazed at how relaxed he felt. How he could have had his whole world flipped upside down just an hour ago, but the thing on his mind wasn't how some people could turn small and fuzzy.

It was how the streaks of gold in August's eyes had lit up—a tiny galaxy, undiscovered and waiting for him to explore.

Jesus. He needed stronger coffee.

"How do you live with being six-foot whatever and having washboard abs?" August finally said.

Sam couldn't help the startled gunshot of a laugh. "And what makes you think I have those?" he drawled, eyebrow raised, more interested than he'd care to admit in the answer.

"Come on, look at you. You totally have washboard abs." August waved that away as if he didn't think it needed to be said. "But, I mean, it's just who you are, right? You don't wake up every morning poking various body parts, wondering how you're going to get through the day with a chiseled jaw."

It was getting harder not to smile; Sam hid it in a sardonic smirk. But he thought he got the gist of what August was going for. "You grew up with it," he surmised.

"Exactly." August shrugged and took a sip of coffee, immediately pulling a face. He hopped up to go and rustle through Sam's cupboards and fridge until he found a container of half-and-half along with the jar of sugar. "Look, if you could turn into a small, admittedly cute rodent, how would that change *your* life?"

Hesitating, Sam's instinctive answer died on his tongue. Because while he wanted to say that *everything* would be different, he wasn't quite sure that was the truth. What would anyone do, if they could change forms? Hell, his own reaction was proof enough that you couldn't exactly do it in public. And why would you want to be a fluffy rodent anyway? To fit into shoeboxes? To dust in hard to reach corners?

"Probably not much," he admitted. August had added enough milk to his drink that it almost matched his skin, all velvet smooth and milky tan. Sam was struck with an almost undeniable urge to go and bury his face in August's neck, to lick and suck that skin until he knew for sure if it tasted of cream and coffee or something else.

Something must have shifted in his tone, his expression. August dropped his eyes to his mug, an awkward hunch seeping into his shoulders. He opened and shut his mouth a few times, as if searching for words, before he nervously took a gulp of the coffee. Sam could almost see him crawl back further in his skin, that painfully held-up smile hiding the way he retreated backward, how he tried to hide.

"I used to be married." It came out, just like that. Sam scowled, arms folding tight across his chest, sitting back in his chair as if he could just dismiss the subject so easily. But August was looking at him, so he forced the words to keep coming. "For almost fifteen years. We got divorced. It was messy."

The phrases were grudgingly dropped, staccato facts that didn't really tell the whole story. Or maybe they did. What else was there to say, after all? They'd been together. Then they weren't.

"I'm sorry," August said into the silence Sam had left. "That sucks."

After a beat, Sam choked out a laugh, rubbing a hand across his mouth. "Yeah," he agreed dryly, but he could feel the way his whole expression softened in a smile, just barely there. "Yeah, it kinda did."

Nodding, August dared to sit back down, bringing his coffee with him. "So, um, yeah." Apparently that had broken the ice enough for the conversation to return to whatever passed for normal. "It's not really a big deal. Hell, tonight's the first time in a couple years I've shifted. Just never have a need to do it."

Really, he wanted to say that was weird, but Sam was having a hard time coming up with reasons why you *would* have to turn into a chinchilla. "So, this case.... You going to have to go all furry for it again?"

"God, I hope not." August rubbed the back of his neck with his nonbandaged hand. "In fact, I'd like to never do the running for my life thing ever again."

"That's probably a good plan." They shared another smile, Sam's held mostly in the crinkles he felt at the edges of his eyes, the way his scowl softened slightly for August. There was a part of him that wanted nothing more than to keep August here. To ask a thousand more questions, to listen to the calm, rolling way August would speak when he relaxed. But the clock over the stove was accusing him with angry red numbers, pointing out that it was far past time any landlord and renter should be talking.

"Let me walk you to your car," he offered, standing awkwardly, feeling as though he should be doing more. The bandage stood out stark-white against August's darker skin, and Sam felt another surge of protective anger. What if that idiot was out waiting for August? What if he wasn't safe?

August was a grown-ass man, Sam reminded himself. And he certainly wasn't in need of a scruffy old guard dog.

"Thanks." August stood as well, rubbing a hand through his hair. "Oh, shit, I left my keys in the car. What if someone stole it? God, I'm so stupid." He practically bolted out the door. Sam followed after, grabbing an umbrella for the rain. The streets were all but deserted now, the rain coming down in a furious tide. Sam shook open the umbrella and stood close enough to August to share it.

"You should be more careful," he scolded, glaring at the street, looking for the shadowy shape of anyone lurking. "What if someone was hiding in the car? What if they just *took* it? Leaving your keys in is a bonehead move."

August's shoulders slumped. "Yeah," he agreed. They picked their way across the street, August's arm warm and solid against Sam's. "I know. I was just thinking it'd be a good getaway plan, but then stuff happened."

Glancing over, Sam noticed August's whole right side was practically out in the rain. With an internal sigh, he wrapped his arm around August, tugging him in closer, sheltering them both underneath the umbrella. August nearly tripped over his own feet before he managed to fall into stride with Sam.

"Well, don't do it again" was Sam's only gruff response. It didn't mean a damn thing, them walking so close, his arm warmed by August. Just that it was stupid for them to not use the umbrella. He kept his fool eyes straight ahead, refusing to look at August, pretending to be far more absorbed in getting them to the car.

August indicated a slightly battered older Beetle parked in front of the dry cleaners. Dear Lord, was he actually trying to be undercover? He was in full view of the plate-glass windows of the shop; no wonder he'd gotten caught. Sam refused to comment on it though. Not his job. August got his rent in every month, albeit late, so obviously he knew enough to get paid. Sam was just his landlord. Nothing else.

They checked out the vehicle, making sure no one was hiding in the back seat. It looked clean. Hell, the keys were even still in the ignition. Like a fucking miracle. "So, I guess I'll, um, see you around?" August was saying. The rain was streaming down, muting the colors and the lights until everything was a shadowy swirl. But Sam could see those golden streaks in his eyes, the soft caramel of his skin, the way his hair fell across his face. The lips that begged to be touched. Everything else in the world was cut off by the deluge. Even the sounds had faded away.

Nothing existed other than August.

Maybe it was August who moved forward, holding Sam's gaze, drawing him in like a kite on a damn string. Or maybe it was Sam who leaned in, his want getting the best of him. Either way, one minute they were separate, simply two people existing apart. And then August's lips were against his like a sigh, the soft brush sweeping away the last hold of his reserve.

Parting, they stared. The light kiss was still lingering like fire against Sam's lips. August seemed just as stunned, his hand going up to touch his mouth as if he could confirm what had just happened.

He should just turn and walk away. This was goddamn foolishness of the highest order. This was *begging* to be hurt.

"Sam—" August started. He reached out to grasp Sam's arm, as if he could tell Sam was about to bolt.

That one touch electrified him. With a groan, Sam dropped the umbrella. He wrapped his arms around August and hauled him in. August's mouth claimed his, greedy and unrestrained. The rain poured down over them as Sam pressed August back against his car, as they kissed until there was no more air left within them. Like molten heat, like a dam had burst, they kissed, they tangled into each other, Sam's leg pushing between August's, August's hands fisting into Sam's hair and jerking him in closer. Sam bent him back against the hood of the car, tongue tangling with his, lips swollen with the force of their embrace.

Jerking away, Sam heaved in ragged breaths, staring wildly. August was sprawled back, soaked and panting. His lip was red from where Sam had bitten him, and his eyes were dark with want. In that moment, he was the most beautiful goddamn thing Sam had ever seen.

Shocked, Sam stood there, rain beating down, warring between desire and common sense. With a hoarse sound, a frustrated noise, he ground his teeth and grabbed the umbrella. Pressing it into August's hands, Sam then turned and walked back to the building. Back to his small, simple life.

And the rain just kept coming.

CHAPTER
FOUR

AUGUST

The alarm was blaring at me, some early-morning talk show just loud enough to be annoying. I'd hit the snooze button so many times I was pretty sure it was about to give up on me. Staring up at the ceiling, I willed my brain to turn off, just for ten more minutes. If I could get even *ten* minutes of sleep, maybe I could face the day.

My hand twinged when I curled my fingers into my palm, and I held it up, examining the bandage. Even seeing that had a little knot of heat whispering into my gut as I remembered Sam's strong fingers holding mine, the careful, deliberate way he had taken care of me. How his eyes had darkened into this incredible stormy blue when he'd gotten close. Sam was this gruff, scruffy, kind of scary guy who towered over life and acted like he was sick of all of it. But yesterday he'd been weirdly gentle, even when he'd thought I'd just been some random chinchilla.

How do you not want to kiss that guy?

I forced myself out of bed, finally, slapping off the alarm and dragging my sorry ass to the shower. I was not going to think about this. With how fast Sam had run away the night before? Apparently kissing me was not something he would ever want to repeat.

Sadly, I was *all* about the repeats. The water streaming over my head just reminded me of the rain the night before, how soaked I'd been, how every breath had been like steam, how Sam had blanketed me, solid and big and fucking *perfect*. I had never had a thing for older guys before, but something about the little bit of gray in Sam's stubble was exactly right.

For those couple of minutes, I hadn't felt like the fat, awkward kid. I'd felt important. I'd felt like I mattered, like I was sexy and strong and confident. He'd made me feel that way. That kiss had been amazing, like world-class awesome. Sam had wanted *me*.

And I was an idiot. Because however good that kiss had been, in the end, Sam had left.

At least I knew he really wasn't straight.

Driving into work, I decided the better use of my brain cells was in figuring out a new angle for the case. Jake was looking pretty damn guilty. Who would waste that much energy chasing after someone digging through their trash? Someone with something to hide, that was who. So I'd just dig a little into Jake's background, see if I could pick up on something that might clue me in on how he was stealing the money in plain sight of cameras and coworkers.

I'd admit to walking a little slower past the steps that lead down to Sam's apartment. I'd clumsily rewrapped my hand that morning and for a moment I considered using that as an excuse. After all, it was hard to tape gauze neatly when you were down to one hand and your teeth. In the end, though, I held strong. I marched purposefully to the elevator and up to my office with nary a sideways glance.

After all, I was a gumshoe. A detective. A private dick. I didn't have time for men who distracted me. Wasn't that always what got them into trouble in the movies? Some beautiful dame with legs up to here would come walking in and that was when everything went to hell. Well, never let it be said I could be swayed by a perfect jaw and blue eyes. I had learned my lesson from countless books and movies. Love only got in the way.

I spread out the information I had in neat piles on my desk. Chin resting on my good hand, I started at the beginning. Three weeks ago, Mr. Petros's bookkeeper had noticed his deposits weren't adding up.

The only explanation he could come up with was that someone was skimming from the nightly till drops, which pointed to one of his three shop employees. None of them closed alone and none of them worked every night. The worst part was, though, they didn't tally up the cash after every shift, so no one knew if it was off until the weekly trip to the bank.

After three hours of staring at the possibilities, my head had started to hurt. I went around and around in circles, but every stinking time, I landed at the same spot. I didn't have enough information.

"I need coffee," I told Cocky, burying my face in my hands. "And a brain transplant."

There was something missing. Some vital piece of the puzzle that simply hadn't shown up yet. Heaving a sigh, I got up to fuss with the coffeepot. Wearily, I poked a finger at yesterday's grounds. The coffee can was nearly empty. If I used fresh today, I wouldn't have any more tomorrow. Glancing around like I expected my mother to pop up from behind the couch and scold me, I put the old grounds into a fresh filter and turned the machine on.

My parents didn't like that I'd moved farther away. They *hated* that I was trying to be a detective. Then again, my father, my grandfather, and two of my great-uncles all worked at the same plumbing business. The Mendezes didn't handle change well. Striking out on my own, starting a business, living alone—all of that might be normal in any other family. But for us, for our tight-knit herd, I was an anomaly.

And now I'd let some outsider see me shift.

Seriously, somewhere my mother was being struck with an urge to shout at me and she didn't know why.

The kiss had overwhelmed the other thoughts about last night. Now that I was refusing to think about that aspect of it, certain other things were becoming clearer. Like that I had to make sure Sam understood how vital it was that he never tell anyone what he'd seen. And that Jake might become a serious problem. He'd recognized me, which meant he was going to be looking for me. Normally I'd just keep my head down and park the next block over, but this case wouldn't let me keep my distance.

I was close to something; I had to be. I just needed a little more information. Whatever had been in those garbage bags last night had been worth chasing me over. Perhaps that was a good place to start.

The building was eerily empty on Saturdays. Normally I'd be at home too, but the dry cleaners were only open a half-day today. I had a perfect shot to snoop around in the nonscary daylight. The problem was, I couldn't exactly just walk over there. What if Jake was around? What if he had a partner he'd told about me? As much fun as my impromptu run was—and as much as I totally still felt it in my calves— without the cover of darkness my last-ditch plan Z was kind of out. I hadn't even gotten away with the chinchilla thing in the pitch-black. No way was I going to pull it off midafternoon.

I didn't want to be standing outside of Sam's door. And no way did this have anything to do with last night. But he was the only person I really knew in the city, and definitely the only one I could use at short notice. Which was why, shifting back and forth, worriedly gnawing on my lower lip, I gathered up my courage and knocked.

It was like he'd been waiting for me. The door flew open and Sam was there, half a head taller than me, scruffy and not quite put together, and totally gorgeous. If you were into that. Which I was not, no sir. He was wearing these faded jeans that hugged his legs like they'd been created just for that, and a blue flannel shirt that really shouldn't be working for him. God, it was.

Again, if that was what you liked. I personally couldn't have cared less.

"August," he rumbled, silky tones hooking right into my stomach and dragging me forward until I was vibrating from them. "Isn't it Saturday?" His eyebrows raised as he glanced down at his watch. "Before noon? I must be hallucinating."

Sam was acting like nothing had happened. Like I'd had some rain-fueled wet dream and we were just our usual selves. Which was fine. Probably smart, really. What did I care that he'd bent me back over my car and kissed the hell out of me? That wasn't, like, a fantasy or anything. It was just a thing that may or may not have happened. We were two grown men.

God, his lips were nice.

Gah. "Yeah, well, I, uh, had case... stuff," I explained lamely. "Actually, can I, um, maybe come in for, like, a second, really? Not long. Just wanted to ask you for a favor."

There was a long beat with Sam staring at me where I was pretty sure he was going to just close the door on me. I wasn't really sure if I'd blame him or not. But in the end he moved aside for me to enter his apartment. It all looked exactly the same. Which, of course it did—I didn't think Sam had gotten up at the crack of dawn to redecorate. It just felt like it should. Like all the fear and the shock and the surprising gentleness, the heat that had turned a stupid crush into something so much more.... It should have taken place somewhere I couldn't get back to. Like the Brigadoon of one-night stands. Our kiss, that moment, it needed to exist in a perfect memory.

"Sorry about the mess." Sam went to the kitchen, where he started busily pushing dishes around in the sink. "I just finished lunch."

"No worries." I tapped out a nervous rhythm against my leg with my fingers as I watched him. He was acting like scrubbing that pan was going to magically erase my presence. "Um, I just needed to... I mean, I know you probably get it. But I really need you to understand that you can't talk to anyone. About me."

Sam switched on the water, his back still to me. I raised my voice a little, hopefully, like volume was going to suddenly make him super excited I was there. "It's just... my herd, you know? Not even only my herd. All of us. It's too dangerous, to have an average out there talking about how some people can go all fluffy. We don't tell anyone. Ever. I think you might be the first person outside the family to know about us in a couple decades. So...."

The guy was Martha freaking Stewart right then, drying off the dishes, putting them away, completely ignoring everything I was saying. Which, okay, fine, we were ix-naying the kissing talk. I got that. Hell, it wouldn't be the first time someone, in the harsh light of day, regretted doing something with me. But this wasn't about some stupid—*awesome*—kiss. This was about my family.

Which could have been why instead of slinking off, I grabbed his arm and forced him to turn around. "Hey," I said, glaring at him. "Look, just *acknowledge* what I'm saying, okay? This might not be a big deal to you, but it's kind of important to me. So stop being a dick for five freaking seconds and tell me you understand."

Maybe that had startled him, because Sam just looked at me. It was like he'd looked at me last night, as if he was really seeing me for the first time. I felt my cheeks warm, but I just held his gaze stubbornly, hand still gripping his arm.

"Sorry," he grunted, which might have been a miracle in and of itself. Sam rumbled out a breath and tossed the dish towel over to the sink, leaning back against the counter. "Yeah, I get it. Your secret's safe with me." He huffed an incredulous laugh, rubbing his hand across his face. "Not like anyone'd believe me, anyway."

I let him go, rubbing my hands together to erase the tingle of his skin. "Yeah, well." Smirking slightly, I shrugged. "Little furry things that turn into people probably will get you an up-close-and-personal tour of a crazy house, true."

"Look, August...." His voice faded into a sigh; all at once he was right there, was standing so close I swore I could feel his heart beating against my chest. He wasn't that much taller than me, really, but somehow when he did that it seemed like he was massive. I had a sudden, vivid memory of the way his stubble felt against my cheek, how his kisses had tasted like whiskey and peppermint. "You can trust me." His eyes were this heavenly blue, and I stared up into them, forgetting every good reason I had for shoving last night into a box and forgetting it. "I wouldn't do anything to put you or your family in danger. I'll keep my mouth shut."

The stupid thing was, I did trust him. I believed he was worth that much.

"Okay." My mouth was so dry. "Thanks." I was the one that stepped back this time, ducking my head, fidgeting with the hem of my shirt. "I guess I'll leave you to your dishes."

I'd turned on my heel and was halfway to the door before his voice stopped me. "Wait. Was that it? The favor?" If I didn't know better—and I did, I *really* did—I'd say there was some rough longing in his voice. He'd moved forward after me; when I looked back he was standing there, all broad shoulders and gray at his temples and strangely vulnerable.

I had forgotten why I was there. Or maybe I'd just thought better of it. Either way, it took me a moment to remember. "Oh, uh, I guess there was one more thing. I'm still on this case, you know, for Mr. Petros? The one I was working on last night too. Well, I can't exactly go over there now." I lifted one shoulder in a shrug, cutting Sam another glance. Surprisingly, he looked thunderously angry just at the mention of what had happened. "With Jake maybe being around."

"What do you need me to do?" Just like that.

I blinked in surprise. Honestly, I'd been expecting to have to beg or promise to wash floors or something. Even then, I'd only half hoped he'd say yes. "There was something last night in their garbage. Jake caught me before I could see too much, but I have this hunch. They threw out two big, black garbage bags, full of, like, lint and papers. I was thinking maybe that was how they were getting the money out."

"You think they'll still be there?" Sam was already tugging on his boots.

"I'm not sure," I admitted. "But it's the best lead I've got."

He cut a little glance at me, but he finished lacing up his boots and nodded. "Stay here. I'll be back." Before I could get out a protest he was gone, shutting the door behind him.

Well. That'd been easier than I'd anticipated. Although now I was left to sit around and, what, clutch my pearls? Just because some big guy had chased me yesterday and I'd barely missed getting my face beaten in didn't mean I was *helpless*. I could have done something.

Puttering around Sam's apartment, I found myself putting away the dishes he'd left, wiping off the counter. It felt stupidly domestic, using the same dishrag as he had, cleaning up after a meal he'd made. Nice, though. His apartment was bigger than mine, and even though the only windows were small ones set high up in the walls, it felt airy and clean. Sam obviously liked to keep things orderly.

Once the last cup was put away, I wandered the room, half snooping. There weren't any pictures of him anywhere. One of a dog, a big shaggy collie, but nothing else.

Divorced, he'd said. I had to wonder if it'd been a man or a woman. Sam hadn't kissed me like a straight guy, that was for sure. Maybe he'd been closeted? It wasn't uncommon. I tried to guess his age from his CD collection. Old-school Metallica, Johnny Cash, and a rather eclectic collection of what looked like foreign folk music didn't give me any answers, though I had to wonder who bought CDs anymore, anyway. That could be my answer.

"See anything you like?"

I jumped, nearly dropping the bookend I'd been examining. Sam was standing there, a bemused smile just barely lifting the edges of his lips. He held two black trash bags. After scrambling to put the bookend back so it didn't tip over, I moved toward him to eagerly haul one of the sacks close, sinking to my knees so I could dig through it.

"I was playing 'guess the age,'" I admitted, wrinkling my nose when I encountered another huge ball of lint. "Unsuccessfully."

That seemed to surprise him. He regarded me quietly for a moment before pulling up a chair, sitting down, and carefully undoing the second bag. "Forty-six," he admitted, looking over at me almost sheepishly. "What am I looking for?"

Huh. "Thirty." I shrugged. "Almost thirty-one. And I'm not sure. There were all these receipts, but I didn't get a good chance to read over them."

Sam nodded. His expression had shuttered off again and I had to wonder if it was the age thing. He just looked so damn *resigned*; I wasn't sure how to even begin to unravel that. So I just concentrated on going through the piles of paper in my garbage bag.

I wasn't thinking about *him* stuff, anyway. Just focusing on the case.

In silence we continued to dig. Every so often one of us would make a soft noise of interest or hold something out for the other to see. Mostly, though, we focused on separating true garbage from something potentially useful. After half an hour we had a pile of carefully uncrumpled yellow receipts, obviously ripped out of a book, and a smaller stack of white receipts.

And I had no fucking clue what any of it meant.

Sagging back, I scrubbed my hands across my face, through my hair, trying to bite back my frustration. All my good ideas and I was the same place I'd been this morning. Sam stretched, hands on the small of his back, and stood. He got the trash out of the way and headed into the kitchen. I ignored him as I picked up one of the receipts and looked at it before letting it drop back to the table, frustrated.

What was I doing? I wasn't a damn detective. I didn't even know where to *start*, much less how to solve this.

I was startled when a mug appeared, as if by magic, in front of my face. It was carried by Sam, his eyes crinkling slightly at my startled expression. "It's coffee," he urged. "With an ungodly amount of sugar and cream. Take it."

I did, slowly, staring at him the whole time like I expected a punch line. But no, just damn good coffee, which I drank appreciatively. Settling in, legs crossed and my back resting against the side of a chair, I gave a baleful glare at the piles of paperwork. "Thanks," I said, lifting the mug slightly, "for this. And for going and getting this stuff. I'm sorry to waste your time."

Sam had sat back into the chair opposite me, the table between us. He seemed more comfortable there for whatever reason. "How do you know it was a waste?"

Like it wasn't obvious. "It's just… junk. A bunch of papers that don't mean anything." I sighed into my coffee, miserable. "I've got a big fat nothing on this case." Shit, and now I'd never afford rent next month. Not that I was going to tell Sam that.

Sam gave a vaguely supportive hum, but he was busy looking through the stack of yellow receipts. "You don't have anything yet," he agreed. "But that's the key. Yet. Come on, your gut told you to dig into this. There might be something here."

"My gut also convinces me that eating cookie dough from the tube at 2:00 a.m. is a fantastic idea," I grumbled. But I did sit up again, picking through the white receipts with a scowl. "My gut is an idiot."

Sam laughed quietly. For some reason, that one noise sent little shivers down my spine. I liked his laugh. It occurred to me, then, that I didn't hear it nearly enough. It broke through some of my bad mood, and I settled in to give the paper more than a cursory glance.

The coffee was nearly gone, the last dregs of it cold, when I got through my stack. Setting them down, I shook my head. "Anything?" I asked him, hopeful.

He hesitated, looking over at me. Grimacing faintly, he set the last handful of receipts back on his pile. "Sorry. They look like normal dry-cleaning tickets to me. A little expensive, yeah, but nothing nefarious."

"Great." Flopping back, I rolled my head on my shoulders, wincing at the sharp pain of a crick forming there. "I am officially the worst detective in the world."

"I wouldn't say that," Sam protested.

"No? This is my first big case that's not 'follow this guy and take pictures,' and what happens? I have no ideas. Less than no ideas. I owe the universe ideas at this point." Picking up one of his papers, I waved it at him. "This is garbage. I just made you spend your afternoon looking through garbage, because I am a crazy person. You know what this is?"

"You had a hunch." Sam wrapped long fingers around his coffee mug, seemingly just for something to do with his hands. "That's what people do when they're investigating. They follow hunches, they gather evidence, until the whole story comes out."

"Yeah, well, I watch TV too. They also *solve things*, which I am failing spectacularly at," I grumbled, reading over the receipt just so I didn't have to look at him. So I wouldn't have to see the kindness in his eyes. I didn't want it. Sam was way too confusing for me while I was having a mental break.

"My ex was a cop." That got my attention. I snuck a glance up at Sam to find him studying his mug like it held the answers to all the mysteries in the world. "He made detective while we were together. Trust me, they don't always solve everything."

He. Well, that answered one question. "This isn't exactly the Lindbergh baby," I pointed out. "I'm missing something. I mean, as much as I enjoyed reading about Mr. Wang's trousers...."

Wait. I knew that name. Frowning, I dug through the pile of white receipts, scattering them as I searched. My heartbeat picked up as I closed my fingers on the right one, eagerly scanning it. Mr. Wang had brought in a pair of trousers for stain removal last week. Ticket number 5406A. Both the receipt and its carbon copy held the same number, the same customer information, the same garment.

The difference was the price.

"Holy shit." I stared, stunned. "I know how they're doing it. Maybe. I know *something* at least."

"What did you find?" Sam slipped over next to me, leaning against my shoulder to take a look. I watched his gaze go between the two, and it took him far less time than it'd taken me to put the pieces together. "This one is about twenty percent higher." He pointed at the yellow ticket. "They're overcharging the customer and, what? Turning in the white copies to the bookkeeper? That way they can pocket the overage."

"I don't know," I admitted. "It could be. In any case, this is definitely not trash."

A smile creased Sam's face. "I would say not. How did you find it?"

Oh. Uh. I could feel a faint blush stain my cheeks. "The name?" I croaked, feeling like I wanted to crawl under the table. "I thought it was funny." Because I was secretly fourteen.

Sam's laugh was unexpected and I found myself grinning at him. "A case cracked by Wang," he intoned seriously around the sparkle in his eye, the amusement in his voice.

"That is going on the business cards," I returned. That wonderful *flutter* was back in my stomach. We were sitting close, Sam smiling at me, and it felt *good*. It felt just as good as getting a break in my first big case.

Twenty percent markup didn't seem like enough money to go through all of this work. I fiddled with the receipts, glancing over the amounts, the dates. It was about a week's worth of sales, it seemed like. "Do you have a calculator?" I had a hunch. And that was what Sam said detectives did, right?

After Sam handed me the calculator, I started to go through the receipts, comparing the price on the yellow to the white, adding up the differences. Sam caught on pretty quickly and began helping as well. As the stack dwindled, the number on the screen just kept increasing.

Two thousand, six hundred and thirty-one dollars. In one week.

Sam whistled lowly when I showed him my calculations. "That's a pretty big payday."

"Nearly two hundred thousand a year," I agreed. And that was just what we'd found. It could possibly be a lot more. "Definitely not chump change."

"Worth going to some trouble to cover it up." Sam nodded. When he smiled at me again, it was like I couldn't stop grinning back. Like I never wanted to try.

"Thanks," I whispered.

"What for?" His eyebrows were doing that thing again, that half raise that meant I'd confused him. They did that a lot.

"If it wasn't for you, I'd have given up. I'm, um." I fidgeted, shrugging. "I'm not very good at this."

"Yet," he murmured. I felt the thrill of that word all down my spine.

Yet. The possibility of more. Of change.

I liked that word. I liked the way he *said* that word. I liked the *yet* that hovered between us.

BACK in my office, I spread the receipts out carefully. One by one, I matched them up until I had a desk covered in yellow sheets with white slips neatly paper-clipped on top. The answer was right here. I had the *how*, at least a part of it, and now that I knew that, the rest of the pieces should fall into place.

Right. Any second now I was going to get a flash of inspiration.

The problem was, this didn't point to some entry-level worker skimming money out of the register at night. This was organized. Thoughtful. This meant management, possibly Mr. Petros himself. But why would he call *me* in? An investigation would just expose whatever he was doing. All I'd have to do is call the Sally family, let them know their manager was stealing, and it'd be over.

It didn't make sense.

My thoughts circled around and around the problem, always winding up at the same spot. This evidence pointed to Mr. Petros. But Mr. Petros had hired me. So it couldn't be him. Around and around I went, but I got exactly nowhere.

Exhausted, hungry, I switched off my light and tugged on my coat to leave. Grabbing my fedora, I headed out toward the elevator. There was something obvious I was missing. There had to be. This was always the part in the movie where the hero missed some big thing, only to have it become obvious later on.

Going out to my car, I glanced across the street. It was nearing dark now, the twilight shadows creeping across the sidewalks. The dry cleaners was empty, no cars parked anywhere. If I knew how to break in without triggering the alarm, now would be a perfect time to take a look around.

Then again, maybe I didn't need a lockpick.

Scurrying back inside, I clomped down the stairs to Sam's door. Knocking briskly three times, I waited, eagerly seesawing from one foot to the other, practically dancing with anticipation. I had an idea. A *good* idea. A Spade-worthy idea.

And it involved Sam. Total A-plus in my book.

Sam answered the door in soft, faded sweatpants, shirtless, a towel slung over one shoulder. For a moment, my brain completely fritzed out. There was dark hair softly curling on Sam's chest, light flecks of gray in it to match his stubble, winding down to his belly button and trailing down farther, disappearing under the waist of his pants. I stared, eyes wide, cheeks on fire. There was an overwhelming urge to reach out and bury my fingers in it, to trace the faint outline of his abs, to catch one nipple between my teeth and feel it harden under my tongue.

Jesus. "Hi." The one word I did manage came out nearly strangled. My pulse was pounding in my temple, blood rushing every which way but up. God, how did one guy have the ability to make me into a complete idiot?

And he knew it too. I could tell by the way he was looking at me, the darkening of his eyes, the rise and fall of his chest. He could see how badly I wanted him right then. If I could have crawled into a hole and died, I think I would have.

"I thought you'd gone for the day," Sam was saying, toweling off his hair. It stuck up in the wake of his assault in damp waves. I itched to tangle my fingers in them, recalling with perfect clarity how they'd felt sliding against my skin, heavy with raindrops.

"What?" Blinking, I had to take a moment to let my brain catch up with the conversation. "Oh, right. Uh, nope, still here. I actually was going to leave, but then I had an idea and I came down here to tell you about it, because it was a good idea, and then you answered the door with no shirt. Which is fine! Totally. You can definitely pull off the no-shirt thing. I just look like a tanned Stay Puft Marshmallow Man, like, attacking the town, who-you-gonna-call-type thing, but not you. You are definitely... shirtless."

Some days I really thought that cutting off my tongue would be a viable option. Sam just looked down at himself, huffing a quiet laugh. "Yeah, sorry. I just got out of the shower."

Bad brain. No mental pictures of water sluicing over all that skin.... Abruptly I turned around, staring wildly at the far wall and definitely not at Sam. "Okay, well, that's totally fine," I managed, voice a bit more high-pitched than normal. "After, you know, everything you've done I really hate to ask you for something else."

He'd moved closer instead of retreating inside to put on a shirt like I'd hoped. I could feel him, heat against my back, hovering there barely far enough away to not be touching me. "Don't worry about it," he murmured, and I jumped to feel his breath against my neck. "What do you need?"

You. That was the only answer that came to mind. If I just shifted back a half a step, I'd be pressed up against him. His lips could trail along my jaw, his hands could settle at my waist....

Where he'd encounter rolls of fat. He could touch my stomach, which was just a big fucking blob, or my arms, which were gross, or realize my *jaw* was more round than chiseled. Sam was standing there, so goddamn comfortable in his own skin. Sure, he wasn't a model or anything, but he was definitely not an eyesore. I'd stare at him, happily, any day of the week. He was *Sam,* with that gravelly voice and the way he smiled, and I thought he was pretty near perfect. I couldn't let him touch me. I couldn't stand to see the disgust in his eyes when he realized exactly what he'd gotten himself into.

I'd fantasized about this. Hell, I'd had a very nice image of the two of us only a minute ago. But in my head, I was.... Well, I was the me in my head. I was the image everyone had of themselves in the body they'd feel comfortable with. The reality, though, now that it was here, now that I felt Sam shift forward behind me, was vastly different.

His hand lightly touched my side, and I flinched. I wanted to enjoy it. I wanted to do a Snoopy happy dance and drag the shirtless Sam back into his apartment. In my head, it was so easy. I'd turn, I'd meet his eyes, and then there'd be a hell of a lot more of that kissing. Before, I'd been stunned, and I hadn't had time to think about anything but the press of Sam, the way our mouths had devoured each other. Now, though, there was quite a lot of thinking. So I flinched.

And I kind of hated myself for it.

I darted away, up the stairs, calling back, "Never mind, we can talk later." I caught a glimpse of his face, some inscrutable mix of relief and longing, before I rounded the corner at the top of the stairs and bolted for the door.

Gulping in the cool evening air, I managed to get all the way to my car before my hands started shaking. I fumbled the keys, scraping marks all around the lock. It wasn't that I hadn't had sex before. There'd been a couple of guys over the years and yeah, I'd been naked and everything. So I'd been there before. But it'd been a while. A year and a half, to be exact, and I'd put on a few more pounds. Or thirty. So where I'd been definitely chubby before, now I was fat. Just fat. And I couldn't stand to let Sam see that fully. Not him. Someone like me, maybe, or someone more my league. Sam was so far out of my league that he was playing football and I was sneaking cupcakes under the bleachers.

All day long I could daydream about this. Sam was worth a few idle fantasies. But when it became real, when it was starting to happen, all I could think about were my flaws. The only possible endings were the worst-case scenarios. Underneath the fat-guy-required self-deprecation, I'd apparently started to loathe my body so much that the immediate prospect of sex with a hot guy made me panic. Just great. Because being me wasn't stupid enough, now we were adding self-esteem issues Dr. Phil would deem overdramatic.

"August." Sam was there, standing outside my car as I finally managed to get the door open. He stopped me from closing it behind me, a frown creasing his forehead as he took in my miserable hunch, the way my hands were clutching the steering wheel. "August, what's wrong?" His voice got so soft and he crouched down so he could try and see my face. "Did someone hurt you?"

Yes, sir. It was Captain Crunch and the infamous Twinkie Twins. They did a drive-by fattening.

I shook my head, not trusting my voice. With a sigh, Sam stood and I thought he was just going to leave me alone, a thought that filled me with both relief and an ache I couldn't even begin to identify. I didn't want him to see me like this, to ask questions I might have to answer. What was I going to say? *Sorry that I eat both my feelings and the feelings of the person at the drive-through window, and the idea of you touching me or seeing me naked makes me want to go have an entire cheesecake. Logic has left the building.* But at the same time, I really didn't want him to go.

There was the creak of the passenger-side door opening, and Sam folded himself into the front seat, leather squeaking under him as he adjusted it back. His long legs barely fit, but he didn't seem bothered. He just sat next to me, calmly watching out the window, while I clung to the steering wheel and refused to look over at him.

It wasn't fair. He shouldn't be in my space. This was my wallowing space; it was clearly marked and he was just sitting there. Being patient. Big, stupid, patient man.

"You worried about Jake?" he asked lowly. I almost laughed.

Yeah. That was it. Not my crippling self-esteem ruining the once-in-a-lifetime opportunity I'd had to maybe, possibly have a moment with someone as great as Sam. It was the giant douchebag. "No," I managed thickly. "No, it's nothing. I'm fine."

I dared to glance at him. He'd pulled on a shirt, but his boots were crammed haphazardly on, one pant leg still tucked into the laces. Clearly he'd run out after me. What was that supposed to mean? He kissed me like we'd been in some romance movie or a music video and then he ran away. He helped me with my case, he answered the door shirtless and had *no* shame, and now he was in my car. I had no fucking clue what was going on.

"You came to me for something," he prompted. "What was that about?"

A sigh escaped me, my whole body slumping forward. "I, uh. I was going to do some spying. You know, since no one is at the dry cleaners. But I needed your help getting in."

He rubbed a thumb across his lower lip, thinking. "I'm not sure I know how to break in," Sam admitted. I had to bite back a laugh. He looked kind of upset to reveal that he was not, in fact, James Bond.

"It's okay. I do." I'd admit to enjoying the incredulous look Sam shot my way. He wasn't pushing me about my sudden hand-wringing drama-queen moment; talking about the case was easier. We worked well together. Being friends was an option, if I hadn't ruined it. I'd like to be Sam's friend. "I just need a ride."

Sam had half turned toward me, filling my car with the tang of his soap, the faint oaky undertone of his aftershave. I could feel his eyes studying me while I tried to look like I wasn't a giant, jiggly ball of issues. "Okay," Sam drawled after a beat. "I'll bite."

Which was how I wound up as a chinchilla, once more riding in Sam's pocket. I'd waited outside his bedroom door while he changed clothes, shifting when he told me he was triple sure the coast was clear. Watching him from what had seemed like a million miles away, Sam had looked kind of enthralled with the whole thing. His fingers were rough with callouses, but he was so incredibly gentle with me when he picked me up, rubbing his thumb along my side. I'd admit to being a total attention whore in my shift. It just felt good, man, to have someone petting me, especially if they scratched just behind my ear. And hey, chinchillas were supposed to be fat! We were fluffy and soft, so no one could judge me.

In his pocket, I felt every step as a jarring bump. Amazing how different everything was when you were six inches long. Sticking my nose out of the side of his hoodie pocket, I watched as we swayed our way across the street, street lamps making enormous pools of light against the darkened sidewalk. I would have just done this myself, but shifting in the alley by the dry cleaner's in the early evening when anyone could be walking by was far too risky. And changing at the office meant a block and a half journey. Where with Sam's long legs, the walk was an easy five minutes. As a chubby ball of fur, it'd be a danger-filled dash across a road filled with rolling death machines. Much safer this way.

Sam's hand rested lightly against the pocket, the warmth of his palm encouraging me to curl up next to it. I nudged him through the fabric, and I felt him breathe out a laugh, stomach rising and falling with the sound. "Okay, hold your horses. We're almost there." He was muttering to me under his breath, and if I could have smiled then, I would have. I could just see him, this big, gruff guy, talking to the fluff ball in his pocket. Probably quite a sight.

The world lurched as Sam knelt, and then he slipped his hand inside to grasp me lightly, pulling me out into the night air. I blinked, head raising, ears twitching to pick up the soft whisper of sound from the street beyond us. It was quiet, other than the wind rustling some old newspaper, the soft slush of traffic, the quick beat of Sam's heart. I looked up at him, nudging my nose against his palm.

"You be careful," he said, raising me up slowly so that we were eye level. "I'm not going in after your hairy ass."

Chittering at him to show him what I thought of that, I stretched my neck out, touching our noses together. His eyelashes fluttered in surprise before his eyes creased in a smile. "Okay, fine. I'd go in. But I wouldn't like it."

Fair enough. Once I'd moved to the edge of his palm, I wiggled myself, indicating I wanted down. Sam obliged, and I picked my way cautiously over to the wall, nosing my way along, looking for an entrance. My chance came at one of the basement windows. There were iron bars over a screen, but the glass was open. The acrid stink of harsh chemicals assaulted my nose. I had to pause, sitting up on my haunches, rubbing my paws over my face, trying to rub the scent out of my fur.

Ugh. I was going to stink for days.

It took me a few minutes of nibbling to get through the screen. It left a terrible stale, dusty coating on my tongue, but I was finally able to squirm through the opening and onto the windowsill. The drop to the floor looked a little bit like BASE jumping into the center of the earth. Crap. If I shifted here, I'd definitely fall off midturn, and from experience I knew that would bruise. Oddly, I was tougher with fur than skin.

Well, no guts, no glory. I waddled right off the edge of the ledge, curling into a ball on the way down and braced for impact. I hit and bounced, dazed, rolling off under a chair. For several shaky breaths, I laid still, heart a thundering beat in my ears. No one was rushing in to investigate the case of the death-defying fluff ball, so gradually I stretched my legs out, experimentally wiggling my paws. Nothing seemed broken.

I was a little wobbly when I stood, but as I went creeping across the cement floor my balance returned. We Chinchas were tougher than we looked. Of course, small babies in knitted hats were tougher than we looked, but the point remained.

Sneezing several times as I got closer to the source of the harsh chemical smell, I sat up and scrubbed my face with my paws again, obsessively trying to clean the stink off my whiskers. This must be where they did the cleaning. I could see, towering above me, a truly terrifying array of machines I could only begin to guess the purpose of.

After darting around the legs of the machines, iron bars bolted to the ground, I found a door. Which was shut. Well, it'd been fun while it'd lasted. Closing my eyes and concentrating, I felt the tickle of fur retreating back into skin, the grind of bones shifting back into place. When I opened my eyes, the world flared with color again. My nose was almost as good as it had been, which I proved when I started another sneezing fit over the dry-cleaning solutions. Jesus, I didn't know how anyone worked down here without getting a migraine.

I had my gloves in my coat pocket and I tugged them on now. It took me a couple of seconds of painful fumbling to get one on over the bandages on my left hand. I jerked it down and nearly fell backward when it finally slid into place. That done, I eased open the door, peering around it, careful not to touch anything I didn't need to. I'd watched enough crime shows to know what a tiny hair could do.

The hallway I found was dark and cramped, filing cabinets crammed in on both sides. I followed the narrow path to the staircase that led up toward the shop, stumbling over a bit of buckled carpet before the first step. My arm shot out to catch my fall against the nearest door, which immediately slammed open, sending me headlong tumbling into the darkened room beyond.

Take that, James Bond.

Rolling over onto my back, I stared up at the ceiling and took a moment to thank whoever was the patron saint of klutzes that Sam had not seen that. I'd already had an embarrassing breakdown, he so did not need to see me tripping over my own feet. With a groan, I sat up to try to struggle back to my feet. I'd landed in some kind of office, filing cabinets crowded around a small desk. On the door was a small, plastic nameplate.

Accounting.

The bookkeeper, Mr. Petros had said, was the one who originally found the discrepancies. I found the light switch and cautiously switched it on. I scanned the office, moving slowly around the room. Each drawer on the cabinets was neatly labeled with a month and a year. I picked one from three months ago, tugging it open to find obsessively ordered file folders. Which actually might even be color-coded. This was not a woman who would miss something as big as a complicated overcharging scheme.

And yet she had. For who knew how many months. The receipts Sam and I had found were from the last few weeks, before Petros had contacted me, so who knew how long, really, the scam had been going on? Yet from all appearances, this woman was organized to the hilt.

Maybe she was in on it? But then why would she even bring it up, much less start an investigation?

Curiouser and curiouser.

Paging through the files, I frowned. Every one of them was the white paper, like the receipts we'd found with the lower prices. They were stapled to a spreadsheet printout showing the cash amounts for that week, balancing at the bottom. So the bookkeeper was getting the fake, cheaper receipts and using them to check that the money was correct. Only, because she was going off bad info, she didn't know she was short what they actually took in. Something had happened to make the bookkeeper notice the discrepancy. But what?

On a hunch, I went hunting for the folder labeled for this past week. We had those receipts in my office, so they shouldn't be here. Sure enough, the drawer that should have been for this week was empty. So someone had tossed out the evidence, but why? Who?

Every time I thought I figured something out, I got three more questions.

Opening a drawer at random, I found the receipts from a year ago. They were the white paper we'd found, folder after folder of them. So that must be what they'd been using for a while. So where did the yellow slips come in? Curious, I flicked off the lights and headed upstairs, more careful this time to not fall on my face.

The only light coming in from the big plate-glass windows was from the street lamps outside. I picked my way cautiously up to the register, waiting for my eyes to adjust to the dark enough for me to see. On the shelves underneath were stacks of receipt books. Yellow. So, they took the cash, wrote out a yellow receipt, and gave the bottom half to the customer, the top half going into the register for the count. Somewhere between the front end and the cramped office in the basement, someone was altering the amounts and skimming money from the tills.

The counter was pretty much bare—the *cash only* sign, a list of services, and a container with pens. The service prices matched what I remembered from the higher-priced receipts. Whatever was going on here, it'd been happening for a while, and it was much bigger than someone grabbing cash out of a drawer.

A shadow outside jerked my attention up. There was someone approaching the door. I was hidden from sight now, in the dark interior, but all it'd take was two steps in and I'd be more than visible.

Panicked, I started back toward the stairs only to realize I had no way out. The window was too high to reach in my chinchilla shift, but the ledge was too narrow for me to stay on in this form so I could change.

Yeah. Apparently my genius plan had one rather glaring hole.

Okay. Plan B. As I heard the key in the front door, I shifted. Faster than I'd ever done it, I focused on that other form, on the instincts itching in the back of my mind. It was strange; I'd never really thought about it before, until Sam had asked, but being what I was really didn't seem *weird* to me. I didn't feel like I was something odd. The chinchilla was just another part of me. I didn't really think of it as something separate. Right then, I was letting myself sink into that form, shrinking rapidly behind the counter.

Without giving myself time to freak out about close calls, I zoomed across the floor toward the entrance. As the door swung open I zoomed out, dodging past brown leather shoes and out onto the sidewalk, catching a whiff of what smelled like strong tobacco as I passed. I didn't give the person time to react to a chinchilla, of all things, escaping like a bat out of hell from the store. I darted into the alley and started squeaking my freaking heart out.

A hand closed around me. I twisted in the tight grip, scrabbling my claws against the wrist. My heart was beating a thousand miles an hour, pure panic overtaking me. I'd gotten caught. The one thing that had been hammered in my head, over and over, since I was a kid was *don't get caught,* and now it was happening.

"Chill out, Mendez." Sam's rumble echoed around me. I was pulled up to his chest, both of his hands cradling me. "It's just me."

Jesus fuck. Slowly I calmed down enough to actually pay attention to what was happening. Sam's scent was that spice of soap, beer, and something else, something deep and masculine. I liked it. He was holding me carefully, letting my heartbeat return to normal, slowly stroking fingers through my fur. I nuzzled into his chest, and he huffed a laugh, the rolling gait of his walking rocking me lightly. Whoever had gone inside obviously hadn't seen me, or cared enough to come looking for an unknown rodent. Sam carried me carefully back across the street, as I snuffled up to his neck, his chin, chittering happily when I felt him laugh again.

That was a good sound. I wanted that to happen again.

In the safety of Sam's apartment, I changed back, flopping down onto his couch with a groan. "Next time I decide to go all furry undercover, remind me that I need an exit plan."

Sam snorted under his breath, rustling around in his kitchen and returning with two beers. "That's probably a good thing, yeah." Handing off one of the bottles to me, he lounged out next to me on the couch. Not, I noted, on the chair opposite. "What'd you find out?"

I was hoping we wouldn't revisit my little freak-out. I liked Sam. I really liked Sam's broad shoulders and chest and the little divot in his chin, sure, but I liked Sam himself, and getting to hang out with him as more than the grumpy landlord was pretty high on my priority list. So if I just put aside my little crush, we'd be good.

"I found the accounting office," I said with a quick grin, enjoying my role as the storyteller. Taking a long drink of my beer, I settled in, turned to face Sam with one leg drawn up on the couch. He was sitting much the same way, his arm casually slung across the back, fingers resting, curled, a few inches from me. If he wanted to, he could reach out and touch my shoulder.

And even if I really wanted him to want to, I had already found out that was a very bad idea. So I wasn't going to think about it.

"And," Sam prompted, one eyebrow rising while he took a drink.

"So, the woman is, like, OCD organized. Everything labeled and the folders color-coded, all of that. She has the white receipts attached to spreadsheets showing the weekly deposits."

Sam made a quiet noise of consideration, nodding slightly. "This is the person who discovered the missing money?" he asked.

"Yeah. When Mr. Petros hired me, he said she'd been the bookkeeper there for years, before he'd started, even, so if she said something was going on, he believed her." I shrugged, rubbing my thumb along the long neck of my beer bottle. "But, get this. When I went up to the front counter, all their receipts are those yellow ones we found. So I'm thinking it's got to be something like someone comes in, gets their stuff, gets their copy of the receipt, and pays the higher price. When Mr. Petros was telling me about procedures, he said that every night, they just bundle the store receipts, the cash, everything, put it in an envelope, and it gets locked in a safe."

"So when the bookkeeper gets the deposit ready—" Sam leaned in, adding to my theory; I could see the interest in his expression, the intrigue over solving a puzzle. "—she gets the bags with the receipts, counts the cash, adds up what she *should* have, and balances."

"Right." I was grinning. I couldn't help it. This felt so damn *good*, taking all the little pieces and finding how they fit. And Sam helping just made it better. "But I looked back a year, and I think she's been getting the wrong receipts, for who knows how long, really. She's balancing off of lower figures, so she didn't notice the higher prices."

"So what changed?" Sam rubbed his thumb across his lower lip, momentarily sending my mind to all the dirty places I was trying to avoid. "I mean, this isn't some new scam. So something happened so that she'd notice."

"Guilty conscience?" I suggested.

He nodded slowly, but neither of us was convinced. "Maybe."

"You know what I need?" I mused. "Timesheets." Sam's eyebrow lifted in a silent question, so I filled in, "The only way those receipts are getting altered and the cash taken is if someone is removing them from the safe."

"And the only way the bookkeeper finds out is if, for some reason, they *didn't*," Sam finished the thought, a smile spreading across his face to mirror my own. "If we see the timesheet—"

"We see if someone was missing the week she reported the shortage." Our words overlapped and we were left, exhilarated, realizing that we really were going to solve this. We were on the right track.

Sam's fingers brushed against my shoulder, lightly, the smile on his face fading into something sharper, eyes darkening into storm-tossed blue. "We should talk to the bookkeeper too," he murmured.

"Yeah," I agreed, throat tightening with anticipation. He was looking at me like I'd morphed into Brad Pitt, like he *wanted* to move closer. I didn't know what to do with that much intensity on me. "Yeah, good idea."

"We can go tomorrow?" Sam suggested. "Maybe get lunch?"

"Sure." I was nodding like an idiot, swallowing hard. "Sounds really good."

We were staring at each other, Sam's fingers warm on my shoulder, tracing tiny circles that were sending shivers all through me. I wanted to lean forward. God, I *really* wanted to close whatever space was still between us, because Sam was sexy and smart and he'd carried me with such gentleness. He was just a *good guy* and I was falling for him.

And that was kind of scary.

He seemed to feel the same, at least about the scary part, because all at once he was pulling back, his hand leaving my shoulder. I immediately missed the contact. "It's late," he said quietly. I turned to blink at the clock in the corner, surprised to find he was right. "You still have to drive home, right?"

"Yeah, uh, I do." I stood, rubbing the back of my neck. "I guess I'll see you tomorrow though?"

He smiled again, sending butterflies doing high kicks sweeping through my stomach. "Yeah. Tomorrow."

CHAPTER
FIVE

SAM

Well, he was a damned idiot. He was standing in front of his bathroom mirror, scowling at himself, wondering if he should have gotten a haircut or shaved or something. Trying to decide if his shirt was good enough. He was acting like a kid on his first date instead of a grown-ass man going to lunch with a friend. He was showered, his shirt was clean, and that should have been enough. He should just walk out the damn door right now.

He didn't. He sighed and shrugged off the faded flannel shirt, grabbing his only decent dress shirt instead. Doing up the buttons, Sam frowned at his reflection. "You are an idiot, Ewing," he declared. His mirror-self seemed to agree. Getting himself all tangled up in knots over a guy when both he and August seemed to realize that it wasn't going to happen. It just wasn't a good idea.

But here he was, primping. Splashing on aftershave. Because he was a goddamn fool.

On the elevator ride up to the fourth floor, Sam nearly changed his mind three times. Yesterday he'd had August show up at his door as if summoned by the intensely dirty thoughts Sam had been having while taking a shower. And Sam had a moment of weakness, of reaching out, which had seemed to upset August. Sam could take a hint. The guy wasn't interested, and that was fine.

Too bad Sam couldn't dismiss his own interest. He knew it was going to end badly, no matter what happened. Unless he got himself over his stupid crush, he was only going to wind up hurt. Again.

As he approached the door to August's office, Sam caught the sound of a woman's voice, of her laughter mingling with August's. Sam's steps slowed, a frown flickering across his face. He nearly left, standing for what felt like forever, trying to hear more than the faint murmur of conversation. Unsure if he should interrupt or not, Sam, in the end, knocked very gently on the door, ready to leave if August was with a client.

The door was opened by a plump, smiling shorter woman, her hair done in an elaborate braid over one shoulder. "You must be Samuel," she said, patting his hand, taking his arm, and despite any protests Sam was ushered inside and crowded to sit on the couch next to August. He shot August a helpless look, only to get an apologetic wince in return.

"Uh, Sam, this is my mom."

Ah. Sam immediately stood again, towering a bit over the woman, taking her hand in both of his. "It's very nice to meet you, Mrs. Mendez," he rumbled. She flashed him another smile, and Sam wondered how he hadn't remembered her immediately. She was the same woman in August's family pictures, and Sam could easily see August's smile in hers.

"Oh, please, call me Maggie," she tutted at him. "Sit, sit." She was beaming at him like she knew a secret, leaning against the desk and studying the two of them. Sam obliged, and her smile widened. "You just missed Auggie's dad, Ramòn. He went out to get the car. We had to park six blocks away; it was terrible. I told Auggie that moving to the city would mean we couldn't come see him as much, but he just had to go off and be a big detective."

"Private investigator, Mom," August said, voice a miserable mumble. Sam glanced at him, lips twitching upward in a smile he was trying desperately to hide. "And Sam and I have some work to do. Why don't I walk you down to meet Dad?"

"He just had to move away." Maggie was ignoring him, instead fixing Sam with light-gray eyes that seemed to see straight through him. She was such a sweet-looking woman, but at that moment, Sam was pretty sure she was secretly some sort of mother bear, smiling at him until she ripped his guts out.

He hated meeting parents. Especially the parents of a guy who gave him as many confusing thoughts as August.

"Mom," August tried again. "It's not even two hours from your house. It's not like I rented an apartment on Mars. And Sam is giving up some of his day to help me out on something, so we really should get going." He even half stood before Maggie gave him a quick glance. Sinking back down, groaning under his breath, August nudged Sam's knee with his own. "Sorry."

"So, I hear you're dating my son," Maggie said, just as chipper as anything.

Sam stared, eyes wide, feeling as though he were a child being scolded in school. "No, ma'am. We're just friends." He could feel August's gaze on him, but he refused to look over.

Maggie cocked her head, studying him a moment before she nodded. "Good. He's still finding himself, but I'm sure he'll find a nice young man to settle down with." Beaming a smile at August, she patted his hand. "Did I tell you that Mrs. Santino's son is single? And he might be gay! I should invite them for dinner next time you come home."

"Okay, Mom," August stood, arm around his mom's shoulders, and hustled her out the door. "Dad's probably waiting for you. Why don't we go down and meet him?"

"It was nice to meet you, Mrs. Mendez," Sam offered, standing as well, feeling incredibly awkward.

"You too, dear." She smiled, waving at him as she left. "I left some cookies for Auggie. Tell him to give you a few, won't you? You look like you could do with some homemade cookies."

And then they were gone, door shut behind them. Sam sank back to the couch, feeling a little stunned. Now that wasn't something he'd been expecting. His answer had been defensive, given before he'd had time to think things over, and Maggie's response hadn't exactly given him any peace. He knew he was older than August, by quite a number of years. It wasn't as if he were some young kid, and he'd long ago stopped being romantic or hopeful. Maybe he was just stubborn, though, because even though ten minutes ago he would have agreed with that entire sentiment, he found himself scowling down at his interlaced hands.

Sixteen years wasn't that much. They were both grown men. And he could be *nice*.

August walked back in with a sheepish look toward him, fiddling with that damn hat he kept carrying around or wearing. "I'm so sorry," he started, but Sam shook his head.

"Don't be. She's your mom. I'm some stranger you met in the big, scary, parking-challenged city." He shared a little smile with August, watching as the man's tenseness relaxed. "It's fine. Besides, she brought you cookies. I can't get mad at someone who bakes cookies for their kid."

Rubbing the back of his neck, August leaned against his desk, still looking unsure. "She's great," he insisted, even though Sam didn't really need to be convinced. "We're just, you know, kind of a close family. Especially with…."

"The fact you can turn into a chinchilla?" Sam nudged his foot against August's. "I said it was okay, August. I can handle a little motherly fussing."

"She doesn't know you know." August shrugged. Which might be why he looked so worried. "I've never lied to my mom before, but she asked me when I said we were going to lunch together, and I just said *of course not* and we moved on, but… you do."

Sam found himself reaching out to grasp August's hand, using their grip to tug him onto the couch. "I do," he agreed. "And you know you can trust me." He held August's hand between both of his, August's fingers curling up against his palm as the man bowed his head, that messy tangle of his hair covering his eyes.

"I know," August said quietly. And then, even softer, "I hated when you said we were just friends."

Christ. Sam opened his mouth to respond, only to have August pulling away, looking vaguely horrified. "I'm so sorry. Jesus." August rubbed his hand across his face, barking out a stuttered laugh. "Unexpected visit from the parents questioning my life choices. No better way to get me to turn into a massive idiot." Before Sam could formulate any kind of answer, August was putting his hat on and shrugging on his trench coat. "Come on, I'm starving."

Sam could have pressed it. He could have said *something*. Because frankly, he hadn't much liked it either. And he definitely hadn't been a fan of the implication he was too old. If one spectacularly failed marriage had taught him anything, it was that he was a stubborn idiot. Telling him *not* to do something usually got him digging his heels in.

Except that couldn't be all of it. He'd wanted August for months, and the past few days had only made that worse. There were moments where it felt as though they had something more, and Sam found himself increasingly looking forward to those.

Bah. He didn't know. It was a bad idea. Then again, he was starting not to give a damn about the consequences. In any case, it was easier to just follow after August, agreeing. "Lunch sounds good."

He was a big damn coward sometimes. Even if it was the smart move.

They wound up at a café a block down. Sam knew they had decent sandwiches, even if they didn't have beer on the menu. The bustle of getting seated, of ordering drinks and looking over the menus, eased the awkward tension between them. By the time the waitress was leaving to put in the request for their meals, Sam could almost forget what August had said completely.

Almost.

"So, this bookkeeper," Sam prompted, leaning back with his iced tea. "Do you know what time she gets off?"

"According to the schedule Mr. Petros gave me, she leaves every day about two." August shook his sleeve back to glance at his watch. "So we've got a little time."

And there was the awkwardness again. They both shifted in their seats, ice clinking against glasses, like two strangers instead of... whatever they were. First August looked as though he were going to speak before thinking better of it. Sam did the same a few minutes later. In the end, both remained silent.

When their waitress set down their plates, Sam almost hugged her in relief. At least then they had something to do. Sam's tuna salad required him to concentrate on eating so he didn't drop any, and August seemed absorbed in putting his burger together. They exchanged pleasantries about how good the food was, how they enjoyed this place, perfectly genial conversation.

It sucked.

"Look, August—" Sam started.

August immediately cut him off, talking slightly louder than normal, as if he could stop Sam from saying whatever it was he thought the conversation was going to be about. "Hey, so I was thinking about dessert. Do you want dessert? They have this great cheesecake here." He twisted in his seat, looking around for their waitress.

Reaching across the table, Sam grabbed August's hand, bringing his attention back to their conversation. As soon as those deep brown eyes were back on him, though, Sam felt every word he could think of simply leaving his head. He'd felt this way about Kyle, a long time ago. Every time Kyle had smiled at him, Sam had forgotten everything else. When things started to go so wrong, maybe that had made it worse. In all their years together, Sam hadn't ever managed to be as open as Kyle had wanted. That was part of it, in the end.

You're a coldhearted bastard, Ewing. The sad thing is, I think you like it that way.

"I didn't like it either." The words came out, almost unbidden. Sam winced, gaze dropping to the table. "Look, it's a bad idea. And I don't know what you're thinking about everything. But yeah, I didn't like cutting us off at the knees that way." A very faint smile touched the corners of his eyes. Sam leaned back in his chair, scrubbing both hands across his face. "Wasn't a big fan of your mom calling me too old, if it comes to that."

There was a long moment of August just staring at him, those big, beautiful eyes tearing him apart as if he could see straight through him. Sam shifted in his seat, glowering down at his hands, at his empty plate. At anywhere but him.

"Have you ever thought about a career in sales?" August's lips twitched upward, the confusion in his expression warring with growing amusement. "Because I really think you have a rare gift."

Yeah, okay. Maybe he wasn't exactly painting a pretty picture here. Sam snorted, ducking his head and rubbing the back. "It really could end badly," he pointed out quietly, gaze darting up to August's, unsure. "In my experience, most things like this do."

"What things like this?" August scooted his chair closer, hands resting lightly on the table, almost as if caught between an urge to reach out and a desperate need to keep himself separate.

"Things where I think about you all the damn time." Fuck it. Dancing around this wasn't doing either one of them any favors, and at this point, Sam wasn't sure he could anymore. "Things where I watch you smile and it makes me want to do fucking anything to see it again. Things that make me want to leave behind all that horrible shit that happened, the absolute open, festering wound my marriage turned into. I want to *try*." Sitting back in his seat, chin lifted almost aggressively, Sam folded his arms as the words trailed off into a scowl.

He didn't just *say* shit like that. And the reason why he didn't became shockingly apparent as August just stared at him, mouth dropped open. He was *bad* at this shit. Standing up, Sam tossed some bills on the table blindly, hoping that it would cover the bill. He was out the door and running away—from August, from his smile and his eyes, from all those things Sam hadn't actually meant to say out loud— walking away from the café at a brisk pace. His head down, his hands in his pockets, Sam wondered if there were enough ways to say *idiot* to cover his actions.

A hand landed on his arm, and Sam was stopped, pulled around to find August standing there. He was practically vibrating nerves, and for a long beat Sam was certain that August would pull away and the moment would be gone.

Sam saw the moment when August drew himself up, when a determination settled into his eyes. August wrapped a hand around the back of Sam's neck and pulled him in, where their lips met in a hard press.

The foot traffic on the sidewalk flowed around them, completely unheeded. Sam wrapped his arms around August as their kiss deepened, Sam's fingers diving into August's hair, their bodies pressed together. Heat flickered under Sam's skin, August's lips parting under his, their tongues tangling together. Sam forgot how to breathe apart from August, all of the reasons *why not* lost in the taste of him.

When they broke away from each other, lips flushed, chests rising and falling in a shallow pant, Sam couldn't help but bark out an incredulous laugh. He slid his thumb along the curve of August's cheek, baffled and *wanting* all at once. This was a bad idea. But so was eating a chili-cheese hot dog or drinking beer. Somehow he found the prospect of August, of being with him, more and more worth the future pain.

"I've never done anything like that before," August said, looking more than a little stunned. He glanced around at the people on the street. Some of them were giving them glances as they walked by; most of them didn't seem to give a shit. All of them, however, made August shrink in on himself again, a mortified expression creasing his face.

"What, kissed a man?" Sam rumbled, arm sliding around August, not wanting to give him room to second-guess. "'Cause I'm pretty sure you have at least once. Been thinking about it since it happened."

Color touched August's cheeks. "No, do the whole eighties rom-com dramatic-running-after, kissing-in-the-street thing. I mean, I don't know why I did. It just… seemed like the thing to do?"

He was so clearly uncomfortable doing any of this in public that Sam had to take pity on him. Nodding toward the office building, Sam walked shoulder to shoulder with him, cutting August little glances as they headed back. The trip took all of ten minutes, and once they were off the street, August seemed to relax slightly.

"I meant what I said," Sam said, crowding August against the wall, teasing fingertips through August's messy hair as he'd been wanting to for months. "This could implode in the worst fucking way."

August's eyes had darkened, even as he squirmed, looking supremely uncertain. "Couldn't everything, really?"

It was true. All of Sam's very valid reasons to walk away seemed so ready to crumble now that he was close. Now that it was happening.

For his part, though, August seemed caught between two extremes. His hand was resting lightly against Sam's chest even as he backed up farther, as though he didn't want their bodies that close. Sam frowned, searching August's face, trying to figure it out.

"Say the word and I back off," he wound up rumbling, bracing one hand on the wall next to August. "I mean, you don't owe me shit. You kissed me, it was…." A grin split Sam's lips unbidden and he bowed his head. "It was great," he admitted honestly. "But that doesn't mean you're obligated. You seem uncomfortable."

Fidgeting foot to foot, August shook his head in a little jerk. It killed him to move away, as if he'd opened floodgates he didn't want to think about closing, but Sam backed off, giving August space. Then again, he kept saying this was a bad idea. He could hardly blame August for agreeing with him.

"I don't understand." August was worrying his lower lip, face caught in a frown. "I mean… shit, Sam, look at you. I don't get it. Is this a joke? Because honestly, if it's a joke…."

Eyebrows rising, Sam gave August a look. "Don't see a damn thing funny about this," he all but growled. Why the fuck would he even think that?

Stepping forward, August dared to raise his eyes. "Look, I'm not going to be all 'oh, beauty on the inside,' because this isn't a fairy tale. I'm just not what I imagined someone like you wanting to, you know."

He waggled his hand between them, vaguely embarrassed. "Do stuff with."

Oh. Sam felt exceedingly stupid for not putting all the signs together earlier. The way August shrank in on himself, the loose clothing, running away the other day... anyone else probably would have picked up on all of that. Sam just was pretty sure he was half blind.

August thought he wasn't attractive.

Which was the dumbest damn thing Sam had ever heard.

Cupping August's cheek, Sam drew him in for another kiss. Softer this time, exploring August's mouth, letting their lips mold together sweetly. Sam let his hand come to rest at August's waist, smiling when he felt the faint jump of muscles under his hand. "I want you," he told August lowly, his cheek resting alongside August's.

"I don't believe you," August returned, just as quietly. "I mean, I can't. You're so, you know, *you*, and I'm me, and I'm a realist. Or, I try to be."

"I don't think you get to tell me what I find attractive." Sam pulled back just enough to meet August's gaze. "So if you want to doubt me, fine. But I'm willing to give this thing a shot, if you are." There was a lurch in his stomach at the declaration, a little warning bell going off. Logic said getting involved with August was stupid.

Sam hadn't ever been that much of a thinker.

"I want you," he repeated, holding August's gaze, refusing to look away. "I'll tell you as many times as it takes to sink in."

Apparently he hadn't fucked this up too bad because August wasn't bolting. The other man just stood there, staring at him as if he'd grown another damn head. Finally, August let out a quick exhale, a little helpless laugh. "Okay," he said, so quietly it ached. "Okay, fine. Crazy, grumpy landlord and the fat chinchilla man. How could that go wrong?"

A smile spread across Sam's face. God knew if he leaned in or if August pulled him close, but the end result was a kiss that exploded between them, a harsh moan getting tangled up in their tongues, and the taste of coffee and peppermint shared between them. Sam all but shoved August back against the wall, August grabbed fistfuls of his shirt, and when Sam's leg nudged between his, Sam was rewarded with a soft little whimper from August's lips. Yeah, he definitely wanted to hear that again.

"Mrs. Dallas," August gasped.

Sam had been busy sucking kisses down his neck, and he only paused long enough to laugh against August's skin. "Never gotten that before," he murmured. "Interesting."

"No, I mean...." The words died in a moan, August's hands sliding up Sam's arms to bury in his hair, to pull him in closer. For a moment August just rocked against Sam's leg, and it was all sweet skin and beautiful friction. But August rallied, trying to pull back. "The bookkeeper. What time is it? We're going to miss Mrs. Dallas."

Dazed, Sam lifted his head, looking around before squinting down at his watch. "Fuck, the bookkeeper," he muttered. "We've got five minutes."

It took that long to get themselves back together, for the painful *rise* of certain things to be manageable again. When they walked out the door in a rush, though, their hands brushed, their fingers laced, just like that. Without any conscious thought, for a moment they connected and Sam squeezed August's hand, August smiling up at him.

They separated when they hit the street. Probably not a good idea to go into an investigation all moon-eyed at each other. Sam wasn't exactly a pro at this, but he was pretty sure that was a good rule of thumb. And he tried, really damn hard, not to miss the contact the moment August's hand slipped from his own.

Mrs. Dallas turned out to be a rosy-cheeked woman with short gray hair, her glasses on a beaded chain around her neck. Bags over her arm, she was juggling her keys out of her purse to open her car door where it was parked a few blocks down from the dry cleaners. August hesitated as they approached her, and for a moment Sam wondered if he'd freeze altogether. Drawing himself up, tightening his jacket around himself, August took a breath and strode forward as Sam lingered behind.

"Ma'am?" August kept a respectful distance, and Sam could see the edges of August's lips easing upward as he gave Mrs. Dallas a polite smile. "I apologize, I didn't mean to startle you. My name is August Mendez."

Mrs. Dallas had paused, halfway to getting into her car, keeping the door between herself and August. Sam saw her look at both of them, rightfully wary, gaze darting over to the foot traffic as if gauging how quickly she could get help. Sam tried for a reassuring look, backing away to lean against the side of a storefront. He was close enough to hear, but August was definitely less intimidating than Sam knew he, himself, might appear.

"Can I help you?" Mrs. Dallas said, voice as tight as a guitar string, no fear showing at all.

August gave her another little smile, nodding. "Yes, actually. I'm working for Mr. Petros. He hired me to investigate the money disappearing and I was hoping you could answer a few questions?"

There was a long pause, Mrs. Dallas staring August down as if she could sniff out a falsehood. But August just met her gaze steadily, the only sign of nerves his fingers fidgeting on the cuffs of his jacket sleeves. Finally, Mrs. Dallas stepped away from her car, shutting her door behind her. "I believe you and I should have a cup of coffee," she told him before turning and striding away, purse in hand, apparently absolutely expecting August to follow.

Throwing Sam a baffled look, August trailed after her, taking two quick steps to keep up with the older woman. Sam stifled a smirk and joined them, nodding to Mrs. Dallas when she shot him a glance. There was a coffeehouse on the corner, and it wasn't long before all three of them were crowded around a table, steaming mugs of coffee in front of them. August had ordered something with caramel and whipped cream that, Sam thought, frankly looked like a diabetic attack waiting to happen. August drank it with such obvious enjoyment, though, that Sam had a fleeting thought about buying his own syrups for flavoring coffee to try and replicate it at home.

Hopefully while serving August breakfast in bed.

"Are you two boys dating?" Mrs. Dallas asked, sharp gaze darting between the two of them. When they didn't answer right away, she waved them off with a careless flip of her fingers. "Oh, never mind. It's quite all right by me. My nephew is gay. Lovely boy. His husband cleans out my gutters every spring."

Sam nodded, as did August, making the required interested sound before returning to their respective drinks. Sam had wanted just a plain goddamn coffee, but such things were too much for places like this. His cup smelled like a sugar cookie. It was disturbing.

"Now, you and your boyfriend," Mrs. Dallas started.

"Sam," August filled in for her.

"Yes, Sam." Mrs. Dallas studied them both with birdlike little turns of her head, a gaze that seemed to miss nothing at all. "The two of you are investigating a theft?"

"Yes, ma'am," August agreed. Sam didn't correct the assumption they were working together. He really didn't *want* to correct it.

"And you say Phillip hired you?" When August nodded to confirm that Petros had, indeed, requested their help, Mrs. Dallas leaned back a bit, considering them. "That is very interesting. Because, you see, Phillip told *me* that it was all a misunderstanding. I had mentioned going to speak with Mrs. Sally, one of the owners. I used to work for her, you know. Anyway, when I brought it up, just the other day, in fact, he made it very clear that nothing at all was wrong."

Sam and August exchanged a quick look, August's surprise hardly hidden on his face. He'd never be a poker player, that was for damn sure. But it seemed to work for them in the moment; Mrs. Dallas was obviously tickled that she'd dropped a rather large twist into their puzzle solving, her lips creased upward, laugh lines around her eyes deepening. "But he hired me," August repeated, slower, as if he could somehow make the pieces magically fit neatly together. "I mean, he *asked me* to look into this."

"Perhaps he's simply keeping it quiet," Mrs. Dallas suggested, folding her hands primly, legs crossed in her perfectly pressed pantsuit. "I really don't know, but I thought I should mention it."

The minx knew exactly what she'd done, and Sam had to admit, she seemed very pleased to have opened this particular can of worms. Not fond of her boss, he'd guess. He knew the look; he'd had it on his face for fifteen years, working for a man who'd been an absolute prick. "What color are the receipts you get?" Sam asked. Both of them gave him a confused look, though August did seem to immediately catch on.

Mrs. Dallas frowned faintly. "I don't understand—"

"When you get the receipts from the front counter," August explained, leaning in slightly. "The ones you use to balance. What color are they?"

"Why white, of course," Mrs. Dallas answered, eyebrows beetled together. "They've always been white."

"Always?" It was Sam's turn to pin her with a look.

Mrs. Dallas tapped her fingers lightly against the table, obviously thinking back. "Except for the week I noticed the money missing." She nodded. "That week they were yellow. I thought Phillip had changed suppliers—he's always looking for ways to cut corners—but he said that it was a mistake. He'd had a death in the family, you know, and was away for a few days suddenly. Such things slip one's mind in times like that. He assured me, though, that it was simply an error."

August was sitting back in his chair, looking more than a little stunned. "Two more questions, Mrs. Dallas," he said faintly. "Who has access to the safe?"

"Myself," she answered promptly. "Phillip."

"No one else?" August's overly sweet coffee confection was forgotten as he questioned her, voice quiet, polite, but never wavering. "Not even for a short time, no one else has had the combination?"

"Not since I started there." Once more, Mrs. Dallas had folded her hands together, shoulders straight, looking more than a little formidable. "I change the combination once a week, after I do the deposit. If anyone else had it, I'd know." Sam didn't doubt it.

August nodded, lips pursed in thought. "And did anyone else miss work that week? The days you had yellow receipts for, was anyone else not there that should have been?"

"No, dear. Just Phillip, gone Thursday and Friday to his wife's mother's funeral."

As Mrs. Dallas gathered her purse and her coat, August ran a hand through his hair and Sam could practically hear the wheels turning in his head. He wanted nothing more than to kiss away the frown at the corners of August's eyes, or to tangle his hand in those messy waves. Instead Sam stood as Mrs. Dallas did, nodding at her. "Thank you, ma'am."

She patted his arm, shaking her head at the two of them. "Keep your heads down, dears. There are two things that people get themselves hurt over. Money and sex. And let's just say Phillip wouldn't be interested in the latter with you."

And with that, she swept out the door and back onto the busy sidewalk.

Staring after her, Sam was torn between incredulousness and amusement. He decided to settle on a laugh, sitting back down, his back to the table. Sam propped his elbows on it and let his fingers drag a light path along August's thigh. "Hey," he murmured. August jerked himself out of his thoughts, those gorgeous brown depths of his rising to Sam's face.

"Sorry," August said, a frown crumpling his expression. "Just... I don't get it. I mean, Mr. Petros, he hired me. He didn't have to do that."

Sam lifted both shoulders in a shrug. "Maybe he was trying to give himself a cover story?"

"But he had to know I would figure it out," August started before stumbling to a stop. His gaze dropped, a miserable curve bending his body in on itself. "No," he amended. "No, he didn't. He thought I'd fuck it up."

"August…." Sam really wanted to protest. But honestly, that did seem like the right conclusion. It was, if he looked at it unemotionally, kind of brilliant. Hire someone you knew would point the finger at the wrong man, and then that would be your cover. Fire the guy or whatever and move on, no one the wiser. August had been part of that bastard's cover.

Sam wanted to kill him.

"Well, he was wrong," Sam pointed out, scowling. "You got him. We're going to get the evidence we need and we'll go straight to the damn cops. See how that fucker likes jail." That didn't seem to ease August's mood. Sam scooted closer, wrapping one of his arms around August, lightly making circles against his side with his fingers. Eventually, he felt the tenseness in August's body fade; the man leaned into him and Sam kissed the top of his head, holding him a little closer.

"Yeah," August agreed, taking a deep breath. "Yeah, okay." When he looked over at Sam, he didn't look insecure or anguished any longer. He looked pissed. Determined.

He looked fucking gorgeous.

"Let's go back to your place," August said, sitting up, pulling his hat on firmly. "We have work to do."

CHAPTER
SIX

AUGUST

So apparently I was the worst detective in the world. I was pretty sure Philip Marlowe had never gotten hired purely because the bad guy thought he'd let him get away. Heck, even Roger Rabbit had gotten more respect, and he'd been framed. Humiliation ate at me, sour and thick down the back of my throat. I wanted to quit. I wanted to just go hide under the covers, to lose myself in a movie or a book, anything but reality.

It'd be easy to do. I could walk away. Change my number, move, ignore anything that reminded me of how big of a fat loser I was. Sitting in misery at that stupid café, hating myself and my stupid hat and every fucking choice I'd ever made that led to that moment, I had it all planned out. I'd go home, I'd pack up my idiotic belongings, and I'd just drive until I ran out of gas. The end. Me being a detective was so goddamn laughable that everyone else had gotten the joke long before me.

But then there was Sam. Beautiful Sam, gruff and growly and stubbly Sam, who sat next to me and glowered at the whole goddamn world like he could personally cut off whatever was hurting me. He'd wrapped one arm around me, he'd refused to sugarcoat jack shit, and he'd looked me in the eyes and told me I could keep going.

He gave me the harder option, the one not based in fantasy. The one that wasn't in the movies, wasn't between the pages of any of my books. It'd be hard and I'd have to swallow what was left of my tattered pride and work, but when he met my eyes, when he said my name, it occurred to me that he didn't expect me to choose anything else.

So what else could I do?

I put my goddamn hat on and I went to work.

We wound up in my office. Both of us scrunched onto my couch, the coffee table in front of us scattered with everything we had so far. Receipts and the security tape that showed nothing, a work roster, and what felt like a thousand sticky notes with everything else. It was adding up to something substantial, but the problem was, none of it was good enough to go to the cops with.

"They'll want something or someone more than what we got digging around in the trash," Sam sighed. We'd been at this for at least an hour, shoving things around in a different order, writing down what we thought was important, trying to find a thread we could pull to send the whole house of cards tumbling down on Petros's head. So far there was nothing. "There's a white-collar crimes division that'll be interested in this, especially since all of this definitely means he's committing tax fraud on top of everything else, but we need something solid. Like what you found when you went through Mrs. Dallas's files."

"I saw it with my own eyes officer, I swear." I mimicked a higher voice, sagging back on the couch in weariness. "When I was a chinchilla, I saw the whole thing go down."

"Yeah, okay," Sam allowed, giving me a grimace. I had to smile; he just looked so *big* and ornery sitting on my couch. But he was there. Like he had just assumed he and I were a team. "So something else."

"Something else," I agreed in my normal tone, staring at the piles of paper scattered across the table. I couldn't think about it anymore right then. Forget seeing the forest, I'd been staring at a tree so long I was pretty sure all I was noticing was bark. "We know he was the one who missed work, we know that the yellow receipts didn't get switched out on those days because of that. So maybe he does it nightly? Or it could be someone else, someone he gives the combination to." I paused, thinking. Something was niggling at the back of my brain, some fact I had that I hadn't put into place....

Tobacco. "The other night, at the dry cleaners, when I had to run out." I looked up, eyes widening, the realization hitting me even as the words spilled out. "It was because someone was coming in. They almost caught me."

"Okay." Sam nodded. "Do you know who? Did you see them?"

"No. Better." I gave him a grim smile, picking up the envelope, the one Petros had used to hand over the information I'd asked for. "I smelled him." Running my nose along the length of the manila envelope, I inhaled, eyes closing. Paper. The faint scent of glue, cleaning chemicals, and ink. But under that, laced through everything else, was the smell of tobacco. "It was Petros. I'm sure of it."

"So now we know." Sam grimaced, sitting back. "It's all circumstantial though." He seemed reluctant to point it out. "I mean, you're right, but it's still not enough."

I slouched back down, deflated. Seeking a distraction, I picked up a pencil and bit lightly at the unsharpened end, studying Sam. He was leaning over the table, broad shoulders stretching his worn flannel shirt, hair curling against his collar. The gray flecks at his temple and in his beard seemed to highlight the strong lines of his face, and I was struck by how freaking handsome he was.

Not so scary now. In fact, not scary at all. Definitely giving me other kinds of feelings though.

"How do you know so much about this?" I asked.

"Remember I mentioned my ex was a detective on the force?" Sam suddenly seemed way more interested in getting a pot of coffee brewing. A very faint smile touched his lips, more rueful than fond. "Might have been a shit husband, but he was good at what he did. I picked up a few things here and there."

I had this sudden image of a strapping man, not unlike Sam, all muscles and flat stomach in a tight cop's uniform. And okay, maybe that fantasy was more based on strippers and pornos than reality, but still, I all at once was very aware that my T-shirt was loose and my pants felt too tight and I had rolls in places you shouldn't. "Why'd you guys split up?" I asked, the question out before I could second-guess the wisdom of it.

Watching Sam's back as he carefully measured the coffee grounds into the filter, I could practically feel the tenseness radiating off of him. He chanced a glance back; his eyes dropped as soon as they found mine. It was pretty clear this wasn't a topic he wanted to pursue. I almost told him to forget it—after all, it wasn't really my business— but he dropped back to sit on the couch, a little nearer to me now, leg pressed against mine.

"We met when the bank I worked at was robbed," he said, voice a low rumble that did funny, achy things to my chest. "He was the first officer on the scene. I was just a teller then, third month on the job, and he had to take my statement." Another smile flickered across his face. "They had to ask if we had relationships. Wives, girlfriends, what have you, so they could do a background check. I told him I had a boyfriend. He told me I should dump him. Totally unprofessional." Smirking, Sam shrugged. "I did, though, two weeks later. As soon as the investigation was closed and I was no longer a witness, he showed up with flowers. We got married a year later."

Those were the good memories, I could tell. Something eased in Sam's face, some of the bitterness that seeped into his voice when he talked about his ex faded. I wasn't sure I liked it. Sure, I got it—he'd been married, *some* of that had to be pleasant. But I was finding that I wanted to be the only one that gave him that tone.

Which was ridiculous and selfish, really.

"It was good at first." Sam shifted, rubbing his hands absently against his knees. "But I wasn't happy in my job, he worked long hours, and somewhere in there... I don't know. We just stopped talking." He cut me a sideways glance, blowing out a rueful little laugh. "I've never been good at that shit anyway. Talking about emotions. But

Kyle, he was a hurricane, and I just couldn't figure out how to keep up. In the end, he said a lot of shit to me. I don't think he meant it; I think he just wanted me to react. To make me hurt because at least then he'd *see* me feel all the stuff I didn't tell him."

One of his shoulders lifted in a shrug. "Like I said, it ended messy. He got the house and the dog. I'd bought this place a few years before it all ended, so I moved in here. And that was that."

What the fuck did I even say to that? Maybe there wasn't anything. I just reached over, curling my fingers tentatively around his. Sam smiled faintly, turning his hand to meet mine, squeezing it lightly once he'd grasped it. "Is it really terrible for me to be happy that Kyle apparently is a very stupid man?" I asked quietly, searching Sam's face. "Because anyone who'd leave you is an idiot."

For a moment I was positive that'd been absolutely the wrong thing to say. Sam froze, staring at me as if the words I'd spoken were gibberish. I felt heat rise in my cheeks and ducked my head, starting to pull away.

Sam tightened his grip, refusing to let mine go. When I looked up, I found him *looking* at me, so much heat in his gaze that it arched through me as well, settling low in my gut. Like I was some guppy out of water, my mouth opened and shut, words completely failing me. There was just an *intenseness* there and it blew away any joke, any flippant remark I could have made.

"I'm going to kiss you." Sam's voice was hoarse, a trickle of smoke over stone, his hand lifting to cup my cheek. His thumb made a slow arc across my skin; I shivered under it, eyes wide, heart throbbing. Unlike our other two kisses, it wasn't Sam hauling me in, it wasn't breathless need and restrained passion colliding. He deliberately met my gaze, moving slowly, giving us all the time in the world to savor each second, each *almost* contact. "And when I do, I want you to know it. To feel it. I'm kissing *you*, August."

A quiet little exhale escaped me just as his lips claimed mine. And I did, I *felt* it, down to my bones, shuddering as he gently parted my lips, as our tongues slid together in an exquisite agony of want. It was soft, *sweet*, achingly so. I'd had sex. I'd kissed. Hell, *we'd* kissed before. This struck me down to my soul. This felt like he was gently unraveling me until all that remained was where we were pressed together, the slide of his hand along my arm.

He pulled away, his fingers trailing across my lips, his chest rising and falling in shallow breaths. The way he was staring at me, drinking me in, it was like I was something worth looking at. We didn't move, inches apart, trembling there on the cusp of something more.

"Jesus fuck," I muttered, hooking my fingers in the front of his shirt and kissing him, hard. He made a muffled noise of surprise and I could feel his lips curving into a grin under mine. Those gorgeously big arms wrapped around me, his fingers curling into the hair at the nape of my neck, pulling my head back so he could mouth hungry, sucking kisses along my throat.

He made me feel so *bold*. When I pushed him back against the couch, when I straddled his lap and caught his lips in a bite, in a slow, deep kiss, I didn't think about how fat I was, how many rolls my shirt was hiding. How I was probably crushing his legs. I just knew I wanted him; I knew that his broad hands slid down my back to dig fingers into my ass, jerking me closer, making me moan against his mouth.

I just felt like a guy who was making out with the person I was falling for. My body wasn't something I wanted to crawl out of or hide behind; it was what was practically humming with want. Sam's hand cupped my cheek, drawing me back in when I pulled away for air. We devoured one another, soft moans and quick, greedy gasps the only sounds.

"I want you to fuck me." Sam's voice had turned into this low, husky drawl that sent flips through my stomach.

Panting a groan, I leaned in, hands braced on his shoulders, sliding kisses along his jaw. "You are the sexiest person in the whole freaking world," I murmured. Christ, I was turned on just from that. "Yeah. Yeah, okay." I stuttered a laugh, biting his lower lip, sucking it to see it flush. "Jesus, *please*, yes." And then, almost as an afterthought, I buried my face in his neck, loving the way his muscles would jump when I sucked hard enough to leave little marks behind. "I, uh, I don't know... I mean, I've never done that part."

It was hard to be embarrassed by my lack of experience when Sam's hands were shoving under my shirt, painting warm trails along my skin, when he growled under my teeth and bared his neck so I could have more skin to cover with kisses. He grinned broadly, predatory as he rocked his hips up against mine, biting the gasp from my lips. "Good," he told me. "My ass is going to be your first."

Jesus Christ, it was hard to think when he decided to talk dirty. Another laugh got lost in a tumbling kiss, Sam practically ripping my shirt off between each hard, deep press of our lips. For a moment I panicked, realizing that all of me, all the flab and rolls and blemishes, was on display. Freezing, eyes flaring wide, I pulled back. I felt the blush starting at my cheeks, creeping down my chest, shame starting a sick knot in my belly.

Sam didn't let me go too far though. He trailed his fingers lightly down my chest, to my round stomach, that heat never leaving his gaze. "You're gorgeous," he whispered. And I believed him. Not that I suddenly felt the need to be an underwear model, but I believed *him*. I believed when he looked at me, whatever he saw was reason enough for that want in his eyes. Which was absolutely incredible.

Slowly, I undid the buttons of his shirt, darting glances down at him as my fingers worked. I found I really liked watching him watch me. For such a big, gruff guy, Sam was so freaking responsive. Right then it was like he was tight with anticipation, each slide of my thumbs along his skin sending muscles jumping under my touch. I leaned in impulsively, leaving a wet trail of kisses behind on each bit of his chest I revealed. He squirmed under me and laughed, hoarse and low, fingers threading in my hair. "God, your mouth is going to drive me nuts." His hands were restless, in my hair, sliding down my back, slipping under the waistband of my jeans to curve around my ass.

Shoving his shirt off his shoulders, I ran my fingers through the soft hair on his chest, following it down to the faint trail that led under his pants. I liked that trail. Fuck, I wanted to spend *days* just on that part of him. And then another week on his arms. And his chest.

Just mark me down for a month of exploring every inch of Sam.

"I don't have anything," I realized in a daze, Sam's lips sucking down my chest, fingers flexing against my ass. "Like, for sex. I have no sex things."

It took him a minute to catch up with me; he was too busy yanking my jeans down, which made me catch a startled whimper in my throat. Blinking, eyes dark with arousal, Sam looked up at me with the cutest damn bewildered frown I'd ever seen. "Sex things?" And then a smile. Christ, that smile was like a leer and the sun coming out all at once. "I found your sex things, August." He dug his fingers into my ass as if to demonstrate, and I yelped, squirming a little, not minding one bit that little jolt of pain with my pleasure. "And I think I'm going to get my mouth on one of them." My cock was standing proud now that my jeans were down around my thighs, and I was pretty sure it got harder just from the promise of that.

"No, I mean lube. Condoms. Things you need for sex." Biting my lip, I let my head fall back as Sam's thumb rubbed across the head of my cock. He actually licked his lips before he turned us, me sprawled on my back while he painted open-mouthed kisses down my stomach, my thighs, yanking my jeans the rest of the way off and tossing them across the room, my boxers following close behind.

And then I didn't care about specifics anymore; I was too busy spreading my legs, one knee hooked over the back of the couch, while Sam's fingers trailed along the length of my dick.

"I do."

It took me several long beats to realize what Sam was talking about. I struggled to sit up, panting, trying really hard not to just beg. "What?"

"I have stuff for sex." A smirk flickered across his face. "You're adorable when I tease. I think we're going to have to do a lot more of that."

"You're a jerk," I managed. The bite of my words, though, was completely ruined when I wrapped one hand around the back of his neck and hauled him in for a kiss. "I don't want to wait." The admission was mumbled against his lips and he quirked a smile.

"Me either. Feels like we've been waiting forever." Another kiss and he was standing, pulling away. "But trust me, I'll make it up to you." He was hard, I realized, my gaze dropping down to the front of his jeans. That was… so goddamn hot.

I curled my fingers into his belt loops, and I yanked him back to me. With me sitting on the couch, Sam standing between my knees, he was at the perfect height. I curled my tongue around his belly button, following that happy trail down until my chin bumped against his buckle. Glancing up, I found Sam was staring at me with such want that I found myself bold. I undid his belt and pulled down his jeans just enough to get his cock out.

Christ, it was big, thick, curving a little to the left as I slid his pants and boxers down his hips. His hands trailed along my shoulders, any talk of leaving forgotten for the moment. I pursed my lips over the head of his cock, and teased my tongue along his slit before I sank down onto him. It'd been way too long since I'd gotten to do this. As soon as he hit the back of my throat I choked, eyes watering, and had to pull back.

Which was just super smooth and sexy.

"You okay?" he asked, so concerned. I just nodded, coughing, waving him off.

"You're big. The last guy I did this to was a long time ago and a lot smaller. Don't you dare move; I'm not done with you yet." Right, okay, I could do this. Like riding a bike. Grasping his hips, I pulled him in closer so I could run my lips down the side of his cock. I buried my nose in by his balls to tease slow, deep sucking kisses along the base.

"You can keep telling me the other guys were small-dicked losers," Sam chuckled, threading his fingers through my hair. "It's doing wonders for my self-esteem."

I decided a much better response was to try again, hand wrapping around his thickness to stroke him as I got my mouth around the head of his cock. My cheeks hollowed out as I bobbed my head in time. The moan Sam gave was like it'd been yanked from deep in his gut. He rose up on his toes, clenching, as I got him deeper.

He was heavy and hot on my tongue, filling my mouth with salty sweetness. I looked up at him, lips stretched around his dick, and I swore he was going to come just from that. He bit his lip so hard it dimpled, and when I tightened my hand around his cock his hips jerked as if they were on a string. I could have done that forever, dragging my mouth up and down his cock, my hand filling in where my tongue and lips couldn't reach. Eventually, though, he gasped, gripping my shoulder.

"Stop," he moaned. "Fuck, babe, stop or I'm going to come."

I didn't want to, but I pulled back, unable to resist giving the tip of his cock soft little kisses while I stroked him lightly. "I want you to come," I told him, voice huskier after I'd had him down my throat.

"Yeah, well, I'm not thirty anymore." It was said ruefully, his thumb rubbing my lower lip, watching me. "And I want to come with you inside of me."

That caught my interest for sure. "Then get some lube and condoms," I ordered, biting his hip. Sam jumped and then laughed, rolling his eyes.

"Bossy."

"Damn straight." I lounged back, forgetting how exposed I was in favor of admiring his tight stomach, the thick thighs, the way his skin was flushed with arousal. "You like it."

"I really do." Sam winced as he tried to do up his jeans again. Cursing, he barely managed it after taking a few deep breaths, and he shrugged his shirt on, leaving it untucked to try and hide his bulge.

"I could go with you," I felt the need to point out. "I mean, you have a bed, right?"

"Or you could fuck me right on this couch." Sam's smile creased his whole face. "It'll take me five minutes."

I was never going to look at this couch the same way again. "I really want you," I told him, gaze traveling up and down his body, knowing already how he tasted, how his chest felt under my hand, wanting to find out so much more.

"Me too," he murmured before kissing me quickly. He practically ran out the door, like he was afraid to look back for fear he'd never actually leave.

And then I was just naked on the couch in my office. It'd been sexy five minutes ago; now I just kind of felt like a perv.

That was when the doubt started. The fabric of the couch was itchy against my ass, it was cold in the room, and my overly-demanding hard-on was beginning to fade. Standing, feeling enormously awkward, I tugged my shirt back on, cursing as I tried to find my boxers. I was hopping up and down on one foot, trying to pull them on, when Sam walked back in the room. When I looked up and saw him I missed a hop, stumbled, and fell back with a loud shout.

"Five minutes," I heard Sam mutter, sounding exasperated. "I was gone *five minutes*, do you think you could not hurt yourself?"

His hand was held out for me and I took it, stumbling awkwardly to my feet. Sam took in my clothes, a little frown creasing between his eyes. "Oh." His fingers touched the collar of my shirt and I could see emotions flick across his eyes before he stepped back. "Changed your mind?"

He actually looked upset. It was impossible for me to wrap my head around the idea that he might actually be bothered by the idea that I'd gotten dressed, but there he was, staring at my boxers with the little lightsabers on them as if they'd magically tell him what had gone wrong.

"No." Taking a step closer, I gently touched Sam's chin, pulling his head up so I could meet his eyes. "Christ, no. I just... I kind of started to feel ridiculous, sitting there naked. Like I should cover up or something." My lips quirked upward and I searched his eyes, seeing the acceptance that had started to settle in there, like he was expecting me to walk away. Like he'd gotten a taste of something he found really good, so of course it wasn't going to last.

Someone like Sam, someone good-looking, who actually had their life together, I never thought about them having issues of their own. That I wasn't the only one going into this with voices in my head telling me all the ways it could fail. "It's my office." I tried to explain, letting my fingertips slide along his jaw, my other hand rest on his chest, wanting him to see how much I wasn't pulling away. If we were going to be the Queens of Insecurity, we might as well take turns carrying the load. "And, you know. My mom helped me pick out that couch."

That got a smile, a quick laugh. Sam's shoulders relaxed and he ducked his head before blowing out a breath and nodding. "I just... I don't know. Figured you'd realized I'm an old, bitter divorcé and decided to get out now."

"You're an idiot" was my oh-so-elegant response. But I wrapped one hand around the back of his neck and hauled him in, close enough to kiss him hard, before pushing him back onto the couch. "Now take off your pants."

We both tumbled out of our clothes. Sam grasped my hip and jerked me in, and I nearly tripped again over the boxers around my ankles. We fell into each other, into deep kisses that had his tongue fucking into my mouth, driving any thought of *clothes* or *leaving* out of our heads entirely.

Lube was pressed into my hand and Sam hooked his legs around my waist, grinning. "Do you know how to get me ready?" he asked, the words slurred into him sucking hop-skip kisses along my chest. "It's been a while, so we might have to go a little slower than I'd like."

I was so not going to point out that I'd run out of lube eight months ago and hadn't bothered to buy any more. I remembered how this part went, I thought. Besides, lube was way more fun to use with someone else, right? Nodding, I carefully opened the tube and spread the clear, slick liquid over my fingers. I braced myself over Sam to catch his mouth in a hard kiss as I slid my hand between us, as I rubbed my fingertip over his hole. He moaned loudly, hips rolling up to meet me. It was incredible how freaking *responsive* he was.

Slowly I nudged my finger inside of him. I'd stopped our kissing to concentrate, brow furrowed as I watched his face, making sure I was doing everything right. I went up to the first knuckle and then stopped, pulling back to see what I was doing. "It's been a while, and I was never all that great at this," I admitted sheepishly.

Sam gently reached down to wrap his hand around my wrist and guided me to push in deeper. "I do masturbate," he murmured. "You don't have to treat me like I'm glass." Slowly he used my hand, fucking my finger in and then out again, short little gasps getting lost in his throat. I watched him, stunned. He was spread across the couch, legs akimbo, head fallen back, body arched, Adam's apple jumping as he swallowed moans. He was a fucking sex god, and I was just there to worship.

I added a second finger then a third, Sam's hand helping me set a rhythm. "Curl your fingers," he groaned. "Like you're telling me to come here."

Doing so, I was surprised to feel his whole body jump. I nearly stopped, but Sam was making this low whimpering noise every time I moved my fingers and I suddenly was *very* invested in hearing it again.

He sat up suddenly, dragging me in, and our lips bruised together, heat racing through me as he reached down and wrapped one hand around my cock. He stroked me hard, leaving me gasping against his mouth, my hand going up to wind in his hair to pull him in closer.

"Fuck me," he growled, voice so low I swear my toes curled. "Right now."

Like I was going to argue.

I stood, grabbing a condom only to have it slip out of my hands. Lube was really, really slippery. And kind of all over my hand. I frowned, looking around for something to use, before I decided to wipe my fingers off on the edge of the couch. Hey, that would wash off, right?

Finally getting the condom on, I looked over to find Sam had knelt on the couch, his arms braced against the back, his ass seriously the most tempting thing I'd ever seen. He was watching me over his shoulder and I grinned at him. "Yeah, okay. You're hot." I smoothed my hand down his back, fascinated by how his muscles would twitch under my touch, how he'd arch up into me. Taking a deep breath, I grasped his hips and tentatively pressed my cock against his hole, watching with wide eyes as I, inch by inch, slid inside of him.

He was gasping, head buried in his arms now, and I had to bite back the urge to ask him if he was okay every two seconds. Those were not unhappy noises he was making, and once I got past the initial nerves I couldn't focus on anything but how he felt. Hot and tight, he gripped my cock as I thrust deeper, my tentative movements growing more confident as Sam dragged out a moan.

"Fuck me harder," Sam demanded, voice doing that low scrape of gravel that sent shivers all down my spine. His hand went back to grasp my hip and I followed his lead, pushing into him until I was gasping with the friction, bottoming out so deep inside of him I swore we'd just melted together entirely.

I moved, then, in quick strokes. First I dug my fingers into his hips as I felt out the rhythm. When Sam moaned my name, though, I lost the last bit of restraint. I blanketed over his back, one arm wrapped around his neck as we moved, harder, the couch squeaking under our rocking motions.

Sam bit my arm. I returned the favor with my teeth in his neck, slamming into him to hear him groan. It was like he was pulling me deeper, clenching around me every time I withdrew, trying to keep me inside of him just a moment longer. Our bodies were slick with sweat, skin burning to the touch. I spread my hand across his belly, jerking him back against me. I planted one foot on the couch, knee bent, so I could change my angle.

It was a good move, judging by how much louder Sam got. Heat was racing through me, arousal jumping under my skin as we fucked harder, as Sam kept begging for more.

And then my foot slipped as I pulled out and I stumbled. I cracked my chin against the small of Sam's back and fell off the couch.

Stunned, I laid there, staring up at the ceiling, brain way too busy draining blood down to my cock to deal with standing up again. Jesus.

Sam started to laugh. I looked up, wounded, sprawled out on the floor with my cock practically squeezing any thought besides *Sam* and *sex* out of my head. "What's so funny?" I grumbled, up on my elbows.

"You are the biggest klutz," he informed me. Instead of me getting up, Sam came to me to straddle my waist and kissed my pout away. "We're going to have to get you some safety gear."

Grumbling, I slapped his ass. "A helmet," I agreed. "Maybe some kind of rope to tie me to you."

"I like ropes." He grinned. He wrapped one of his hands around the base of my dick. Before I could figure out what was happening, he'd lifted himself up only to sink back down on my cock, prompting a highly embarrassing level of moans from me.

Sam braced his hands against my chest, and he began to move, hips rolling in tight little circles, just barely giving us the friction we were both desperate for. He was grinning, still, head thrown back, looking entirely too pleased with himself.

It was always easier in movies to turn someone over, to switch places with that kind of passionate grace. I did my best, though, even if I did wind up knocking my shoulder against the desk. Sam was on his back, legs wrapped around my waist, while I fucked into him hard and deep. I didn't let up, didn't give him a second to breathe. Braced over Sam, I watched his eyes darken and glaze, felt his legs shake, knew he was getting close. I was pushing him there. His moans were for me; those breathless little noises he made when I moved just right were mine. My own tightening arousal was almost forgotten in favor of watching him, breath barely more than a ragged pant against his lips. We shared open-mouthed kisses, messy and desperate, his hands latched tight to my back.

"So close," he whispered, and I fumbled between us, wrapping a hand around his cock, trying to keep some kind of symmetry. It was hard to do when everything seemed completely soaked in need, in how tight he was, in the way he shuddered and shook.

"Come on, Sam," I murmured restlessly. "I want to see you."

His head fell back, gaze distant, focused only on the wave of pleasure I saw working through him. It started as he clenched around me, his body tightening, a string on a bow, curving up and taking everything I could give. Sam gasped, nails biting into my skin, jerking twice, and I felt his come hot against my hand. I kept moving and he moaned, long and drawn-out, legs wrapping more firmly around me. It didn't take much more for me; Sam flexing around my cock, the look in his eyes, the way he sucked kisses along my neck, and I was coming. White heat flashed behind my trembling eyelids, like someone had wound me up tight and then let me fly. I could feel every inch of me, every inch of *him*, and for a moment it was so overwhelming I thought I might come apart.

Sagging down on top of him, dazed, I couldn't catch my breath. We were tangled up together, Sam's arms around me, my hand buried in his chest hair, my face pressed to his shoulder. I couldn't even think about moving.

"That was fucking incredible," I finally said in between heaving gasps of air. "Seriously."

His fingers were sliding lightly along my back. I could feel him relaxing with every breath he took. I hadn't even noticed how tense Sam was normally until right then. He looked five years younger. "That was amazing," he agreed. Turning, he kissed my jaw, smiling against my skin. "*You* are amazing."

"Even if I'm clumsy?" I asked in a happy murmur. All I wanted to do right then was curl into a ball and cuddle. My inner chinchilla was relishing the warmth and connection and the petting. I wanted more of that.

"Especially because you're clumsy," Sam corrected, threading our fingers together. "You're pretty much amazing all around."

"You're sappy after sex," I teased. Not that I minded it.

"Yeah, well." Sam tried for a gruff look and completely ruined it by kissing me softly. "Don't tell anyone. I have a reputation to maintain."

"Your secret is safe with me." Nuzzling into his neck, I breathed out a happy sigh, letting my eyes fall half closed. We lay there in silence for a few minutes, Sam's hand dragging soft patterns against my side.

This wasn't bad at all.

EVENTUALLY we made it downstairs to his bed, where we curled up and fell asleep practically immediately. I ached in really good places, Sam was like a freaking furnace, and we were tangled together. This was pretty damn close to bliss.

I woke up drooling on Sam's pillow, hogging every blanket on the bed. Eyelashes fluttering, I groaned, rolling over and reaching out before I even processed where I was. Sam's side of the bed was empty, but I could hear him moving around out in the kitchen, and I caught a whiff of cinnamon and coffee. Breakfast. Peering over at the clock, I had to huff a laugh. Breakfast for dinner, then. Totally up my alley.

I tugged my T-shirt on and padded out to find Sam. The floor was chilly against my bare feet, my boxers were hanging low around my hips, and I was positive my hair was sticking up everywhere. I didn't particularly care, though; first priority was wrapping my arms around Sam's waist and kissing his shoulder. He'd neglected to put on a shirt, and I let my fingers play along the waistband of his sweats, smiling when his stomach hitched in a quick breath.

"Hey," he rumbled, leaning back into me. "You're up."

"And you're cooking." I smiled, kissing his neck, feeling so freaking *good*. He was dipping bread into what looked like eggs before putting them into a hot pan.

"French toast." He turned his head and kissed my ear, grinning. We both were grinning like idiots and I, for one, didn't want to stop. Sam looked so *relaxed* like this. That gruff scowl that had permanently creased between his eyes was gone now. When his gaze caught on me, his whole expression softened. "I know it's not really our first breakfast, but I wasn't sure what you'd want for dinner, and french toast is kind of a universal crowd pleaser."

"It smells fantastic," I assured him. So did he. His hair was still damp, he smelled like soap and aftershave and *us*, and, under all of that, the sharp spice I associated with Sam.

"There's a fresh towel and toothbrush and stuff in the bathroom," Sam told me. "If you wanted to wash up. We've got another ten minutes before this is ready."

"Sounds fantastic." I hesitated, though, worrying the inside of my cheek. "I just have to run up to my office."

After putting the last piece of bread in the pan, Sam turned, frowning, to rub a hand down my arm. "Everything okay?"

See, this was why I'd never done well at dating. What should have been a simple thing—have a romantic shower together—I now had to search for a plausible explanation as to why I was going to be different. Why I couldn't just hop in that easily. I'd come up with some weird-ass lies over the years. Except with Sam, I could just... tell the truth.

Huh. This was going to be interesting.

"I have to take a dust bath first," I sighed, rubbing the back of my neck, giving him a sheepish glance. "It's a thing. You know. A Chincha thing. Normal soap and shampoo and stuff don't really get me all the way clean."

Sam made an intrigued hum, lips pursing a little in thought. "Okay. So you have... dust in your office?"

"It's this really fine sand stuff." I shrugged. "I mean, ideally I'd have a pit in the bathroom I could use." That sounded weird; Sam was just kind of staring at me as if I was some kind of strange thing he couldn't quite wrap his brain around. "It's really fun to roll around in it. Like, my parents have a separate room for dust baths, with like almost a sandbox built in the middle?" I gestured with my hands, mimicking a square shape. "And you can actually get in and rub the dust into your hair and skin and roll around. I don't know how to explain it, but it's super relaxing."

Sam turned to flip the french toast over, nodding absently. "Do you do it every day?" he asked.

I rubbed my lower lip with my thumb as I watched Sam warily, trying to figure out if he was freaking out or not. "No. Couple of times a week. We use this special shampoo, really gentle, because our hair—"

I stopped as his fingers slid through said hair. A smile, so achingly fond, touched his lips. "It's so soft," he murmured. His other hand went up, combing through my messy waves and pulling me in close again. I relaxed, my shoulders slumping, raising my own hands to cover his.

"Yeah. It gets super brittle if I don't take care of it, so if I'm going to use your shampoo, I have to do the dust bath first." I wrinkled my nose up at him. "Is that… okay? I can wait and shower at home if that's too weird."

He kissed the bridge of my nose. "Where's the dust?"

"The bathroom in my office." My mom had taught me to always carry supplies with me. You never knew when you'd need chewing sticks or dust or a nail file. "It's in a big blue jar."

Sam pressed his lips softly to my forehead, my eyelids, my chin. Accepting me. Like he was processing through that new information and deciding he was okay with all of it. I slid my arms around his waist tightly. I sighed into his jaw, rubbing my cheek against the prickle of his stubble. "I'll go get it," he told me, sliding his fingers down my spine to tease at the dip of my back just above the band of my boxers. "I made coffee, if you want any."

He turned off the flame on the stove and then put the pan into the oven to keep warm. Before I could protest, he tugged on a flannel shirt, not bothering to button it, and moved to toe on his shoes so he could head upstairs. For whatever reason he wanted to be involved in my odd little quirks. And that was… incredible. *He* was incredible.

Dear Diary, I think I might be in love.

His bathroom was a decent-enough size, clean and, like the rest of his place, not suffering from an overabundance of personal touches. There was a towel on the sink, a clean washrag, a toothbrush still in the packaging. Smiling, I touched the pile lightly, wondering how on earth Sam had hidden the marshmallow center under the grumpy-guy image for so long.

Brushing my teeth, I heard the door open and shut, Sam's steps crossing the apartment to the bathroom. His gaze met mine in the mirror, corners of his eyes crinkling, and he held up the jar. I grinned around the toothbrush. "Victory is yours," I informed him and he laughed.

"Okay, so what do we do?" He set the dust down on the counter next to me while I rinsed out my mouth. "Is it just your hair?"

Wait. "What?" I paused, wiping my mouth and turning toward him. "Sam, you don't have to...."

"I know." He unscrewed the top of the jar to poke a finger in curiously. "But this is something you do, right?"

"Well, yes, but—"

"So I want to be here."

Watching him for a moment, unsure, I finally let out a breath and rolled my eyes. "You humans are so weird," I teased.

"Says the furry guy about to dump dust in his hair." Sam leaned in and kissed me, and I found myself grinning.

"Okay, so." I had that moment of fear before I tugged off my shirt. Even now, even after I'd seen the way Sam had wanted me, I was still ashamed. Like earlier, though, he didn't let me wallow in it. Sam kissed my shoulder, taking the shirt and tossing it away. "Basically I just put some in my hands and rub it through my hair, my arms, legs, uh...." I blushed. "Anywhere with hair."

There was a beat and then Sam laughed. I still couldn't get over how much the expression transformed his whole demeanor. "I know all the places you have hair." He smirked, thumbs hooking into my boxers and tugging them down.

I tried to give him a stern look, which totally didn't work when he was standing there with that little leer, when he wrapped his arms around me and all but picked me up to turn and deposit me into the tub.

I gave a—very manly—shout, startled, before bursting into laughter. "Oh my God, you're insane."

"I am simply trying to keep the mess contained," he informed me innocently, eyes dancing. "Is that a problem?"

I leaned up and bit at his lip. "Give me the dust, Ewing."

"Yes, sir." He pressed the jar into my hands. I was standing in his bathtub, naked, while Sam watched, about to rub dust over myself. This was quite possibly the weirdest first date ever. Then again, after what we'd done earlier, I wasn't sure we could categorize this as something like that. First dates were awkward kisses good night on the doorstep. We were way beyond that.

I shook some of the dust into my palm. I rubbed it through my hair with quick little motions. My face was next, then my arms, small amounts of the dust massaged into my skin and hair. I felt Sam's hands on me then, mimicking my movements, rubbing the dust over my chest. He knelt to do the same for my legs, and I couldn't help the happy little noises I was making. I relaxed into it, wriggling into his touch, that same languid pleasure seeping through me as if I'd decided to take a nap in sunlight.

Our fingers tangled together as we rubbed dust in around my cock, Sam happily giving the head a soft kiss as we finished. He stood then, seeing how blissed out I was, sliding his arms around my waist to tease his lips across mine.

"I am definitely going to remember this," he murmured in a rumble that hooked into my chest. "You look like you enjoyed it."

"It feels good," I agreed with a lopsided grin. "Never had anyone else do it to me. Well, when I was a kid, but this was *definitely* not like that." Thank God. "It's a thing that mates, you know, will do with each other…."

Shit. I'd said the infamous *M* word. Sam's expression didn't change, but I started to freak out. *Mates.* Partners. Whatever you wanted to call it, I'd just done a *dust bath* with Sam, and that wasn't exactly casual. Sure, it didn't mean we were soul mates or anything—I wasn't expecting this to turn into *that*—but it'd been kind of a big deal, and I hadn't even thought about it.

It'd just felt *right*, having Sam there.

"Do you think about it like that?" Sam asked me lowly, those smoky-blue eyes studying my face. I couldn't read him, couldn't figure out if I was supposed to say that it was just a term, an archaic one, that I was far more modern and hey, what was a little dust between friends?

Or, "Yes." Which was the truth, I realized. Shit, he was going to leave. "Or, uh, I mean *mate* sounds so weird, I know. But it just means *partners* or, you know. People who have a connection."

"People who are in love?"

We were both standing there, staring at each other. There was this cliff we were trembling at the edge of, this unbelievable drop that I didn't know if we'd survive. One foot over the brink, one more breath and we'd fall.

"Yeah." I barely got the word out, throat thick. "Yeah, people who are in love." A beat then, and I was pretty damn sure I was going to bolt. There had to be a handy hole I could go hide in. The silence dragged onward, Sam's expression never changing, and I was pretty sure I'd just ruined everything. No one talked about *love* the same day they got together with a guy. Well, no one who wasn't a crazy stalker. "But this doesn't mean anything. I mean, we normally don't *tell* anyone about the whole Chincha thing until we're married or partnered up, so."

Crap, was that making it worse? I talked faster, babbling to cover up how *scared* I was getting. "Not that I think we're... I mean, obviously, you're just different! You don't have to say anything or... we're just us, you know? We just started and that'd be crazy to expect something—"

"I think I love you." Sam stopped me with just those words. He looked so *unsure*, jaw clenched tightly enough that it had to be painful. It was like they'd been dragged out of him. As they hung there between us, me gaping like a freaking idiot, he turned and stalked away. Running his hands through his hair with a growl, he was already dismissing it. "Forget it. You're right, it's too soon, and I'm not going to be the one—"

It was my turn to stop him. I scrambled out of the tub, bare feet skidding on the mat, and grabbed his arm. "Me too." Searching his face, I reached up to cup his cheek. "I think I do too. Love you. I mean, it is, it's nuts and it's too soon, but…."

But.

"But it's you and me," Sam murmured, lips curving upward slowly, honey on hot toast as he melted into my touch. "It doesn't make sense."

"Maybe it does," I said softly. "For us, it does."

When Sam kissed me, it wasn't fire. It wasn't need. It was desperate and soft; it was all that strength, that gruffness, that hurt that lined his eyes, pouring into our connection. Sam was trusting me. As much as I'd trusted him with my secret, he was believing this time wouldn't be like before. When we pulled back he smiled faintly, shaking his head. "I knew you were trouble," he sighed. "Second I saw you."

"That's me," I intoned seriously. "Trouble is my middle name."

Man, I'd always wanted to say that.

"Go shower," Sam said. "I'm going to finish cooking."

Tugging him in for another kiss, I grinned against his lips. "Give me fifteen minutes and I'll be out."

Sam ran a hand through my hair, nudging our foreheads together. We stood like that for a few beats, my hands resting on his shoulders, just looking into each other's eyes. Which, okay, was incredibly gag inducing and overly sweet, but also just about the best thing I could imagine.

We finally did separate. I took a shower, Sam did cooking kinds of things, and we met back out in the living room to eat. French toast and coffee, the television on in the background while we talked about movies we liked, the piles of books I had at home, where we'd go on a dream vacation. Just stupid stuff that seemed so important when it was him. All those little pieces of his life that were mundane, that made up all the moments I hadn't seen yet, I was desperate to know.

I was leaning against him, legs out on the couch, his arm around me, and our fingers tangled together. Every so often he'd kiss my temple; every so often I'd rub my cheek against his shoulder. We finished eating, it got later, but I wasn't even thinking about leaving.

"What are you doing tomorrow?" I asked, rubbing absent circles against the back of his hand.

"I have some errands. Have to go to the hardware store for supplies, and there's a couple of maintenance things to do. Not much though. Why?" He took a sip of his coffee. "Do you want to go pick out paint with me?"

Smiling, I tugged his hand up and kissed his knuckles. "Yes. But I was also thinking of how we could get the evidence we need against Mr. Petros."

That caught Sam's interest. He looked down at me, one eyebrow arched. "Oh yeah?"

"We need proof, right?" I was half thinking out loud. The vague idea of a plan had occurred to me; I just wasn't sure how to pull it off. "So we need to get something we can show Petros, force him to retire."

"Retire?" Sam sat up a little, turning to face me. Concern puckered his lips and he scowled at me. "What happened to going to the police?"

"I'm just some guy who claims to be a private detective," I pointed out. "I mean, sure, I'm licensed, but come on, no one is going to believe me. Mr. Petros has been around for years. The Sally family trusts him. I don't know what I could do to convince the cops to investigate him or the owners to turn on a guy who's been running their business since they expanded. Besides, we'd have to explain how we got anything we brought in. And *going chinchilla* isn't really a recognized investigation technique. As much as I'd like to see him go to jail, this way at least he'll have to stop embezzling."

Sam still didn't look happy. "So you're, what? Going to go confront him?"

"Kind of." I fiddled with his fingers, lightly threading mine with them, the connection reassuring me when he got his incredibly irritated face on. "First, though, we're going to get your jacket cleaned."

A pause then. I was looking at Sam expectantly, but he didn't seem to catch on. "My jacket is fine," he grumped at me. "What does that have to do with anything?" Even as he said it, though, his eyes went wide. "Because we know the bookkeeper."

"And we'll have proof that they're charging more than they wind up depositing." I nodded. "You go in and get the customer copy. We'll get Mrs. Dallas to give us what she winds up with. And then we go see Mr. Petros."

Sam leaned back, considering. "It's a good plan," he agreed finally. "But you're not going to confront this bastard alone."

"Sam." I gave him a look. "He's a dry cleaner. I mean, sure, he's a thief, but it's not like he's some crime lord. I'll be fine."

"I know you will. Because I'm going to go with you." There was a stubborn tilt to Sam's jaw. I considered arguing, but in the end I just sighed and nudged my shoulder in under his.

"Fine. Overprotective."

"I can live with that." He slipped his arm back around me, kissing my temple. "So." That smile was back, the one that slipped across his face and sent little shivers of heat straight to my gut. "How do you feel about going back to bed?"

"We're both full of good ideas tonight." I grinned, tipping my chin up to catch his lips. He laughed and I felt it all through me, the soft thrill of knowing he was *happy*. With me.

Everything was going fucking awesome.

CHAPTER
SEVEN

SAM

So, apparently he was in love.

After Kyle, after his whole marriage had turned into fights and slammed doors and nights spent sleeping on the couch, Sam hadn't wanted to feel this way again. He'd done the whole *giddy in love* thing, he'd heard the bells on the fucking hill, and it'd all ended in a flaming pile of shit. So he could do without. He hadn't flirted, hadn't looked twice, hadn't even wanted to *start*. Not for a hell of a long time.

But then there was August. With his big brown eyes and that messy hair, the way he walked a little taller when he gained a bit of confidence, how he smiled, and Sam swore he'd cup his hands around that and do anything to keep it going. There was August, all but demanding Sam get over his own shit because here was something good.

So Sam was in love. Again. And part of him thought he was pretty much the world's biggest idiot.

But a bigger part knew that August wasn't Kyle. That this could really be *good*. If he let it. If he didn't get his head stuck up his own ass. So yeah, it was fast, and it was scary, but Sam had, a long time ago, stopped trying to put how he felt on any kind of timetable. His heart never listened, anyway. He'd hung around for Kyle long after he probably should have called it quits. And now he wanted August, wanted that *maybe*, that start, faster than Oprah might say was wise.

Then again, fuck Oprah. This was his damn life.

They'd woken up together that morning, August all rumpled and sleepy and totally useless for anything but grunting until Sam had fed him breakfast. And Sam was... happy. They'd eaten together in companionable silence, Sam rustling through the newspaper, August content to poke at his eggs and slowly wake up. By the time Sam had jumped in the shower, he was feeling pretty damn pleased with everything.

"So," he said as he walked out, pulling a towel around his hips, "why don't I go do my errands and then we meet up for lunch?"

August was obviously staring at him, coffee forgotten lifted halfway to his lips. Which, admittedly, Sam had been hoping for. It was damn nice to get a reaction. Sam knew he was getting older. Hair going a little gray, things getting stiff, but August looked at him like there wasn't a damn thing he'd change. Sam knew the feeling. August in the morning was something he'd like to get used to.

"I thought I was going with you." August stood and went about putting his dishes into the sink, darting little looks at Sam over his shoulder, like he was being sneaky. "Come on, I'm great at picking out paint."

"You sure?" Sam purposefully let the towel slip a little farther down his hips. "It's going to be boring."

August gave him a look. "You are trying to kill me." He fit so well into Sam's arms, August's own wrapping tight around Sam's waist. August kissed Sam's chest, his shoulder, the warm press of his lips sending happy shivers under Sam's skin. "And yes, I'm sure. I have to stop at home for some clothes first, if that's okay?"

"Yeah, sounds good." Sam was busying himself kissing down August's neck, tugging the collar of his T-shirt aside to reach more skin. "Soon as we get dressed we can go. You can call Mrs. Dallas from the road, make sure she's on board?"

"Hm?" August had that glazed look on his face, the one Sam was beginning to love. He'd arched his head to the side, moaning softly when Sam's teeth scraped lightly against his skin. "Yeah. Good."

"Or we could stay put." Sam grinned slyly, letting the towel fall away entirely. "You look very tired, August."

"Someone kept me up late," August grumbled, eyes narrowed. His hand slipped between them, wrapping around Sam's cock. The long, slow strokes were definitely getting Sam interested. "*Someone* likes to tease."

"Someone didn't seem to mind last night." Sam was backed up against the counter and he very happily spread his legs, ghosting almost-kisses along August's mouth. "Or early this morning."

"Who sets an alarm for 5:00 a.m.?" August dropped kisses to Sam's chin, his throat, down his chest. He sank to his knees and Sam's eyes went wider. "There is no reason to get up that early except to have morning sex."

"I will keep that in mind." At the first warm press of August's lips against his cock, Sam moaned, digging his heels into the floor and grasping the edge of the counter. "Shit, August...."

Sam could almost feel the smugness coming from August's smirk. August stroked Sam's cock slowly, sinking his mouth down, the wet heat sending arousal pounding through Sam's veins. Really, Sam thought he remembered being able to be much more composed during these things. Now, though, with August, Sam was reduced to a pile of whimpers, groans, and white-knuckling the counter.

Watching August was almost as good as the physical sensations. His lips stretched around Sam's cock, his hand moving in time with his mouth, and his eyes locked on Sam's face with this look of pure bliss. It was one of the sexiest things Sam had ever seen. August *wanted* to do this; he liked getting his mouth around Sam's dick. Sam got that. There was something addicting about getting to suck someone off, but he hadn't really expected to find someone who approached it with the same kind of enthusiasm.

August did this thing with his tongue. He sucked hard enough that his cheeks hollowed out, and Sam was barely able to keep his legs from buckling. His head fell back, his body arched into August's mouth, a low groan rumbling in his chest. August's free hand went up and laid on Sam's chest, his fingers curling into him, and the bite of nails warred against the intense pleasure of August's mouth.

Sam lost all track of time, of place, as if he'd been born and lived and died only in the feeling of August taking him deeper, of the tight stroke of his hand, the way his tongue pressed and teased. Sam barely had a chance to gasp a warning before he came, August licking him clean when he sagged down, little jitters of pleasure still trembling through his muscles.

"Jesus fuck," he managed, dazed. August was kneeling between his legs where Sam had sprawled on the floor, looking entirely too pleased with himself.

"You are so hot," August practically purred. His tongue darted out to swipe at his lips.

If Sam had been fifteen years younger, just the sight of that would have been enough to get him up and interested again. As it was, he grabbed August's hips and hauled him in, August's knees sliding on the linoleum floor. Sam grinned broadly at August's startled yelp. The noise quickly teased into a moan, though, as Sam mouthed his cock through his boxers.

"I believe this is called revenge," he informed August archly. He sucked the line of August's dick, burying his face between August's legs, digging his hands into those deliciously round cheeks of his ass. August was gasping, body rocking in little shockwaves, his hands slamming out to grasp the counter above them.

Sam had no intention of going slow. The front of August's boxers was wet and clinging to the outline of his hard cock. Sam slid down farther so he was half lying under August, his back pressed against the cupboards, sucking August's balls through the thin fabric. Above him, August was making that short little whimper that had driven Sam so crazy last night, as though he were begging when no words would come.

After dragging the boxers down, Sam happily sucked August's dick into his mouth, swallowing around him, getting him as deep as he could. He dug fingers into the full curve of August's ass, pulling him forward, encouraging him to rock into Sam's mouth.

August was tentative at first, his movements unsure. It occurred to Sam then that August might not have had anyone let him do this before. Which was just damn sad in his opinion. "Fuck my face," he growled, pulling away for a heaving breath, lips shiny and swollen.

Looking down at him with wide eyes, August barely managed a nod. August's chest was heaving low, shallow breaths, a flush curling along his skin. Christ, how was he so beautiful? Sam wanted to forget everything else, to spend *hours* just learning the path of his blush, the way goose bumps would spread across his arms, the rhythm of his heartbeat. Sam grinned up at him, slowly pursing his lips around the head of August's cock, sliding down until his nose was buried into the soft curls. August's moan was hoarse and drawn-out, his eyes falling half-shut, goddamn music to Sam's ears.

August rolled his hips and Sam swallowed around him, grasping his ass to encourage him. The salty weight of August's cock slid nearly all the way off his tongue before he thrust it back in, Sam moaning around it, sucking eagerly as August withdrew it again. August increased his speed, gasping, and Sam took the bruising thrusts, losing himself in the hard, heavy bliss.

"Sam," August moaned, his arms braced against the counter, face twisted in rising pleasure. "Christ, so good. You're so fucking good, babe, I'm gonna come."

He couldn't exactly respond, though Sam did have a momentary wish he could take a picture. August wasn't hunching in, trying to be unseen now. He was this gorgeous, free creature, given over to arousal, and Sam would never get tired of seeing him just like this.

A few more rolls of August's hips and he came. Sam swallowed it eagerly, wrapping his arm around August to keep him in close. When they finally broke apart, both panting, both spent, they collapsed to the floor in a messy, grinning puddle.

"I really like breakfast at your place," August mumbled with a slow smile, burrowing into Sam's arms, resting his head against his shoulder.

"Yeah." Their fingers laced together and Sam kissed August's knuckles, utterly content. "Me too."

THEY eventually did get off the floor, after Sam had gotten August off one more time. A nice slow hand job while they made out like teenagers was just what they needed. If Sam could get it up faster, he probably would have just dragged August to bed and forgotten the rest of the whole damn day. So maybe getting older was good for something—late forties meant he had to wait a lot more than twenty minutes between orgasms, which left time in his day for doing something other than August.

"Crap."

Sam was in the bedroom getting dressed when he heard August's miserable sigh. Poking his head out, tugging on his shirt, Sam gave him a look. "Something wrong?"

He was still naked, which Sam was never going to argue with, standing there with his boxers in his hand. "Yeah, uh. My boxers are just kind of... wet."

It took every ounce of control Sam had not to start laughing. August just looked so disappointed in his unwearable boxers. "Get your clothes. We can throw them in the washer while we're out."

August glanced down at himself, wiggling his bare toes against the floor. "Uh, while I appreciate your vote of confidence, I kind of think the good townspeople would frown on me going out like this."

"Well, then they're all idiots." Sam gave him a little smile, went over, kissed August's cheek, and took his boxers out of his hands. "But

I have some things you can wear for now. We'll stop at your place first, even, if you want, so you can get into something of your own."

While Sam gathered up August's clothes for the washer, the other man was surprisingly quiet. Sam shot him a glance to find August looking worried, a palpable air of shame in the way he had curved his shoulders inward, curling his stance smaller. His mouth opened and closed a few times, no words actually making it out, and Sam's heart broke. He didn't even know why, but August was breaking him.

"What?" he asked, frowning, concerned. "What did I do?"

August barked out a quick, helpless laugh, scrubbing a hand through his hair. "Just… I really like the idea of wearing your clothes, but…." He waved a hand at Sam and then back at himself with an anguished twist of his lips. "Nothing you have would fit me."

Sam didn't understand why he looked so crestfallen. "I know what you look like, August," Sam pointed out, confused. "I'm not blind."

"It's like this thing, you know? Wearing your boyfriend's clothes. Only I can't. Because I'm a giant fucking hippo." August was spiraling a little, and Sam went over to him to grasp his shoulders and ducked his head to meet August's eyes.

"August," Sam said, torn between a frown and a reassuring smile. "I have clothes that will fit you. And you never have to feel bad about what you look like. I am attracted to you. Okay?"

After a beat, August nodded, and Sam rubbed his hands down August's arms. He personally wanted to go kick the ass of everyone who'd ever looked at August and seen anything but perfection. Only knowing that it wouldn't make a difference stopped him from starting an ass-kicking list right then and there. Sam kissed August softly, then took his hand and led him to the bedroom.

"Okay," Sam said, hands on his hips, scowling at his messy closet. "The box is in here somewhere."

"What box?" August asked, peering curiously at the disorganized tangle of clothes and whatever else Sam had thrown in there for storage.

"Kyle's old shit. There were some of his clothes I never bothered to give to the thrift shop." Frowning, Sam carefully pulled one box aside, trying not to start an avalanche. "Several years out of style now, but they'll be clean."

Ah, there it was. Shoved all the way in the back, of course. Sam dug it out and deposited it on the bed. He flipped open the top and rifled through it. There were a few shirts, a pair of jeans, several boxers, and some old photographs. Sam wondered when he didn't feel the same pang of loss and anger and bitterness he normally got when he saw photos of him and Kyle. Then again, that might have everything to do with who was sitting there with him.

"I definitely am not going to fit in your ex's stuff," August said, sounding weary. Sam had to assume at this point that August thought Sam was completely visually impaired.

"Yeah, you're probably right," he mused. "Kyle was bigger than you."

The shock on August's face was almost worth it. Sam showed him a picture of Kyle, taller than Sam, blond hair, big grin. It was a photo of the two of them at the zoo, near the start of the relationship. Sam's hair had been dark then, no gray in sight, and he'd been kissing Kyle's cheek. Happy.

If only he'd had a fucking crystal ball.

"That's Kyle?" August asked, sounding stunned.

"Yeah." Sam put the picture aside and moved to shaking out a T-shirt to consider it. It had the logo of a pub they'd liked, a long time ago, but it looked like it'd fit August without being too large. "Why?"

"That is so not what I pictured."

Sam cut him a quick glance, eyebrow raised. "Oh yeah? And what did you have in mind?"

"I don't know." August took the boxers Sam handed him, then tugged them on. They slipped a little lower on his hips than August's others, but Sam didn't count that as a bad thing. "Like you. Fit, good-looking."

"He was good-looking," Sam said lowly. "August, I thought Kyle was hot. He and I did not work out, at all, but it wasn't because I didn't find him attractive. What, did you think I didn't like bigger guys? It's kind of my type."

"I thought you were just being nice," August admitted, taking the offered T-shirt and pulling it over his head. The jeans followed, August hopping up and down, foot to foot, to hitch them on.

Sam paused, face creasing into a frown. "Really? You thought all that… you thought I was just, what, pitying you?"

August's shoulders raised in a shrug. "I don't know. Yes?"

He had to take a deep breath, trying to force back his irritation. Sam knew he had a temper. Kyle had liked to poke his buttons, to make him lash out. August wasn't Kyle, wasn't *trying* to start a fight. He was just… really, really wrong.

"I'm not," Sam said shortly, packing everything back up into the box. "You are hot. God, you have no idea. The first day I saw you, I couldn't stop thinking about you. This is what I like." Sam ran his hand down August's back, studying his face. "This is what gets me going. If you lost weight, I'd still want you. If you gained weight, I'd still want you, because you're *you*. But if you're talking pure body types? Yeah. I like bigger guys."

This seemed to not be the answer August had been expecting. He was fiddling with the hem of his shirt, looking down at the jeans, which were almost covering his feet in length. He looked a little ridiculous in Kyle's clothes, but Sam didn't care. He was August. He was beautiful. End of the goddamn story.

"You're kind of incredible," August told him lowly.

Sam just laughed. "No. I just know what I like." But they smiled at each other, and August kissed him sweetly, so Sam wasn't going to argue too much.

"Come on," August said, finding his shoes and shoving them on his feet. "Let's go run your errands. I want to call Mrs. Dallas on her lunch break to make sure she's in."

"Do you know when she normally goes?" Sam asked, finding his jacket.

"Every day at twelve thirty." August nodded. "It's on the schedule Mr. Petros gave me."

"Okay." Their hands joined together easily as they locked Sam's door behind them, as they walked upstairs and out onto the street. It'd been forever since Sam had held someone's hand. He'd forgotten how nice it could be. "So, your place first, then the hardware store, and then to the dry cleaners?"

"Sounds perfect."

Yeah. It really did.

THEIR morning went well. Sam sat on August's couch and paged through one of his detective novels while August changed. They spent half an hour play fighting over what color Sam should paint the hallways—August won with a light tan over Sam's pick of plain white—and they got lunch at a local diner. They'd held hands over a plate of fries, and hell, they'd shared a freaking milkshake. If it'd been anyone else, Sam would have gotten diabetes just hearing about it.

But it was him and August. So they'd laughed, they'd talked, August had pulled Sam away from giving a scowling lecture to a bunch of kids who were flicking cigarette butts onto the ground. They worked, the two of them.

While August called Mrs. Dallas, Sam hauled the paint and brushes inside and put them into his storage room. That would be a whole-weekend job. Maybe he could convince August to help—it might be fun, to see August paint covered and smiling. There were a couple of things on Sam's to-do list for the week: a walk-through to make sure there weren't any problems he didn't know about, cleaning the carpets in 301, repairing some trim in the second-floor hallway. Nothing urgent, and nothing that couldn't wait.

"I'm not sure when I became your junior detective," he grumbled at August, putting up a scowl as August kissed him.

"Hey, you help me solve this and you get an honorary trench coat." August flopped down on the couch and kicked his feet up on the coffee table, said trench coat making him impossibly adorable. "So, you ready for your big show?"

"Mrs. Dallas is going to help out?" After putting the last can of paint on the shelf, Sam shut the door and sat down next to August. He reached out and pulled August's legs over his lap. He rubbed his fingers absently along August's knees.

"Yup. I'm going to call her with your ticket number so she'll know which receipt to pull. She's going to get into the safe first thing in the morning. We'll have what we need tomorrow."

August looked so damned pleased with himself. Sam liked that confidence, the way he held himself. If this was what working a case did to him, Sam wanted August to have a lot more work.

"Okay, so I'd better get going." Sam pressed kisses to the tops of August's knees, smiling faintly. "Don't want to let you down, boss."

They tumbled off each other, though Sam couldn't resist pulling August in for a slow kiss. The smile he left behind was worth it. Sam found an old suit in his closet to take in to be cleaned and they set off, Sam's arm around August's shoulders. At the corner, August stopped him.

"I can't go in," he explained. "They know me." Sam could see the flicker of worry on August's face, hidden quickly behind a smirk, a joke, as if Sam wouldn't notice. "And I'm not exactly Jake's favorite person."

Yeah, it probably would be best to keep August out of the Sasquatch's sight. Jake might recognize Sam as the scruffy, grumpy guy who shouted at him to get out of the trash, but Sam could handle him. Hell, it'd been dark enough that it was more than possible Jake wouldn't remember him at all. August, however, had made a more lasting impression. Sam squeezed August's shoulder and nodded. "I won't be more than ten minutes."

"I'll be in my office." August gave him another smile, this one more genuine, and headed back across the street. Sam watched him as he went, making sure he got in the building all right. August might be willing to blow off Petros as just a crooked manager, but Sam wasn't about to let his guard down until this stupid case was behind them. Men had done a lot dumber things for money than hurt the guy who could bring them down.

The bell above the door jangled as Sam walked inside. Sure enough, Jake was at the counter, sausage fingers jabbing at his phone. He didn't even look up as Sam waited patiently. For about five seconds.

"Hey." Sam whistled sharply. "Look alive. I want to get this done before I collect social security."

Jake looked up, an ugly scowl creasing his forehead. "Yeah, looks like that's not too far off, grandpa." There was a brief glare, a moment when Sam was sure Jake would remember him, but in the end Jake's expression settled into vague annoyance and nothing else.

"So you better move quick, kid." Sam put his suit on the counter. "Just need this cleaned. You can get back to cruising for porn in no time at all."

Jake grunted, grabbing a stack of receipts to start scrawling down information. Sam gave his name and address, signing where he was told to, and then it was done. "We'll call you when it's ready," Jake muttered, attention already back on his phone.

"And you have a *great* day." Rolling his eyes, Sam turned and walked out, carefully folding his copy and putting it in his pocket. That was that. They'd call Mrs. Dallas with the ticket number and tomorrow morning they'd have what they needed to confront Petros. And, if all went well, this whole thing would be done. Simple.

AUGUST

Nothing was ever simple. Nothing ever just went like it was supposed to. I'd gone home, mostly so if I decided to stay over again I wouldn't have to keep wearing Sam's ex's clothes, but also because I didn't want to crowd him. What we'd started was kind of incredible. The last thing I wanted was to smother him with my intense need to be near him all the time.

Turned out that I was going to be the kind of guy that missed him ten minutes after I left. Awesome. I'd just add *insanely clingy* to my list of good qualities, right under *nonexistent self-esteem* and *hogs the blankets.*

Still, I was pretty proud of myself. I managed to keep from calling him. Instead I tried to keep busy. I dusted. I did dishes. I even cooked dinner.

Well. *Cooked* is such a strong word. I opened a can of soup and made toasted cheese sandwiches. But a stove was involved!

I got myself settled in on the couch, flipping through the channels absently. Once again, my phone beckoned to me, but before I could give in and punch in Sam's number, my attention was caught by the opening credits on the screen.

The Maltese Falcon. Oh hell yes. Only one of the greatest movies ever made, starring my favorite fictional character. This was more than enough of a distraction. I settled in, the familiar soundtrack washing over me, the reassuring black-and-white frames like coming home.

My phone going off made me jump ten feet. Didn't help that I had set "The Imperial March" as the ringtone. Heart hammering like a drum, I punched the Call Accept button without even looking at the number. "Hello?"

A moment of silence and then Sam's low, gravelly voice. "Hey." He sounded as surprised as I was that he was calling. "I, uh." Another long beat of quiet before I heard him exhale a muttered oath. "Fuck. I missed you."

I was pretty sure an entire tidal wave could have crashed into me, flooded my apartment, ruined my computer, and rendered all of my books unreadable, and I *still* would have been grinning. Curling up on the couch, I turned the volume of the movie down, trying not to let the ridiculous smile show in my voice. "Oh, really?"

"Yes," he muttered, sounding entirely too grumpy. That just made my lips stretch further, my cheeks hurting with how hard I was smiling. "Shut up."

"I missed you too."

Now it was Sam's turn to sound pleased. "Is that a fact?"

"Yes." Burrowing down under the afghan my mom had crocheted for me, I leaned my head back, eyes closing, just listening to the timbre of his voice. "You are kind of addicting."

"Right back at you." I could hear the faint rustle of his couch, a click, and the background noise of the television faded away. "So, what are you up to?"

He sounded so unsure, so out of his depth at this, that I had to bite back a laugh. It was adorable—well, as much as *Sam* could ever be called that. "I was watching a movie." Normally I would have left it at that. My enthusiasm over old-school film noir and detective flicks was not normally a great conversational topic. But I went on, because it was Sam, because he got to know about my geeky tendencies. Because I trusted him to like me—*love* me—even if he made fun of my deep, abiding crush on Humphrey Bogart. "It's *The Maltese Falcon*. One of my favorites. Have you ever seen it?"

Sam huffed out a laugh. "God, not for years. *That's* one of your favorite movies?"

"What's not to love?" Bogart was on the screen as we spoke, that intense gaze needing no color at all to burn straight through the set. "Murder, mystery, treasure, unrequited manlove…."

"I must have missed that part," Sam hummed. I could practically feel the warmth of him through the phone. "Where was the homoerotic subtext again?"

"Oh, please. The whole film is basically him taking revenge for his partner's death. Spade totally was in love with Miles Archer."

"Didn't Spade sleep with Archer's wife?" Sam pointed out, an amused little drawl in his voice.

I was not deterred though. Snorting, I waved that off. "That was how men showed their love in 1950s movies," I informed him. "You couldn't just be gay. So you slept with their wife or pined after their girlfriend or whatever. It's like a code."

"I stand corrected." Sam really did laugh at that, soft and low, and it hit me like a shot how much I already cared about him. How deep that new love had already taken root. I'd say it was just like a story, that you could meet someone and *feel* that much, except nothing much in my life adhered to the good side of such tropes.

"What channel is it on?" I could hear the rustle of Sam moving. I imagined him settling further into the couch, that far too sexy sprawl he had taking up most of the room. "Wait, never mind. I found it."

"Are we going to watch it together?" I asked, feeling ridiculously pleased by the prospect.

"It's your favorite movie," he answered, like that was all the explanation he needed.

The movie went on, Sam asking me questions to catch him up, the both of us commenting softly as the plot progressed. It was... comfortable. Even though we were separated by a few blocks and even more buildings, it was strangely intimate. Just the two of us on the phone, going long moments in silence with no awkwardness or me feeling the need to babble on. We simply watched the movie.

"I love this part," I murmured as the last scene began to play. "Just that line. And the look on his face."

The stuff that dreams are made of.

"What is it with you and this stuff?" Sam asked. The music faded, commercials rolling, and I flicked off the television. "I mean, your books, your favorite movie, hell you even *became* a detective. Why do you like it so much?"

No one had ever asked me that before. I sprawled back on the couch, staring at the ceiling, considering the question. "I don't know," I admitted slowly. "I mean, I guess I like that it's not just bad guys and good guys. Everything makes you think, and you could argue that there's no real hero. Just someone trying to figure shit out the best way they can." Rubbing my thumb across my lip absently, I sighed. "And I think... everyone in my family, my herd, we're all so timid. I mean, not weak, but we live pretty quiet lives. I don't know, I guess I just want someone to look at me and think I have guts, you know, that gumption they're always talking about. The audacity to not follow the rules."

Sam was silent for a long moment. I actually got worried he'd found that whole thing too weird sounding. But then, very softly, "You're kind of amazing."

A faint smile flickered across my lips. "I wish you were here."

I could hear the creak of the couch. "I can be there in fifteen," Sam pointed out.

"You're not going to get sick of me?" I looked around, wrinkling my nose at the piles of books and my laundry still in the basket. "I'm kind of a slob."

"Fifteen minutes, babe." Sam's voice had dropped to a low little growl. "Not one second longer."

Then he was gone and I was left grinning giddily up at my ceiling.

Oh shit, my bed was a disaster.

I spent ten minutes running around like an idiot, shoving dirty laundry in the closet, changing my sheets, dithering on whether or not I should light candles. That was solved by the fact I didn't *own* any candles. When the knock came at my door, I froze, staring, heart thundering wildly.

God. Sam was going to spend the night. Somehow that made everything so much more real.

He was smiling when I opened the door. Sam leaned in to kiss me hello in that way he had, and all my nerves turned to happy butterflies.

Standing aside, I let him in, watching as he filled up my apartment, all that intense masculinity turning the place I stayed into *where he was.*

Shutting the door behind me, I studied him. He was in the middle of my living room in jeans that hugged his legs, a T-shirt that stretched tight across his shoulders. And he was mine. God, right then, it was like I just realized it. Sam and I were together. This was actually happening.

"Take off your pants," I told him hoarsely.

He blinked, and my momentary flare of aggression died a little into worry. I shouldn't have bothered. In the next moment Sam's expression turned sharp and hungry. He immediately unbuckled his pants, the clink of his belt sending a little hook of want through me. Eyes locked on mine, Sam stepped out of his jeans and kicked them aside, boxers following to puddle down at his feet. He stood still then, watching me, waiting.

"Shirt," I whispered.

He ducked out of it and let it fall as well. He was so beautiful naked, long lines and soft hair and his cock just starting to get hard. I let him stand there for a long few moments, admiring the view.

"I… I don't know what to do next," I admitted. I liked how his eyes had darkened when I told him to undress. I liked how Sam's want was so clearly seen in the way he stood, in the way his gaze hadn't broken from mine. But this was kind of out of my depth. I'd wanted him naked, which had now happened, so after that I was kind of lost.

"I could undress you," Sam suggested lowly.

Yeah, I definitely liked that idea. I moved closer, then ran my hands down his chest to his hips, absorbed in the feel of warm skin under my fingers. "Bedroom is that way," I murmured. "But I still don't have any, uh…."

"Sex things?" Sam finished for me with a grin. "Don't worry, I brought supplies. Though we really are going to have to go shopping soon."

"Later." I kissed under his jaw, his throat, smiling when I felt him rumble a low moan. "Come on."

Hand in hand, we went into my bedroom, Sam looking totally out of place next to my dinosaur sheets. Then again, it wasn't a bad thing, him there; my sheets could use something this amazing on them. Dinosaurs were cool, but naked Sam was pretty hard to beat.

His hands went to my shirt to undo the buttons carefully. When I dropped my eyes with that familiar flare of nerves, he paused, waiting. When I looked up at him, he smiled at me, softly kissing my lips. "You're gorgeous," he murmured. "I want to see you naked. I was going to dream about you tonight."

Flushing, I didn't look down again. I watched him as he undid my shirt, as he slowly eased it off my shoulders. My pants were next, his hands so gentle against my skin, sliding across my hated stomach, my side rolls, the thickness of my thighs, as if each part were important. As if he wanted to explore all the parts I kept hidden. He knelt in front of me and kissed my stomach He leaned in to let his tongue touch the head of my cock. When I gasped he grinned, nuzzling in to suck my balls with soft, wet kisses.

I was pretty much done for.

"Get on the bed," I told him, voice sinking into a hoarse moan.

He took his time, lightly running his lips down the length of me. When he sprawled back on the bed, I followed him eagerly, blanketing him and catching his mouth in a slow, achingly bottomless kiss. I buried myself in his mouth, our tongues twisting together, his hands flexing against my back.

"Do you want me to fuck you?" Panting, I pulled back, searching his eyes. "I want to make you feel good, Sam."

"Hell yes." His lips curled into a grin, and he hauled me back in, our kiss turning into breathless pants. "My bag, in the living room."

I bit his lower lip before sitting up next to him. "I want to do something... I don't know. I want to try something new." I'd seen a lot of porn. I had some ideas. "Okay?"

Sam sat up, catching my hand with his where it was playing through the faintly curling salt-and-pepper hair on his chest. "Babe, I'll try anything. Whatever you feel comfortable with."

I kissed him, harder, before forcing myself to climb out of bed. "I'll be right back."

Sam's bag held clothes, shampoo, a toothbrush, and a large bottle of lube. There was a box of condoms as well, and I took both of them back to the bedroom. Sam was sprawled back, one knee bent, his fingers wrapped around his cock as he stroked it slowly. When I stuttered to a halt, eyes wide, he smirked at me.

"I'm not very patient," he informed me. Dropping the lube and condoms on the bed, I climbed up next to him. Straddling his waist, I kissed him hard enough to press his head back against the wall. My hand joined his, tightening our joined grips, stroking him harder. That smug look turned into a loud moan. I rocked forward, my cock rubbing against his.

For a few moments, there was nothing but that. We shared groans, hissed in breaths, eager strokes that drove us higher. He rolled me with a muffled growl, his free hand grabbing my hair, teeth nicking my lip. I grabbed his ass with greedy hands, hitching him in even closer. Right then, I was perfectly happy to do just this. Arousal was arching through me, white-hot flares under my skin.

"You keep this up, I'm going to come," Sam gritted out.

"Shut the fuck up. You're not that old," I muttered, wrapping my legs around his hips and shifting my hand so I was stroking us both in one grip. "We're going again."

He might have protested if he wasn't so busy kissing me. We inhaled each other, his hand joining mine, our hips rocking together in a desperate, hungry dance. When he came it was with a soft gasp, my name lost in the air shared between us. And then I followed, grasping him, biting my lip as I swallowed back greedy cries for more.

We lay together, panting, his fingertips painting loose trails up and down my arm. "God," I mumbled, dazed, staring at the ceiling from under heavy lids.

Sam kissed my neck. "Yeah," he agreed, a low drawl in his voice catching at the very bottom of my gut. "You're so fantastic."

It was beyond amazing to get to lie there like that, limbs tangled together, Sam's breath a heavy exhale along my chest. We kissed softly, murmured happy words that got folded into lips and hands and shared pants. I turned us, sprawling on top of him, and honestly, in that moment, I didn't feel like the fat kid. We were just Sam and August, and my body was the thing that I was in instead of the thought at the back of my mind, the disgust or the shame that rounded out every thought. I was just *with him*, and it felt so goddamn good.

We half fell asleep curled up together, dozing lightly, Sam's hand occasionally running along my hip. "I love you," he murmured.

"Love you too."

His hand found mine, fingers tightly threaded with my own. I kissed his cheek, his shoulder, whatever part of him I could reach. This felt better than I thought something like this could—not just the sex, although as my tongue mapped the dips and curves of his collarbone I was already starting to get interested in more of that. It was how he smiled at me, when he didn't smile at anyone else. How he said my name. How he'd jumped in and helped me on this case, for no reason I could see.

We just *fit*. Nerdy, awkward, babbling, chinchilla-shifting me fit with him so well it was a little scary to think about.

"Have you ever done rimming?" I blurted into the stillness.

Sam had been mostly asleep, chest rising and falling slowly. He cracked open one eye to look at me, huffing out an amused breath. "That's a little random," he mused, grunting as he stretched himself back to wakefulness. "Uh." Scratching his chest, he yawned. The gaze that turned on me then, though, was definitely intrigued. "Yeah. I've rimmed. Been rimmed. Why?" A slow little smirk spread across his face. "You interested?"

"It's that thing I was talking about. That I want to try." I lightly bit at his shoulder, hop-skipping kisses up to his neck. "Is it, um, is it something you like?"

Eyes lighting up, Sam ran his hands down my back. His fingers lightly curved around the crease of my ass, one of them rubbing gently against my hole. "Yeah," he rumbled, ghosting his lips across mine. "I really do." I smiled as he kissed me, a surprised moan at how good even just the light touch felt. "Were you wanting to try giving or receiving?"

"Both," I mumbled, too busy kissing him back to bother to give a better answer. I'd never felt comfortable even bringing up the idea to past boyfriends. Sam was just so eager, though, about everything we did. Now seemed like a good time.

A startled yelp escaped me when Sam suddenly flipped us. He grinned, pinning me lightly, nuzzling light bites against my throat. "How about I show you how it goes?" His voice was low against my ear.

What else could I do but nod? Sam nudged me to roll over before tucking a pillow under my stomach. I bent my knees, ass in the air, and felt like an absolute idiot. Pretty sure he was making fun of me, I looked over my shoulder, a flush starting on my cheeks. But Sam was crouched behind me, pure heat in his gaze, and my words died in my throat. He kissed my shoulders, my back, down to the dip above my waist. I was silent, eyes wide, watching as Sam's teeth closed on one ass cheek. He sucked a reddened mark there, leaving me reduced to low moans.

His tongue flicked across my hole, and I jerked a little in surprise. Apparently Sam was expecting that response—he went slowly, licking up and down my crease, applying light pressure against my hole, the wet heat of his tongue feeling so odd. As he nuzzled his face in, I felt the scrape of his stubble against my skin, the pressure of his tongue gradually stroking me into a collapsed puddle of whimpers.

What had started out foreign became a teasing flame of want, every slide of his tongue rendering me almost incapable of noise. I was gasping, nearly soundless, fingers twisting into the sheets. His tongue fucked me deeply, the hard press of his finger following, and I spread my legs wider, desperate for it. He laughed when I moaned, the sound ripping from some low register I'd never reached before. I was hard, aching, pressing back against his face with greedy, wanton rolls of my hips.

When Sam pulled away, I was too dazed to do anything but protest. I felt his lips softly sucking a path up my body, and Sam then rubbed his tongue lightly under my ear. "Do you want me to keep going?" he asked. "I'm more than happy to."

I'd had a plan. It had been a very good plan. It was slightly hard to *think* about said plan when Sam's finger was buried in my ass, nudging my prostate with gentle rocks, when his mouth was nibbling a path down my neck. But I managed a strangled, "Wait," and he paused, watching me.

"Get on your stomach," I told him, and like before, he seemed all too happy to follow orders. "I want to do that to you. And then—" I took another deep breath, steadying myself, trying to ball up that insistent press of arousal so I could focus on him. "I'm going to fuck you."

He groaned just from my words. I could feel the smile like it'd started in my toes and crept up to curl on my lips. Sam was like a freaking sex god, flushed and sprawled out on my bed. Those dinosaur sheets had never looked so damn good.

Tracing a path down his back with my teeth and tongue, I hesitated when I reached Sam's ass. This wasn't something I'd done before. And as hot as it'd been to have it done, *doing* it was a little overwhelming.

Gumption, Mendez.

I started with slow, sucking kisses against his thighs, the small of his back, the round curve of his ass. I pressed my thumb lightly against his hole, rewarded by his encouraging moan. Sam was being more vocal than before, guiding me with sharp intakes of breaths, his groans, the way he arched his back against my touch.

I slid my tongue along his crease, down to the soft skin at his balls and then back up again to his hole. As I pressed the flat of my tongue there, Sam gave a strangled whimper, spreading his legs, muscles jumping. Just the sound of it sent heat ripping through me and the last of my reservations went up in smoke. I *wanted* him. I wanted that sound again. I wanted him to come undone under me.

I fucked my tongue into him, my face buried between his cheeks, hands grasping his hips. Whatever I lacked in technique, I made up for in enthusiasm. I dove in eagerly before pulling back to swirl my tongue around his hole, to lap lightly and then fuck in hard, responding to every shake and moan and begging gasp.

I flailed out blindly to find the lube and hurriedly slicked up one finger. It joined my tongue, sliding in deep, stroking out, faster until Sam was writhing under me, slowing down until he was cursing for more. It was heady, to be doing this for him, to be so *in tune* with him. It was like I knew just how fast to go, when to pull back, when to return to teasing licks, and when to add another finger just from how he sounded, how his muscles were flexing.

"Please, babe." His voice was strung out, thready, a hitch to every vowel. "Please, I need you. God, Aug, fuck me, fuck me now, *please*."

Yeah, like anyone alive could have resisted that.

Fingers shaking, I dropped the condom twice, once losing it completely under the bed. Cursing, I grabbed another foil packet, ripped it open with my teeth, and slid the condom over my cock. Just that contact and I had to pause, breathing deep.

"You're doing good, sweetheart." Sam reached back to grasp my leg with his hand. His incredible blue eyes were darkened with need, were so kind that I had to stop and kiss him. I grasped his shoulder to turn him onto his back, the kiss turning into famished breaths, wicked little pops of desire.

I pushed my hand through his hair, holding his gaze as I slowly slid into him. He was so tight, so perfect around me, and I almost couldn't get any air despite frantic inhales. His legs wrapped tightly around my waist, and I moaned against his lips, slowly rocking in almost languid rolls of my hips. The friction was teasing and slow. We were both so wrapped up in each other, in deep, eager kisses, that it was like it was more than just fucking. Every inch of us was touching, stroking, grasping, and grinding together.

His fingers found mine and we twisted our hands together. I moved faster then, our eyes locked, our exhales mirroring. I said his name in a soft groan, and he said mine under a drawn-out noise of need. Grabbing his leg with my free hand, I moved to hook his knee over my shoulder and thrust into him harder, faster, the change in angle making his back arch up as he tightened around me. "Fuck yes, Aug."

"God, Sam." I dug my fingers into his leg, and I leaned over him, hips pounding a rhythm we both were desperate for.

Head pressed back into the mattress, teeth gritted, Sam came. He was fucking *gorgeous* when he came, a flush sweeping across his skin, the way his stomach would clench before he sagged back, spent. Watching that, I almost forgot everything else, my own orgasm hitting me like a wave.

Sprawled out, panting, sweat-slicked skin pressed against skin, I realized vaguely that our hands were still clasped together. Smiling, lazy and sated, I turned my head and dragged kisses along Sam's shoulder.

"I love you, Sam."

"Love you too."

THE blare of my phone shattered my sleep. Jerking awake with a bewildered grunt, I rolled over, thrashing the sheets and windmilling my arms as I tumbled out of bed. Dazed, I sat on the floor, comforter tangled around my legs, completely unsure of where I was or what was happening.

"Phone," Sam's muffled plea rose up from his side of the bed.

"Yeah. Yeah, got it, sorry." I managed to shake the sleep from my brain, staggering to my feet and searching for it. My pants were in a pile at the foot of the bed. Digging through the pockets, I finally grabbed my phone and offered a breathless, "Hello?" just before it flipped to voice mail.

"August? Dear, it's Mrs. Dallas."

It took me a minute to figure out who was calling me. Hopping up and down on one foot, I managed to tug my boxers on. I stepped out into the living room to hopefully let Sam keep sleeping. "Mrs. Dallas? Oh, right, sorry, yes. Mrs. Dallas." Cracking a yawn, I shuffled over to the kitchen and went absently poking through my cupboard for coffee. "What's going on?"

"I'm afraid I have some bad news." Her voice wavered and I paused in my fussing, a frown creasing my forehead.

"What is it?" This couldn't be good. My eyes went to the clock— barely even seven in the morning. Nothing good happened this early.

"Phillip fired me last night."

I blinked, stunned. For a moment I couldn't even think of a response. "He what?"

"Last night, he called me and told me not to bother coming in this morning." She sounded equal parts angry and upset. "I don't know what happened."

I did. She'd met with me. Petros must have an idea we were on to him. Or at least he thought he knew what his weak spot was. Without Mrs. Dallas, I'd have no way of getting the evidence we needed. "I am so sorry," I told her thickly.

"Yes, well." She sniffed a little, obviously drawing herself up. "Such things happen. I'm just sorry I won't be able to help you boys take that bastard down."

I bit back a quick, inappropriate laugh. She just sounded so *prim* while she cursed. "Me too, ma'am. I just…." Wait. "Where would yesterday's receipts be?"

"In the safe, of course," Mrs. Dallas said. "What are you thinking, dear?"

"If I could get into the dry cleaners without being seen, would you have a way for me to get in that safe?"

She paused. "I could give you the combination," she finally said slowly. "Phillip can hardly change the register tape, much less mess with the electronic safe. He'll bring someone in to change the combination for him, though. That's his way. So you'll not have much of a window."

Enough of one. I looked at the clock again. They were open for the before-work crowd, but no way could Petros get someone in for the safe until later. "Give me the combo, Mrs. Dallas. I'll take care of the rest."

I could hear her hesitation, but in the end she sighed and gave in. "Seven, three, two, two, nine."

"Thank you," I told her, hastily jotting down the numbers. "Thank you so much."

"Be careful, August," she ordered me before hanging up.

Right. Careful. That was practically my middle name.

I got dressed quickly. Sam had fallen back asleep, and I nearly woke him. But I'd be back soon, and it wasn't like he could go in with me. In the end, I left a note on my pillow and headed out. I'd bring back coffee and muffins from the bakery, and he wouldn't even know I was gone.

Sam,

Don't worry, just went out to get the evidence. I'll be back soon.

You were awesome.

-A

Nothing ever was simple.

Ducking into the alley next to the dry cleaners, I nervously looked around. I couldn't remember the last time I'd even heard of a Chincha shifting in full daylight without it being some kind of dire emergency. But this way I could get into the building the same way I'd done before, and it was the only chance I had to get into that safe. So, ducking behind a dumpster, I gave one last wary glance toward the street and began to change.

Shifting never really *hurt*, per se. It was how my body was supposed to work, and honestly, as much as we might never admit it, there was something that felt so right about changing into chinchilla form. Still, bones were sliding, my spine rearranging, my ears moving, and it felt a little like when your leg fell asleep and you tried to walk on it. Prickly and numb both at once.

My eyesight sharpened, my hearing and sense of smell picked up, and as soon as I got my legs under me I zoomed off toward the window. The screen was still gnawed open where I'd left it, and with a mighty squirm I forced myself through the gap. The drop to the ground was as far as I remembered. Before I dove off, I froze, ears twitching as I tried to figure out if I was alone. No one was moving in the room. There was the faint sound of voices, but it seemed as though the machines used to actually clean the clothes were standing empty and abandoned for now.

Screwing myself up, haunches wiggling, I jumped from the window ledge to the ground. Rolling, I hit the wall, dazing myself. Jesus, I was going to be happy to never have to do that again.

I'd learned my lesson this time. Freezing in a far corner for several minutes, I made sure I was alone. And then, hastily, I shifted back. Still in a crouch, I was moving as soon as my legs had changed, grabbing a long ironing board and propping it up against the window. It made a ramp from floor to exit route, perfect for a chinchilla.

There were footsteps outside the door, and I shifted once more, scampering to flatten myself against the wall. No one entered, thank God. I'd been planning on turning human to open the door when I found it was just barely cracked open. More than enough room for me to squish myself through. I had to pause to rub my cheeks and whiskers vigorously with my paws. That chemical stink was overwhelming. Out in the hallway it was stifled a bit, although overlaid now with dust and body odor and burnt popcorn.

The trip twenty feet down the hall to the door of Mrs. Dallas's old office was nerve-racking. I kept squeezing myself in behind cabinets, whiskers trembling as the thunder of footsteps passed me by. Never in my life had I wished more to be a mouse. At least then, if someone spotted me, their first thought wouldn't be to call in the exotic pet handlers. There was a logical reason to see a mouse in an old building. Chinchillas weren't exactly native here.

Still, I managed to get to my target without any screams or shrieks of discovery. Score one for the fat, furry guy. The door was open here too, and I nudged my way inside. Slipping along the wall, I made my way forward to disappear behind a bookshelf. The lights were on, voices louder. I peered between a crack and saw Mr. Petros and my best buddy, Jake, having a heated conversation.

"I don't care if you *are* my sister's kid. I'll fire your ass if you don't keep your eyes open." Mr. Petros had seemed like a nice old guy when he'd hired me. Now he was scowling, the whiskers of his mustache quivering. I could smell the nearly overwhelming stink of his tobacco from here. "I'm done cleaning up after your goddamn messes. One thing, Jake. *One thing* you were supposed to do. Take out the trash. Keep your head down. Now this fat fuck playing detective is talking to my *bookkeeper*."

"I said I was sorry," Jake muttered, head down. I almost felt bad for the guy. Almost. "I didn't know what was in the bags."

"Yeah, well, that's none of your damn business, is it?" Petros's hand slammed down on the desk. "Just make sure no one else comes nosing around. Okay? Try to get *one* thing right."

Mr. Petros blew past Jake, storming out the door and slamming it behind him. Jake lingered. I could see his jaw working, frustration lining his features. "Fuck!" he exploded, grabbing a lamp and throwing it against the wall. He strode out of the room, door rattling as he shut it behind him. I didn't move, terrified, whole body shivering as I pressed myself farther back.

In human form, sure, those two would have been scary as hell to run across, especially that mad. But like this? They could break my neck with an ill-timed kick. There was no way I could let them see even a glimpse of me if I didn't want to end up like that lamp.

Eventually I was able to force myself to move. On shaky legs, I waddled across the floor, ears perked for even the slightest hint someone was approaching. Long moments passed with me hunched under the desk, gathering my courage, the clock in the corner pulsing through minutes, the second hand clicking off the time. Finally, I took a deep breath and focused on changing to human form.

My back was pressed against the desk, my head bumping against the corner of it, and I unkinked myself from the uncomfortable position to hesitantly stand. No one seemed to be around; even the whisper of footsteps in the hallway had ceased. My heart hammering in my ears, I moved quickly across the room and crouched down by the safe to punch in the combination.

There were a few zippered bank bags inside. My fingers were shaking as I picked up the topmost one and struggled to get it open. It was stuffed with white receipts and cash, each pile clipped to separate it. My thumb felt like it was ten times larger than normal, clumsy and too sweaty to flip through the paper properly. I'd memorized Sam's receipt number, and I muttered it to myself as I turned the thin slips of paper, searching.

Every second, I was so sure I was about to be caught. Fumbling, I nearly dropped the stack, barely managing to keep the papers in my hands. I cursed, jerking my arm across my forehead to try and wipe away nervous sweat. Just as I was about to give up and move on to the next bag, I saw it.

AC-24703.

Sam's ticket. Grabbing the receipt, I let my gaze dart across it looking for the price quoted. It was a full fifteen dollars less than what Sam had on the paper he'd been given. Rocking back on my heels, I let out a shaky breath.

I'd done it. I had proof.

Shoving the receipt into my jacket pocket, I hastily jammed the paper and the money back into the bag. I tossed everything back in the safe, slammed it shut, and headed to the door. I'd intended to just crack it open an inch or two, check to make sure the coast was clear, and then go chinchilla to get out of here. I only realized how screwed I was half a second before the door handle started to turn.

There wasn't time to think. Faster than I'd ever tried before, I focused on the shift. I cleared my mind, I pictured how the world looked when I was six inches tall, and I tried really damn hard not to freeze in panic. The familiar prickle-numbness of the shift swept over me. I was crouched behind the door, quivering, waiting.

A boot slammed down not inches from my nose. My haunches tightened like a spring, and then, with a burst of flurried movement, I took off running, darting around the person's startled dancing feet, zooming off down the hallway.

"Holy fuck!" I heard behind me, Jake's voice, and then the thunder of his chase. Ears flat, I sped up, banking up on a wall, jumping nearly to the top of a file cabinet, and scrambling the rest of the way up. Nails clicking on top of thin steel, I ran along the top of the cabinets until I reached the cleaning room's door and darted through the opening.

All four legs splayed, I leapt. I clattered to the ground. Then, with a flick of my tail, I went careening up the ironing board. Jake's hand slammed down behind me, too slow. My plump body easily squeezed, liquidlike, through the opening in the screen and I was gone.

If chinchillas could laugh, I would have. The chittering bark I gave was close enough though. Slithering along the edge of the wall, I followed the alley past the bakery and down the block to the corner. I couldn't risk shifting where I had before. Chances were too high Jake was going to come out looking for the strange animal he'd found.

Luckily, the bakery had a dumpster in the back. I followed the smell of stale bread around the building and took cover behind it. A few minutes later, the chinchilla was gone, and I was walking out onto the sidewalk, smoothing wrinkles out of my trench coat. I could see Jake down the street, looking around with a dumb, puzzled scowl. As the flow of foot traffic surrounded me, I crossed at the light, back toward my office building. I did laugh then. Probably scared the old lady walking next to me, but fuck, right then, I didn't care.

I'd solved the case. I'd found the evidence. And I'd outrun the giant moose. This was a good goddamn day, and it wasn't even nine in the morning yet.

Sam was in my kitchen when I walked in, coffeepot in hand. From his expression, I was kind of guessing he wasn't in the same giddy mood I was. "Uh. Morning," I offered, trying for a grin.

A grunt was all I got in return. Sam was getting cups out of the cupboard with all the serious violence of a Bond villain, his glower held in the crease between his eyes. For a moment I nearly apologized for breathing, walking, talking, wearing shoes, whatever it was that had Sam looking so angry. Instead, though, I took a deep breath and walked over. I gently took one of the mugs from his hands.

"Hey," I said lowly, watching his face.

At first he wasn't even looking at me. Every grain of coffee he was measuring into the maker seemed to be laced with C-4 or something for as much attention as he was giving it. After a few beats, though, he sighed and glanced in my direction. "You were gone when I woke up," he muttered, halfway between an accusation and actual hurt.

"I know." Worrying my lower lip, I waited. I'd handled it wrong. My euphoria faded and guiltily, I started to apologize, only to have Sam stop me with a shake of his head.

"I appreciate the note, at least. But, uh, next time, could you kiss me good-bye?" It was said grudgingly, but not, I thought, because Sam thought I couldn't handle it. It was just who he was. It was why he'd slept with his arms around me, why yesterday at the store his hand had been at the small of my back, why he opened the doors for people. He wanted to protect. Barring that, he wanted to be the one fretting over you.

"Okay," I agreed softly. "I am sorry though. I just… didn't want to bother you."

"Bother me," he told me, without a trace of reservation. "I always want you to bother me." That settled, Sam turned back toward the coffeepot, waiting for the sweet, caffeinated nectar to be dispensed. And really, I knew that he cared about me because he poured me the first cup of coffee, which, in my book, was practically a proposal. He kissed me hello, and I nudged my forehead against his affectionately. "You okay?" he asked.

"Yeah." And then, with one hand hooking around the back of his neck and pulling him back in for another kiss, "I should have woken you. I'm sorry."

Sam shook his head and let out a slow breath, the last traces of tension easing from the brackets of his mouth. "Stop apologizing, August. You were working. I just... I didn't like waking up without you."

A smile touched my lips. "Softie," I teased.

Sam growled again, this time more playful, arm wrapping around my waist and tugging me close. "Shush. I have a reputation to maintain."

We took our coffee to the couch. Sam pulled me in to sprawl against his side, his arm still tucked tight around me. He kissed my shoulder, and I threaded our fingers together, surprised all over again at how easy this was. How it felt like home.

"So," he prompted after a few minutes of silence. "Are you going to draw this out or what? Did you get the goods?"

I tried to look serious, like I was giving bad news. It's possible I failed utterly, considering the big grin that crept across Sam's face. I pulled out the white receipt and held it up with a triumphant, "Ta-da!"

"Mrs. Dallas came through." Sam reached out, taking the paper from me. "Now you have what you need."

Oh. Crap. "Uh, kind of. I mean, she did. Just... she got fired last night." I shifted a bit to face him. Double crap, that scowl was creeping back across his face. Sam was a smart guy. He probably already knew where I was going with this. "She was the one who called this morning. I, uh, got the combination from her and went in to, um, get it." My voice trailed up, almost like a question.

Sam's arms folded across his chest. "Is that right?" he asked, voice very bland. That was probably not a good sign.

"Yeah. You know, I just went in. It was good. I can be pretty sneaky, you know." Nervously laughing, I rubbed the back of my neck. "Not many people look down by their feet!"

Jaw jumping a little, Sam appeared as if he wanted to say something. He forced it back, though, giving me a nod. My stomach sank. "Did anyone see you?" was what he finally asked.

"No." I hesitated a moment, wincing. "Yes," I corrected myself miserably. "That, uh, Jake guy. He saw me when I was shifted. I got away though."

With a low, aggravated noise, Sam stood and paced. I hunched over, drawing my legs up under me, watching him with an agonized expression. "Okay," he said, nodding, though he seemed anything but agreeable. "Okay, so you went out, alone, without anyone knowing where you were going."

"I told you," I tried to correct weakly. He shot me a glower, and I fell silent again.

"You left me a note. I was… goddamn, I was *sleeping*." He actually sounded angry at himself for that. "That's not backup, Aug. That's the guy the police talk to after you go missing."

Worrying my lower lip, I looked down at the floor. "I'm sorry," I whispered. Any enthusiasm I'd had over my win was gone now. Sam just looked so *mad*.

The couch dipped beside me, and I heard Sam let out a slow breath. "Don't apologize," he grumbled. His arms went around me, though, pulling me into a tight hug. "I just…." Another heavy sigh. "I don't like being useless."

I raised my head, eyebrows winging up. "What?" Okay, that had not been what I'd thought this was about. I'd thought Sam was going to give me the *you're overweight and weak and shouldn't be going and doing things alone* speech. But Sam just looked uncomfortable, worried, and more than a little *sad*.

"You can handle yourself, I know." Sam brushed a strand of my hair back, studying my face. "But if you're going in someplace, I want… I don't know." Scrubbing a hand through his hair, he looked frustrated. "I want you to be smart about it. And maybe let me be a part of it."

None of that was what I'd been expecting. Eyes wide, I just stared at him, stunned. "You think I can handle myself?" I asked, a smile threatening on the crease of my lips.

"Well, yeah." The tense lines around his eyes eased slightly, that worried look fading. "You're incredible."

He said it so easily, like he was commenting on the color of the sky or the fact we were both using oxygen. *Of course* I was capable, like it was assumed. Like he hadn't even had to think about it.

I loved my parents. My herd had been with me my whole life. No one had ever had the simple confidence in me that Sam had. It was different than my parents, my family, my herd, because it didn't feel like it came from a place of *obligation.* I knew my herd cared about me. They cared about me *because* they were herd. Sam didn't have to be this supportive about anything about me. And yet here he was, worried about me. Wanting to be a part of the things that I did. No judgment, no trying to fix me, because, I was beginning to realize, Sam honestly didn't think I needed to be fixed. I didn't even know what to say. "You're not useless," I told him softly, searching his face. "God, Sam. I just didn't think. I didn't even... it never occurred to me you'd want to get up at the crack of dawn just to go stand outside and wait for me."

Sam seemed to be struggling with a response. "I think," he finally tried, "that the reason Kyle and I wound up being what we were is that I... I'm not very good at the talking thing. I show up. That's how I show everything, you know? I show up. But it wasn't enough for Kyle. Or maybe he didn't get it. I don't know." His thumb rubbed along my arm. "I don't want us to turn into that."

I nodded, teeth catching my upper lip, concerned. "Me either," I admitted. The idea of all the emotions we had, this new idea of love and want, turning sour was kind of terrifying. "So... what do we do?" My complete lack of experience in anything this serious was, all at once, incredibly worrying. "I don't want to make you feel like that ever again."

He huffed out a laugh, leaning in to kiss me, fingers sliding across my cheek, touching the corner of my eye. "I'm so proud of you," Sam murmured.

It wasn't exactly on topic, but I grinned anyway. "Yeah?"

"Yeah." Another kiss, this one slower. "Maybe next time, you could just tell me? Even if you think you're bothering me."

"I can do that." Smiling against his lips, I slid my arms around his neck and pulled him back in close. "I want you there. Trust me, you showing up sounds just about perfect."

I caught his laugh, teasing my mouth against his, sharing one of my own as he leaned me back on the couch. His hand slipped under my shirt, and we just collapsed into one another for long, ageless moments. Christ, I loved the way Sam kissed me. His stubble scratched lightly against my skin, he was greedy and demanding, and it sent little shivers rippling through me.

"We should go see Mr. Petros," I murmured, nuzzling in along his jaw. "I want to wrap this case up."

"Sounds good." He pulled back just enough to nudge our noses together. "There's some work I need to get done today. Why don't I go shower, we'll confront the bastard, and I'll buy you lunch to celebrate?"

Biting lightly at his lower lip, I nodded. "Awesome. Go get ready. I'm going to head to the office, get things together."

One last kiss and Sam moved away reluctantly. "I'll meet you over there in half an hour?"

Rolling over, I very happily watched him walk away. "Sure. You can walk a little slower if you want."

His laugh slid over me like sunshine and I grinned at him. Sam obliged, slowing down his gait, hooking his boxers off and kicking them away as he got to my bathroom. So not fair. If we didn't have anything else to do, I would have been after him like a shot. Stupid responsibility.

My office was sadly lacking in Sam. Which also meant my productivity would be up, because while he was awesome for a thousand things, my concentration was not one of them. I'd signed a contract with Mr. Petros that said I got paid if I could find proof of who'd been cheating him. Obviously he hadn't expected me to figure out it was *him*, but that wasn't really my problem.

I made copies of the receipts on my printer and put them into my office safe, just in case. I had a couple of phone calls to return, some e-mails from potential clients. Two potentially cheating spouses and an insurance fraud case later, I had next week all booked up, which was a great sensation.

Even if Petros tried to stiff me, I'd still be able to make rent. Which was awesome, because I had a feeling being late was going to be even more awkward now.

There was a knock at the door. Sam poked his head in. "Ready to go?"

I stood and grabbed my hat, shrugging on my jacket. "Absolutely." The proof was in my messenger bag, I had Sam there—Mr. Petros could scream all he wanted; it wouldn't change anything. We'd caught him red-handed.

"What's the plan?" His hand found mine as we headed toward the elevator. I squeezed his fingers lightly. For such a burly, grumpy guy, he was a fan of the hand-holding, or his arm around me, and I definitely wasn't going to complain. Sam lightly tugged my hat brim. "You going to put the screws to him?"

"Yeah, see." I grinned, giving him my best Cagney impression. "We're gonna make him squeal, see."

"I'll be your bruiser." We headed out onto the sidewalk, Sam not fazed by anyone who gave us a second glance as they walked by. "Have you thought about what you'll do if he tells you to go fuck yourself?"

"I really thought that was your job," I told him with wide, innocent eyes.

The laugh he gave was more like a loud snort, Sam ducking his head, an actual, honest-to-God flush hitting his cheeks. "I think I can handle that, yes," he murmured.

"Tonight?" I let go of his hand to slip my arm around his waist.

Another startled little laugh from Sam, but he was smiling. "I've got to get up early for a meeting tomorrow," he told me, obviously disappointed. "But how about I pick you up from your office after and we go out for dinner?"

"It's a date." We crossed the street, heading down toward the dry cleaners. "And I'm going to tell Petros to pay me, then he has a week to retire. If I don't see notification in the paper, I go to the Sally family and then to the cops." It was a good plan, I thought. Worthy of Phillip Marlowe for sure.

"You're so badass," Sam teased, but I saw that same pride in his eyes he'd had earlier. It made something warm tighten in my chest. I just wanted him to smile at me like that for the rest of our lives. All too soon, though, we got to the door of Petros's dry cleaners, and we disentangled to head inside.

Jake, of course, was at the front counter. This time, though, instead of running away and flashing my furry behind at him, I strode up to the counter and met his eyes. "I need to see Mr. Petros."

"What the fuck?" Jake glared at me, his attention leaving his phone to fixate on us. "What are you doing here?" And then he turned to Sam, his eyes narrowing further. "Hey, you came in here the other day."

"Observant, isn't he?" Sam rumbled, arms folded tight across his chest. "I believe the gentleman said he needed to talk to your boss. Why don't you scamper off and find him?"

Jake looked like he wanted nothing more than to take a swing at Sam. In the end, though, he obviously thought better of it. He disappeared into the back, and I gave Sam a little sideways smirk. "Easy, Kujo," I murmured.

He just grinned, all too pleased with himself.

Mr. Petros appeared, short and stout, his mustache carefully waxed. "Auggie, my boy." He smiled a greeting, arms wide in welcome. "I didn't expect you this week."

"I have some information for you." His affable act wasn't working on me. It might have, if I hadn't seen him earlier. But now I could see the tense lines around his mouth, the way his smile didn't touch his eyes. "Can we go back to your office?"

His gaze darted to Sam and then back to me, that tight smile never wavering. "Of course, of course. Follow me."

We made our way down the narrow hallway, through his door and into a cramped little room. Sam had to practically fold himself in half to fit into the folding chair while Mr. Petros got himself situated behind his desk. We declined the perfunctory offer of coffee, and Mr. Petros steepled his fingers, watching us over them. A still-smoldering cigar was burning in an ashtray right in front of us. I rubbed my hand across my nose, trying not to sneeze at the smell. "You said you found out who is stealing from me?"

I pulled out the receipt Sam had gotten when he'd dropped off his suit. "Do you recognize this?"

Mr. Petros glanced at it. "Yes, of course. That's the customer copy of our tickets. When we take in a garment, we get the top half and the customer gets the bottom."

"Then the top half goes in your till for the day, and then to your bookkeeper, correct?" I kept my voice even, trying to sound professional. Was it really bad that I wished there was a way to take a picture of this moment? My first big case, I kind of wanted a souvenir.

"Yes." Mr. Petros was frowning. "Where are you going with this?"

"It's just strange, because if this is the bottom half of your receipt"—I pulled out the white ticket from the safe—"I'm not sure how the top fits."

There was a long beat of silence. "Where did you get that?"

"That's really not important." I turned them over to read the prices. "Funny how you're charging the customer so much more than the bookkeeper is depositing. Now, I might be fairly new at this, but I'm guessing that's where your problem is."

Mr. Petros's lips were twitching, rage clearly boiling behind his bland expression. "Yes, that sounds like a problem." He sighed, leaning forward. "What are you suggesting, Mr. Mendez?"

No more *Auggie*, apparently. "I'm suggesting that you're embezzling, Mr. Petros."

For a moment I was pretty sure Petros was going to come across the desk and deck me. Sam shifted in the seat beside me, his glower radiating off the tense line of his shoulders, and Mr. Petros darted a glance over at him. "That's a mighty big accusation for a few slips of paper."

"Maybe," I mused. "But Mrs. Dallas seems to think we're on to something." Just the mention of her sent a thunderous look across Mr. Petros's face. "And I'm sure the police have a whole division that would be interested. And once the Sally family gets involved, I have to think it'll just explode. The tax fraud alone should be enough to get you tied up in this mess for years. I might only have a few slips of paper"— which I tucked safely back into my bag—"but that's more than enough to go forward with."

Clicking his tongue against his teeth, obviously irritated, Mr. Petros considered me for a long moment. "Yet you haven't turned me in," he observed, tone sharp now. Gone was the agreeable old man. He was looking at me like I was a bug he really wished he could squish. "So what do you want?"

"I want to get paid." I shrugged. "And once that happens, I want you to retire."

"You are out of your damn mind." Petros stood then, jerking his chair back and looming over his desk. "I will destroy you. I will—"

"You are going to retire," I repeated, jaw tightening. I didn't admit to the fear that went flashing through me. Holding his eyes, I refused to look away. "You have one week to walk away or I will go to the cops and the owners. Oh, and I'll take my payment in cash. Right now." A beat and I added, "And hire Mrs. Dallas back when you leave, if she wants her job. That was a dick move."

I really did think he was going to slug me. Slamming open the desk drawer, he pulled out a cash box and unlocked it. He furiously counted out the bills and tossed the money at me with a sneer. "Get out of my office."

I took the cash and tucked it into my pocket. Then I stood and straightened my coat. "Nice working for you." I tipped my hat and walked out, Sam trailing after me. Only when we'd gotten back out onto the street did I let the satisfied smile touch my lips.

Holy shit. I'd done it.

CHAPTER
EIGHT

AUGUST

When I'd decided to take Pop Pop's inheritance to open a detective agency, I'd dreamed about a day like this. Figuring out a hard case, confronting a bad guy, walking away with cash in my pocket. This was exactly what I'd always wanted.

Except my dreams hadn't had Sam. So in this case, reality kicked fantasy's ass all over the place.

"So, painting this weekend?" Sam had insisted on taking me someplace nice for lunch. We were in a steakhouse, full from an excellent meal and sharing a slice of apple pie for dessert. "I have to do the hallways, so it'll probably take both days." He reached over to steal a bite of the whipped cream. "If you just want to supervise, that'd be fine with me."

Picturing Sam all sweaty and working with paint smeared across those gorgeous arms was definitely a nice little daydream. "Count me in." With a grin, I batted his fork aside and licked the cream off the tongs of my own. "Uh, I could stay over?"

"I would be sad if you tried to leave." Warmth settled into the pit of my stomach at the way he was looking at me, those sea-storm-blue eyes that I could drown in crinkling just at the edges. "So, tomorrow, dinner?"

"Definitely." I took a drink of water before clearing my throat. "Hey, uh, I was thinking. My mom's birthday is in two weeks. Why don't you come home with me? The herd usually gets together, has a big dinner."

Sam looked for a minute like he wanted to decline. He pointed out, softly, "Your mom wasn't my biggest fan."

I reached across the table to lightly hook my finger around his thumb. "Yeah, well, she doesn't know you. And she's protective." I raised my shoulder in a half shrug. "Herd is important. But come on, I love you. They're going to love you too."

Sam snorted softly. "That's not actually how that works, you know," he sighed. But he turned his hand to catch mine and nodded. "But yeah, okay. We'll go meet the family."

I grinned. "You sound like I suggested a fun trip to the executioner's."

"Your mother is scary," Sam told me soberly. "So I wouldn't joke. She probably could take me."

"She definitely could take you," I informed him. "But don't worry, the chances are very slim she'll kill you over dinner. That would be rude."

I succeeded in teasing a smile out of him. "Oh, well, so long as Miss Manners would approve."

We finished our pie and walked back to our building, hand in hand. He kissed me good-bye at the door of my office, and I swore to God I actually *sighed* as he left, like I was a heroine in a romance novel. How in the world I'd gotten lucky enough to be with someone like Sam I'd never know. But he definitely made even the prospect of painting all weekend something I looked forward to.

I did some work, research on my next jobs, and the afternoon passed quickly. There were a few stakeouts in my future, and I was already wondering if Sam would be interested in keeping me company. By the time the sun had gone down outside my window, I had several new folders, neatly labeled, and papers all over my desk.

There was a knock on my door. Surprised, I looked up. "Come in?"

It was Sam, carrying a desk lamp. He didn't say anything, just set the lamp up, plugged it in, and flicked it on. He kissed me, smiling, and murmured, "I'm going to watch the news before I head to bed. If anyone is interested."

"I do like to keep up-to-date on current events." Happily leaning into the kiss, I lightly pulled him in closer. "How could I say no?"

"I made tuna sandwiches for dinner. Nothing fancy, but if you're hungry. I figured we'd rain check our night out." Sam pressed our lips together one last time before he pulled back. "See you in a bit?"

"Yeah, just let me finish up here."

After Sam left, I couldn't help but reach out, touching the shade of the lamp, unable to dim my grin. That was probably the most romantic thing anyone had ever done for me. It was sitting on my desk proudly next to Cocky, the ceramic rooster seemingly very pleased with his new roommate. After clicking the lamp off, I went to gather my things and headed downstairs to see Sam.

We ate sandwiches off paper plates, curled up together while we decidedly did not watch the news. It turned out making out wasn't just for teenagers, and Sam was easily distracted when I kissed just under his jaw. He had sucked reddened marks against my neck, my darker skin showing the bruises faintly. He'd been very pleased with his handiwork.

I had very detailed plans to get him back this weekend.

When Sam finally headed to bed, I reluctantly left him. It was insane to me how much I just wanted to be around him. Not just the sex—although I was pretty sure I was living the dream there—but just hanging out with Sam was more satisfying, somehow, than anything else I could imagine. I wanted to fall asleep next to him and wake up to him in the morning, share the paper, watch TV, go grocery shopping.... I just wanted to *live* with him, all the mundane little pieces that made up a day. I'd never considered that before. In my mind, relationships were the things you had while you went about your life, what you talked to your friends about, what you tried to fit in to who you already were.

That wasn't what I wanted with Sam. He wasn't some extra piece that came alongside. I wanted him to be part of all of it, of my movie nights and TV marathons. I wanted to take him to my favorite bookstore, to introduce him to all the things I liked. I wanted to know what he did on Saturday afternoons when no one else was around. I'd learn about sports, even, just to have something we could share. Not because I needed us to be the same, but because I didn't want any parts of me to be something he couldn't have.

We might be months away from that. Years away. A lifetime away. But I knew I wanted it, however fast or slow we got there. I wanted him in my life. It was scary, yeah, but I had a feeling he was going to be worth being a little afraid.

I drove home, music up, singing along, in a damn good mood. I'd had my win, gotten paid, and I was in love. I was pretty sure most of the songs on the radio were written about me right then.

My apartment still had signs of Sam spending the night. His mug was still in the sink, and the towel he'd used was hanging in the bathroom. I liked that. It made the place feel lived-in, like a home. Curling up on the couch, I plugged in a movie, deciding that a veg-out evening was the perfect cap to my day.

There were explosions and robots and spaceships, excellent mindless entertainment. My afghan was tucked around me, the glow from the television the only real light, and I was almost dozing by the halfway point. I wasn't sure what woke me up—the scrape of something against the door, the click of the lock, the soft slide of a muffled footstep—but all at once I was jerking upright, heart throbbing.

Someone was in my apartment.

After rolling off the couch and biting back a hiss of pain when I knocked my knee against the coffee table, I backed up quickly on my hands and knees. The movie flickered blue light across the room. I saw the man silhouetted against the doorway to the outside hallway. He was moving around the other side of the living room slowly, clearly looking for something. Or someone.

Moving as fast as I could without standing up, trying desperately to be silent, I scrambled down the hallway toward my bedroom in a crawl. The couch was between the intruder and me, my only saving grace as I tried to make it unseen to my room. My phone was sitting on the nightstand, my lifeline to calling the cops. All I had to do was reach it.

A silent whimper stuck in the back of my throat. I tried to ignore the way my pulse was throbbing in my ears, fear a sick, heavy load in my gut. I just had to get to my phone. I reached the bedroom, breathing a harsh pant that sounded far too loud. But I was almost there. A few more feet.

The tight grip of a hand on my ankle dragged me back just as I reached for the nightstand. I twisted around, kicking frantically, a wordless shout escaping me. The man pulled me back and grabbed my shirt, hauling me up by the collar.

It was Jake. He had on leather gloves and a ski mask pushed up over his head. He scowled at me, slamming my head back against the wall, his fingers around my throat. "Jesus, you're a fat, pathetic fuck," he hissed. "Shut up."

I'd been whimpering, I realized, actual *terror* hitching in my chest. With difficulty I tried to get my breathing back on the right side of hyperventilating. "What do you want?" I managed, trying to sound bolder than I felt.

Instead of answering, Jake slammed his fist across my face, sending me reeling. He heaved me back up again for another punch, a third catching me in the jaw. I felt the warm, sticky slide of blood from my nose, my eye throbbing in pain. "Jesus." My voice had turned to an agonized plea. "What the fuck do you want?"

"You have something my uncle thinks you shouldn't." Jake's fist hit my gut and I doubled over, swallowing back bile. "You're nosy, fatty. That's a dangerous thing to be."

Shit. They were looking for the receipts. I had a sudden, frantic flare of panic about Sam. What if Jake had gone there first? I had to get to him. I had to make sure he was okay.

First, though, I had to get away from the Sasquatch before he broke my face.

"I don't know—" I started, which only earned me Jake's fist in my stomach again. Wheezing, I doubled over, standing only by virtue of Jake's hand grasping my shirtfront.

"Don't waste my time," Jake hissed. "You've got some paperwork. I'm going to take it. Simple as fucking that. So start talking before I get really irritated."

Holding up my hands, I put on my best scared whine. It really wasn't too hard to create a convincing performance. My face was throbbing, I could taste blood on my lips, and I was pretty sure my stomach was going to have some giant bruises. And if I wasn't fast enough, I was pretty sure Jake was going to just beat me to a pulp for annoying him. So yeah, I was scared. "Okay, okay. There's a safe in the back of my closet. Everything's in there."

Jake considered me, eyes narrowing. "What's the combination?" he growled.

"Eight, three, five, zero, seven," I stuttered. "Please, just don't hurt me."

His fist rose again, threatening me, and I flinched back. He seemed satisfied, though, and shoved me away to stumble myself toward the living room. "Sit your ass down and be quiet," he barked at me. "Or I will break your fucking legs."

I complied, hands raised, shuffling back toward the couch. I really didn't need to *try* and look meek or helpless, but I did my best to keep my head down, shoulders hunched in, completely nonthreatening. With one last look back at me, Jake disappeared into the bedroom.

And I shifted.

Chinchillas were pretty mild creatures. We liked warmth, good food, comfort, all that sort of thing. A nice dust bath, maybe a scratch behind the ear, a dark place to sleep, and we were content. We were small and fluffy, pretty damn easy to underestimate. Hell, we underestimated *ourselves* most of the time. But as I flattened my furry body down along the floor, nails scratching across the wood as I darted toward the closed door and the freedom of the hallway beyond, I knew one thing for sure—I was better like this. Right then, in this situation, even injured, I was faster, more limber, all around *better* in my shift.

"There's not a safe, you fat fucking liar." Jake's voice boomed out from the bedroom, his footsteps echoing as he came charging out toward me. "You must really like pain, because—" He came to a stop, apparently noticing I wasn't where he'd left me. "Shit." He lunged for the door, nearly kicking me in the process, to rip it open and look down the hallway. I ran faster, and my haunches bunched as I sprung forward, so close to escape.

Jake's boot caught my side, knocking me off course. He cursed loudly, reaching to try to catch me. When thick fingers closed around me, I squirmed frantically, twisting my body over and sinking sharp teeth into Jake's wrist.

With a shout, he threw me, the world a blur as I flew through the air and came to a sudden stop against the wall. For a few long beats I was too dazed to move, my heart beating so hard I could feel it shake me. There was cursing somewhere above my head, and a huge hand zoomed down to grab me.

Pushing off from the wall, I leapt across the room, legs churning. Leaping several feet straight up, I banked off of a bookshelf, coming back around and grabbing my claws into Jake's leg. He howled, hopping up and down, but I refused to be shaken off. I climbed his jeans, burrowed in under his shirt, and bit his sides, digging in deeper as he thrashed.

Chinchillas were mild creatures, sure. But we had teeth, we had claws, and we could fucking jump. And I was pissed.

I let go as he spun around, knocking into a bookcase and sending the whole thing crashing to the ground. I jumped from him and raced across the room, Jake tearing after me in blind rage. My haunches tensed and I leapt, higher this time, scrambling up onto the countertop.

When he came near, I jumped onto his shoulders, using the height to bite his ear until he howled.

My fur was matted with specs of his blood. I dug my hind legs into his neck and kicked, hard enough to leave long, shiny scratches behind. When he swung one meaty hand up to slap me, I jumped from his shoulders, landed heavily on the ground, and took off for the doorway. Skidding through to the hall beyond, I didn't stop. My short legs churned under me, propelling me down the stairs, each step feeling like I was launching myself off a mountain.

But I got away. The front door was opening, one of the tenants carrying in groceries and far too busy with her bags to worry about one small rodent. I zoomed through that crack like an X-wing through a trench, scurrying out into the night air.

I could have found an alley and changed back, but, honestly, I was a better runner in this form. I wouldn't be setting any land speed records or anything, but I was able to dart around the forest of feet and legs around me, following the crowd across the cold asphalt of the street and to the next block. Keeping my head down, trying to avoid being stepped on, I ran toward the safety of the office building.

The alley behind the building was becoming way too familiar. Crouching behind some trash bags, trying to keep out of the light, I focused on changing back. My face was on fire, and it hurt to breathe too deep, but I was alive. I was mad as all hell, but I was alive. Limping a little—I must have knocked my knee against something—I shuffled over to the alley door.

My phone and my keys were both back at my apartment. So I did the only thing I could do. I banged on the door, shouting Sam's name, until he yanked it open with a scowl. "What the fuck—"

The flare of light from the hallway caught me and Sam's eyes went wide. I'd obviously woken him. He was still tugging on a T-shirt and his feet were bare. "Sorry, I… my keys. I don't have my keys."

"Shit, August." Sam grabbed my arm and hauled me inside, looking around the alley with such a dangerous scowl I was kind of surprised the trash cans didn't run away in fright. He hustled me down into his apartment to get me settled on the couch before he disappeared into the kitchen. "Start talking," he barked at me, returning with a bag of frozen peas.

"Well, I feel very macho right now," I informed him, pressing the freezing-cold vegetables to my rapidly bruising eye. "I've always seen this in movies. Hey, you wouldn't happen to have a steak, would you? That would be awesome." Fighting guys in movies always put meat on their black eyes. This was the closest I'd ever get to butch.

"August." Sam said my name with a sigh, settling down next to me, a soft frown creasing his forehead. "What happened?"

Fidgeting a little, I exhaled, some of the adrenaline dying a bit as I relaxed into his couch and his company. "I was at home, watching a movie, when, uh, Jake showed up."

Actual freaking thunder crashed across Sam's face. I'd never seen so much murder in anyone's eyes who wasn't, you know, on a documentary about death row. "That bastard hit you?"

"Yeah. Apparently Petros wasn't too happy with me. He wanted the receipts and Jake wanted to introduce his fist to my face." I shrugged, letting the hand that was holding the frozen peas to my head drop. My skin felt numb now. "It wasn't a big deal."

"That is a fucking big deal," Sam growled. He grabbed the peas and mashed them to my face again, his big hands not really so great with doing the gentle thing. But he tried, cupping the other side of my head like he was cradling a baby bird. "He hurt you. I am going to rip his goddamn balls off and feed them to him."

"Hey," I said, reaching up to touch his wrist. "Look at me. I'm fine." I gave him my best smile, only wincing slightly. Okay, so I was a wuss. But that didn't mean I wasn't fine. "I got away."

"How?" Sam shifted closer, rubbing an absent thumb along my unbruised cheek. "Did he get what he was after?"

"I Luke Skywalkered him." Sam's expression was blank. I sighed and explained. "You know, in *Return of the Jedi*? When he was in the Rancor pit?"

"You threw a skull at him and crushed him under the gates?" My eyebrows must have rocketed right off my face because Sam gave me a slight smile. "I have seen the movies, August. You aren't the only geek in the world."

"That is so hot." I settled back on the couch, grimacing when I twisted my torso the wrong way. Sam immediately lifted my shirt to inspect my stomach, muttering curses under his breath and going to fetch more frozen things. I was going to turn into an icicle at this rate. "No, I, uh, I tricked him into going in the other room and then I shifted." My teeth were bared in a slight grin. "And when he tried to catch me, I attacked him."

"How is that like Luke Skywalker?" he asked, distracted as he pressed a bag of corn to one side and a frozen container of juice mix to the other. I was turning into a walking grocery store.

"You know." I waved my hand. Sam caught it and pressed it against the juice can, giving me a look until I held it in place. "He was really big and stupid-looking and I beat him."

This logic made Sam pause, gaze cutting up to me, the barest flicker of a laugh in his eyes. I counted that as a win. He just looked so goddamn *mad* and worried, like he wasn't sure if he should start swinging or give me a hug. Apparently he decided to do neither. He wound up just sitting beside me, eyes on me as if he wasn't sure I could be trusted to breathe without his watchful concern.

"You have to go to the police," he pointed out.

I rubbed the back of my neck, nose crinkling. "Yeah," I agreed heavily. "I know."

This was going to be tricky. Not to mention Jake was going to be talking about a wild, rabid animal in my apartment when it was pretty obvious I didn't have any pets. But Sam was right—this was way beyond me now. And while the Dick Tracy school of thought said that most ordinary coppers were the problem and I should strike out on my own, be my own man, I didn't live inside a movie. Being a renegade detective wasn't going to end well for me.

"I know a few people on the force I could call," Sam offered, his hand making gentle circles against my back. "I still have a few favors to cash in."

I didn't need my detective skills to figure out what that meant. Those were people he'd known back when Kyle had been in his life. "Sam, no, I can't ask you to do that." The last thing I wanted was for Sam to dredge up bad memories of his ex just to help me.

But Sam, stubborn idiot, already had his phone out. "Too late, I'm doing it." He squeezed my leg briefly and got up to pace around the room, phone to his ear. I could hear a faint, tinny voice picking up. "Yeah, uh," Sam cleared his throat, arm crossed across his chest, staring up at the ceiling as if willing strength down on himself from on high. "Is Detective Stacy Meddows in?"

Apparently she was because there was a long silence and then another voice saying hello. Sam practically mumbled, "Hey, Stace. It's, uh, it's Sam. Portello. Or, Ewing, now, actually."

Sam turned his back on me slightly, the rest of his conversation punctuated with sighs and long pauses, the occasional, "Yeah, I know," and, "I'm sorry," getting thrown in. But he sketched out what had happened and seemed satisfied with the conclusion when he finally hung up.

"Old friend?" I asked, curious.

"Kyle's first partner." Sam kicked back on the couch, looking vaguely like he'd just run a particularly grueling marathon. "We were best friends for a while, though, her and her husband, Kyle, and me. Kyle got them in the divorce." It was a bad joke, said dryly. Sam rubbed a hand across his jaw, shrugging. "She, uh, wasn't happy I haven't called in a while."

"How long is a while?"

Sam gave me a sheepish glance. "Eight years."

Oh. Well, then, yeah, I could see how she might have had something to say about it. "She's got another call in the area, so she's going to stop by here first. Shouldn't be too long."

"What am I going to tell her?" I wondered, slouching down on the couch. The rapidly thawing peas were getting gross and mushy in the bag. I set them aside, cracking my jaw experimentally. "We kind of try to avoid talking to cops, honestly. Too many questions can be a very bad thing."

"You tell them the truth." Sam gently took my chin between two fingers, wincing as he examined my eye. "You were home; Jake broke in and attacked you. You lied to get him to go to the other room and you ran here."

"And when he starts talking about the chinchilla from hell?"

Sam's eyebrow rose slightly. "What chinchilla, officer?" he mimicked in an overly innocent voice. "I don't have any pets."

"He's going to have bite marks," I pointed out.

"And he can have fun explaining them. You don't have to. For all Jake knows, you weren't anywhere around."

"The second time he saw a chinchilla when I seemingly disappeared?" My stomach was in knots. I stood, pulling away from him and going to pace nervously. "This is so bad. I can't talk to the police."

Sam was beside me in a moment, strong arms wrapping around me. "Hey," he whispered, kissing my temple. I rested my head on his shoulder gratefully. It was good to have him here. All the adrenaline was gone now. All I had left was aches and pains and my quickly approaching panic attack. "It's going to be okay. Look, worst comes to worst, and he, what? Tells the cops you turn into a chinchilla? Who the fuck would believe that? He'll just look nuts. So long as you keep your head down, no one is going to believe him."

He was right. I nodded, stealing my own arms around him. We were content to stand like that, Sam's fingers running soothingly through my hair, while I tried to relax.

"Okay," I agreed softly, pulling back enough to meet his eyes. "Just... could you be there? While they take my statement?"

"Like to see you try and keep me away." Sam kissed me softly, his lips ghosting across my bruised eye, his hands gentling down my sides, as if his touch could magically make me all better.

We headed up to my office. I figured it probably looked more professional to hand everything over to the police there, even though I'd much rather stay curled up in Sam's apartment. The safe behind my desk held the originals of the receipts, along with all my notes about the case. Sam sat on the couch, watching me as I fussed, arranging the paperwork over and over on my desk. I was gnawing on a pencil, practically biting it in half, my nerves not calming as much as they usually did at the action. Then again, I was turning someone over to the cops after having been assaulted. So yeah, maybe a little bit of wood chewing wasn't going to cut it.

"I want a drink," I told Sam mournfully.

"After," he promised me. "I'll give you a dust bath, you can have a beer or three, and pass out in my bed. I'll even let you sleep in."

All of a sudden it hit me. "Oh my God." I looked at him guiltily. "You have a meeting. An early meeting. And now it's"—I shoved up my sleeve to look at my watch—"it's *one* in the *morning*. Oh my God, Sam, I'm so sorry."

Sam just waved me off. "Don't even think about apologizing. It's just sleep, August. I'll blow off the rest of my day and come home to you and a nice nap. That's better than a full eight hours any day."

I still felt like shit. "I'm cooking you dinner tomorrow night," I told him earnestly. "Anything you want. Name it. I will hold a séance and channel Julia Child if I have to."

His teeth flashed in a grin. Leaning forward, he caught my flailing hand and squeezed it briefly. "August. It's okay." The smile turned into a quick leer. "Although I do encourage nude cooking. I even have an apron you can use, if you're worried about splashing."

Rolling my eyes at him, I couldn't help the smile that threatened my lips, worry washing away into amusement. "You are impossible," I told him archly, but I couldn't keep up the pretense. Even my guilt felt a little silly. "Just think how you're going to feel when you come home and I'm making naked pancakes."

"Horny," Sam answered promptly. "And hungry. I'm already considering new and exciting uses for the syrup."

Well, that was an interesting and heretofore unexplored line of thought. Before I could get too excited, though, there was a knock at the door. Sam had been very successful at distracting me from what I was going to do, but as we both looked over toward the doorway, I was pretty sure my stomach sank into my toes. If my life had a soundtrack, this was when the minor-chord foreboding music would start.

The herd didn't go to outsiders. We avoided hospitals, and we didn't involve cops unless it was absolutely necessary. We kept to ourselves. It was too risky, I'd been told over and over again. One wrong move, one human who got too curious, one question answered badly, and it wouldn't just be me in danger. It would be all of us. We protected the herd above everything else. And here I was, having just *attacked* a human while in shift, changing in the middle of alleys, in daylight, talking to the police.

My mother, right then, was being overwhelmed with the urge to scold me, I just knew it.

Another knock, then. While I'd been frozen, staring, apparently our visitor had gotten restless. Sam glanced at me and I swallowed hard before nodding. Okay. Ready or not.

Well, I wasn't ready. At least, I wasn't ready for who was at the door.

The gun was what I noticed first. I didn't have much use for guns; they weren't really part of my whole thing. Trench coat, check. Semi-ironic fedora, check. Gun? Not so much. So when confronted with one, all I could think was that it was so much smaller than I would have imagined it. Just this little bit of metal, really, held in a meaty hand.

Jake was standing there, scratches on his neck still standing out in bright relief, dried blood on his skin. I would have felt proud if I wasn't so busy trying not to piss myself.

"Sit down," Jake barked at Sam, waving the gun between both of us. I cringed at the careless way he moved it about. It seemed like he should be a lot more responsible with that thing. I was pretty sure Charlton Heston had a whole safety video about that very subject.

Sam, hands out, did as he was told. "Calm down," he said, voice a low, calm rumble. "Just everyone calm down. There's no need for you to use that."

"Fuck you," Jake spat. "This stupid motherfucker is going to give me what I need or I swear to God, I will blow your goddamn brains all over that wall."

There was a faint buzzing in my ears, panic scratching at my skull, so close to boiling over. I'd been brave, back in the apartment. Fists and name-calling I could deal with. Sure, it'd hurt, but I'd been able to think. Now? Now there was a *gun* being aimed at Sam. Beautiful, grumpy, brilliant Sam, who should be in bed right now.

I was going to be sick.

"Absolutely," Sam was saying calmly. "We're going to get you whatever you need, bud, okay? Why don't you just put that gun down?"

"You are both goddamn *insane*, you know that?" Jake's voice raised louder, his grip tightening on the gun. I was staring at it with wide eyes, still frozen, breath barely moving in my chest. "And you have some freaky-fuck *attack* rat—"

"Chinchilla," I corrected faintly.

Jake's attention turned to me. "What the fuck did you say?"

Shit. Shit, shit, double dog *shit*. "Chinchilla," I said, louder, wishing for once I could just keep my mouth shut. "Not a rat. It was a chinchilla."

Jake's arm drooped a little. He was staring at me like he was trying to figure out if I had brain damage. I kind of thought I might be giving myself the same expression, were such a thing possible. "What the hell are you even talking about? Jesus, whatever, your attack *chin-fucking-chilla* and I'm going to stomp that motherfucker into the ground. Both of you are just fucking *batshit*. Now give me the goddamn receipts."

I nodded. "Okay," I managed, fingers shaking as I moved to gather the papers. "Okay, sure. Yeah. Right here. All of it's right here. Do you have a bag? Um, it's fine, you can borrow one of my folders. They're blue, but I have green ones too." I couldn't stop talking, like all that fear was just spilling out of my mouth like an unhinged faucet of random words.

"Yeah, whatever," Jake barked at me. "Jesus, just hand them over."

I didn't notice Sam moving. The gun was pointed at the floor, Jake's other hand held out for the papers, when all of a sudden Sam's fist was slamming across Jake's face. I all but jumped backward in shock, Jake making a grunt of pain and trying to get the revolver up. Sam's hand slammed down against Jake's wrist hard enough that I swore I heard something snap. With a loud cry, Jake dropped the gun, fingers nerveless.

Sam scooped up the gun and aimed it at Jake, steady and calm. "Sit the fuck down." Every word was clipped off, his tone more than a little murderous. "Now."

Jake sat.

So did I. Sinking into my chair, pillowing my head in my hands, I realized I was almost hyperventilating. "Sam?" I managed weakly.

"Yeah, babe?"

"Two drinks. At least two. More like four."

There was a pause. Without even looking up, I could hear the smile start to curl in his voice. "Sounds like a plan."

CHAPTER
NINE

SAM

"You're an idiot, Ewing."

Well, he couldn't exactly disagree with that. Stacy had arrived with her partner, George, five minutes after Sam had managed to subdue Jake. Walking in on Sam holding a gun on a guy whose face was all scratched up hadn't even fazed her. She'd just pulled her own weapon, ordered everyone to put their hands up, and called for backup.

Her summation of his actions was just as succinct. Sam had given his statement to George while Stacy had spoken with August. Sam kept cutting worried looks over at him, but despite being a bit pale and shaken, August seemed fine. Which, considering the night he'd had, Sam figured they'd mark as a win.

"I mean, you are an actual idiot." Stacy had come over to where Sam was sitting, watching as a beat cop bagged up all August's paperwork on the Petros case. Her hands were on her hips, impeccably pressed suit making her all that more imposing. "Did you seriously *karate chop* the perp's hand, and I quote, *like a ninja?*"

Sam snorted, glancing over at August. Who promptly gave him a smile and a sheepish shrug. Yeah. A ninja. "I would say it was less ninja and more self-defense-class training, but that's more or less the gist of it, yes."

"You attacked an armed man." Stacy did not sound amused. "I guess we can rule out wisdom coming with age. Do you have any idea how dangerous that was?"

"Yeah, well, it seemed like a good idea at the time." Sam gave her a hangdog look; it never had worked on her before, and now she just rolled her eyes at him, crossing her arms and refusing to give even an inch.

"You got lucky. Next time, don't try to be a hero." Her sour expression softened, and she squeezed his shoulder. "I should be kicking your ass for dropping off the map like you did. Instead, I'll just let you make it up to me this Friday. You're taking me and Cody out for dinner." The corners of Stacy's eyes crinkled. "Someplace expensive. With a good wine list."

"So your husband can eat me into bankruptcy?" Sam scoffed. "Come around to my place. I'll cook you dinner and Cody can remind me why Steelers fans are all head cases."

"It's a date." Stacy glanced over toward where August was being checked over by a paramedic, one of the cops taking pictures of his injuries for the report. "Bring your new boyfriend too." Sam must have looked startled that she knew. Stacy laughed at him, an easy smile crossing her face. "Please. I'm a detective and you're the most obvious person in the world. Give me *some* credit."

Stacy was called away. Sam watched her go, the bustle around August's office fading as everyone began to wrap up their work. Jake had been led out in handcuffs, statements had been taken, and now came the cleanup. August was slumped back in his chair, looking exhausted. Sam couldn't blame him. He felt like he could sleep for a week himself.

The last time Sam had seen Stacy was the last time he'd seen Kyle. They'd been divorced for just under two years, and Sam had bumped into them at a restaurant. Kyle was with whatever new flavor of the month he'd been fucking, and Sam had made himself stand there, make polite small talk, smile, and when he'd finally made his escape, he'd never wanted to see anyone from that life again. Having to deal with Kyle was like scraping off his skin over and over. Stacy and Cody were wrapped up in that emotion.

He'd expected to feel it again. All that anger, all the bitterness, Sam had been prepared for the sight of Stacy to bring it roaring back. But all he felt then was a little sad. He missed Stacy, he missed Cody, and maybe all those years that were between him and Kyle, now, let him just have *that* instead of balling friendship up with the crapfest of his failed marriage.

"Hey." August plopped down on the couch next to him, shoulder nudging against Sam's. "Tootsie Roll for your thoughts?" He offered out the candy with one of those stupid, adorable smiles that seemed to demand Sam return the expression.

"Just glad you're here," he replied, wrapping one arm around August's shoulders. There was no part of him that wanted to go back in time. His marriage had turned into something so toxic it'd infested all the other parts of him. He'd lost two good friends over it. Hell, he'd nearly missed out on August because he'd been so convinced it'd just be a replay of Kyle. But this was good. *They* were really good. Thinking about his ex, maybe Sam could summon up some emotion other than bitterness.

August leaned into Sam's side, and they watched the police bustling about the cramped office. "Right back at you."

THERE was something wonderful about having breakfast outdoors, sitting at a little table on the corner, outside of a bakery, drinking coffee and watching the world wake up. August was all bright eyes, head swiveling eagerly to follow everyone passing. Not that Sam blamed him. No, the upcoming show was something August had definitely earned.

Yesterday was a blur. Sam had dragged himself to his meeting with the tax accountant far too early, had returned home only to crawl back into bed with August. Then they'd both been summoned down to the police station to verify their statements. It turned out Jake had been quite willing to flip on his uncle. He hadn't known about the embezzlement scam, but Jake had been his uncle's hired heavy. Between his testimony, the evidence August had gathered, and Mrs. Dallas, the cops had a pretty damn good start. Mrs. Sally had stormed in, all perfectly pressed pantsuit and permed hair, and immediately demanded to start pressing charges. She'd been like a really awesome poodle on the attack, and Sam had been thrilled that all that ire wasn't directed anywhere near him. Mrs. Dallas was even considering bringing a wrongful termination suit against the company, which Sam thought was the perfect icing on the cake.

They'd picked through the mess in August's apartment just long enough to pack a bag. Until they knew Petros was cooling his ass behind bars, Sam didn't want August spending nights alone. It was gratifying how quickly August had agreed. Then again, maybe Sam had stopped holding his breath for the other shoe to drop. Sure, this might still all go to hell. For now, though, it was damn good.

"Here they come."

Sam looked up from his coffee in time to see what August was staring at. Three cop cars cruised up the street before parking in front of the dry cleaners. Sam could see Stacy getting out of one, her partner, George, taking a few of the uniformed cops around back. Stacy, of course, strode right in the front door. It was quiet for a long time, the rest of the world shuffling past them, unaware. August was watching, though, practically vibrating nerves.

Both of them let out huge exhales when Petros was marched out the front door in a shiny pair of handcuffs. August turned to Sam with a huge, infectious grin, shoving his phone into Sam's hand. "Take a picture, take a picture," August enthused, standing so that the sight of Petros being led to a squad car would be in the background. "This is so going on the wall."

Sam had to roll his eyes, but he couldn't say no. Of course he couldn't. August had just solved his first major case. "Channel your inner Spade," he instructed August, getting the shot lined up.

August gave him a brooding look, fedora on, the wind whipping his trench coat around his legs, black eye worn like a badge of honor.

Sam snapped the picture and smirked, turning the phone around to show August the result. "You look good," he murmured, his hands finding August and tugging him in to sit closer, abandoning August's chair on the opposite side of the table in favor of August sitting on Sam's lap. Who wanted to be that far away, anyway? "The bruise isn't my favorite thing, but other than that."

"I look like a marshmallow man," August sighed, puffing out his cheeks in imitation of how he thought he appeared. He perked up, though, peering down at the picture, "But nice shot of Petros's perp walk. Maybe we can just blow up that part of it."

"August." Sam waited until August looked back up, those impossible brown depths, warm and sweet, finding his own eyes. "You look good," he repeated, softer, voice firm.

Heaving out a breath, fidgeting slightly, August's gaze returned to the picture. Sam could see all the arguments, the denials, flicking across August's expressive face. In the end, though, he just laced his fingers with Sam's and tried for a shy little smile. "Fine. We'll put up the whole thing."

"Damn straight we will. This is your moment."

Together they relaxed back into their chairs, sipping coffee and watching the show. It was satisfying, seeing the end of something they'd worked on together. Sam thought he could get damn used to this.

"So," Sam drawled, turning his attention back to August as the last police car sped away. "I have some work to do, but it should only take me an hour or so. How's the rest of your day looking?"

A Cheshire Cat grin spread across August's face. "I think I could free up some time. How about I make you lunch?"

"Deal." Sam leaned over and kissed August, gentle at first, until August's hands slipped up to tangle in his hair. It was hard not to lean in, to want more, with the way August's lips parted under his own. When they pulled away, breathless, Sam ghosted soft brushes of his mouth along August's. "Walk me back?"

They went, hand in hand, Sam perfectly content. Right then, at that moment, he was gloriously, simply happy.

His work went quickly enough. Just some basic handyman stuff, some paperwork, nothing that required too much brainwork. He even took some time to cruise through information online about various maintenance companies. It'd be good, he thought, to plan a long weekend trip with August. Something in the bed-and-breakfast variety, maybe up the coast. He could get a temp company to keep an eye on things while he was gone and devote several days just to relaxing.

Or maybe they could get a lake house that summer. Sam hadn't been fishing in ages, but he thought kicking back with a cold beer and the hot sun might be just the thing. There was even a small part of him that was wondering what a trip overseas might be like. When he factored August in, the world seemed so much more inviting. Even the idea of a night spent at home seemed better. He could teach August the finer points of football, make some of that neon-orange cheese.

Just a few months ago Sam would have balked at the idea of sharing his solitary rituals. They seemed emptier, though, now. Nights spent alone, days spent with his head down, avoiding every living soul, it didn't appeal as much.

Shit, the Grinch's heart was growing three sizes.

Clicking off his desk lamp, Sam stretched, glancing around his tiny office. When he'd first bought the building, halfheartedly dreaming about a nice retirement nest egg, it had just been supposed to be that. But the night Kyle had kicked him out, he'd wound up here, sleeping in his desk chair. Then it'd been a camping cot he'd manhandled into the narrow room. Where he now lived in the basement had, at the time, been nothing but a storage room. The project to convert it to an apartment, though, had been his salvation for a while. He'd needed something to take his mind off his shattering life.

And it'd been enough. Roof over his head, a job, a television, and he'd called it a day.

Now he was thinking about houses, about whether or not a dog would get along with a guy who spent time being a chinchilla. Sam was honest-to-God thinking about rebuilding his life. He hadn't even known he'd lost it, but now....

Well, now it seemed like it was about time to try to start over.

Sam headed into his apartment, absently kicking off his shoes at the door. "Hey, babe? I'm home." There was the distinct scent of pancakes, and Sam turned toward the kitchen, a smile starting.

Sure enough, August was busy at the stove, the bow at the back of Sam's *Kiss the Cook* apron sitting neatly just above that biteable curve of August's ass. Gorgeous light-caramel skin was on display, and Sam's gaze traveled over all of it with hunger that had nothing to do with food.

It turned out August made pretty good pancakes. They warmed up nicely hours later, although Sam found a much better use for the syrup. And when they finally fell asleep, sated and blissed out, Sam wrapped his arm around August and he dreamed of a house, a picket fence, and this man.

Yeah. He was planning on getting used to this right there.

AUGUST

So, it turned out that catching a criminal could, indeed, make you a minor celebrity. If you counted a thirty-second spot on the local news and a few inches in the paper in which your name was misspelled. Which I absolutely did. In the week and a half since Petros had gotten taken in, I'd had more calls for work than I knew what to do with.

"Hey, can you grab Cocky?" I used my knee to push the box in my hands back up. It kept sliding down. Or I kept nearly dropping it, because the only lifting I normally did was with a book, whichever. I was blaming it on slippery cardboard. "And the lamp."

"I got 'em." Sam came up behind me, giving me a sideways glance. "Although next time you ask me to grab your Cocky, I really hope it has a different connotation."

Snorting, I leaned up and kissed him, resting the wayward box against the wall. "Just you wait, mister. We're going to break in my new office like you wouldn't believe."

All the jobs I was getting, I could afford one of the newly vacant offices one floor down. Well, I was pretty sure I couldn't *actually* afford it, honestly, but Sam had insisted I needed more room, and he refused to tell me how much of a discount he was giving me. Apparently I was good for business. The building had been featured right alongside me in the news, and Sam had gotten renewals from all of his leases along with an Internet start-up that wanted my former space on a short-term basis.

So now we were carting the last of my stuff down the elevator. The office was the center one on the left of the hallway, it had a huge window, and my stuff all fit without having to knock my hip on the desk every time I slid past the couch. It was so *adult*.

After heaving the box in and letting it drop next to the bookshelf, I collapsed back onto my chair. "Moving is hard," I groaned. "Next time, let's just teleport everything."

"Agreed." Sam slouched onto the couch. "I'll get right on inventing that."

"Would you? That'd be fantastic."

He huffed a laugh, nudging my ankle with his foot. "Oh, hey, I got your mail out of your old box. It's on the desk."

Perking right up, I wheeled the chair over to rifle through all the piles of paperwork to find the stack of mail neatly held together with a rubber band. There were a few signed contracts for work, some solicitations, and one thick manila envelope. I sliced that open first and looked through the papers and photos that fell out.

It was a case. Frowning, I leaned back in my chair, reading through the letter. The owner of a large local grocery chain was sure that his business partner's daughter was stealing. She was the head of their procurement division, in charge of buying stock for his stores, but lately he'd been worried that the quality of their merchandise was going down while costs were rising. He wanted me to take the case and help him get enough proof to quietly force her to resign.

All for the sum of more than I'd made in a year. The last three years.

"Holy shit."

Sam had been putting books away. His head came up at the sound of my voice though. "What is it?"

Numbly, I handed him the letter. I gathered the rest of the information, then went over to the couch, using the coffee table to spread everything out. There were work schedules, photographs, inventory lists, enough to get me started. Resting my chin on my hands, my elbows on my knees, I studied it all.

Sam whistled lowly. I assumed he'd gotten to the fee. "This is amazing." He sat next to me, those perfect clear-blue eyes already darting over the evidence we'd been given, that brilliant brain going straight to work.

"It's too much." I shook my head, worrying at my lower lip. Shit. All my pencils were packed. I really needed something.

"What? The fee? August, never argue with someone who wants to overpay you." Sam saw me patting my pockets, looking under folders and books, and he suddenly got an incredibly sheepish expression on his face. "Hold on."

"It's not the fee. Although that would be more money than I've ever had at once." Damn it, how could I not have *one* pencil around? I went to my desk to dig through the drawers with increasingly frantic movements. "The *job* is too big. That guy owns seven stores in this area. He's a multimillionaire."

"So?" Sam was looking through the last box he'd brought up.

"So?" I repeated, voice going a little higher-pitched. "This isn't just one guy, this is… this is big. Huge. This is an actual case. Like, what a professional would get."

"You are a professional, August." Sam crossed the room, hands behind his back. "So breathe." He presented me with a bouquet of sticks, twice as long as my finger, the perfect width for chewing. They smelled heavenly, the sweet scent of applewood unmistakable. He'd even tied a ribbon around them. "I, uh"—he shifted his feet, actually looking *shy*—"I did some reading about what chinchillas liked to chew on, and that seemed to be the most popular choice. I was going to leave them on your desk. You know, as an office-warming present. But you seem like you could use them now, so." He thrust them out farther, awkwardly. "Here."

Touched, I took them and buried my nose in the soft wood to breathe deep. Pulling one out, I carefully set the rest of the bundle down next to Cocky and my desk lamp. Just the action of gnawing on the wood soothed my frayed nerves, and the taste was so much better than the pencils I normally used.

Sam drew me in to sit again, both of us budged up on the couch together. "We'll do it together," he offered, nodding toward the papers on the coffee table. "If you want me to, that is. I'll help, however I can. You *can* do this." He looked so damn confident in me I wanted to cry.

"I was thinking," I said, playing our fingers together, lightly rubbing my thumb along his palm. "I need a name. For the detective agency."

Sam took my conversational swerve with aplomb. "Okay. Any ideas in mind?"

"Well, I kind of liked *Mendez and Ewing Detective Agency.*" Thank God for the chewing stick, or else I might have bitten through my lip in nerves. "How does that sound?"

For a long beat, Sam didn't respond. In movies, the score would have told me exactly what he was feeling, a soaring upbeat for *impending romantic moment* or a kazoo slide for *wow, that guy is a dumbass.* Since I got neither, I was reduced to worriedly searching Sam's face, wondering if I'd overstepped.

"I mean, I know you already have a job. Obviously you're not just going to drop everything for me. But, uh, you're... you're my partner, right? I mean, you're going to go meet my family tomorrow, so you obviously are fearless." It was a weak joke, given with an even weaker laugh. "If you hate it, then I was totally just kidding, you know."

"We should get those letters," Sam mused.

I stopped, blinking in confusion. "Letters?" I tried, totally lost.

"Yeah, on the door. Not a plaque, but in the films, they always have the agency name up in letters on the glass. I can probably do it." Sam peered over at the door, considering. "Bet it'd be easy. I can have it done for you this weekend, so when you meet your clients in your new office, you'll be all ready."

I could have said any one of the hundred things pinging around in my head right then. Instead I hauled him in to kiss him. Our lips met in a clash, in that wonderful, sweet exhale I craved so much, and I felt a smile twitch under my mouth. Sam pulled back, grinning at me, and dragged me up onto his lap so he could kiss my jaw, the corner of my lips, my shoulder.

"I take it you like the idea?" he drawled.

"I take it you like the name," I returned before pressing my lips to his forehead.

Sam's arms settled around my waist, comfortable and secure. There was rain slapping against the window, clouds making the early-afternoon sky dark. And here we were, together, my fedora and coat hanging behind the door, our latest big case spread out in front of us.

Who said movies were better than real life? Not for even one second of black-and-white glory would I trade this. This was my path.

Thanks, Pop Pop.

"You really think I can do this?" I asked him softly, fingertips playing through the hair at the nape of his neck.

Sam picked up the letter again, studying it. "Yeah," he told me. "I really do."

"Why?"

His smile was better than the sun breaking through any storm. "Because, August. You've got gumption."

ALEX KIDWELL, confirmed geek and bibliophile, lives in the Midwest with partner Robin Saxon. Alex relaxes by slaying dragons in MMOs, listening to music that can be sung along with in the shower, and enjoying BBC programming.

Other than writing, Alex enjoys knitting and is currently attempting to learn how to knit in the round. There are plans for a future of cat hats, which Alex is certain will go over well with household-running felines, Starsky and Hutch. Alex also indulges in too many cooking shows, while owning only one pan.

Visit Alex's blog at http://saxonkidwell.blogspot.com/, Facebook at http://www.facebook.com/profile.php?id=100002270719608, and Twitter @kiddingalex, or e-mail Alex at alexkidwellwrites@gmail.com.

Also from ALEX KIDWELL

http://www.dreamspinnerpress.com

The Sanguis Noctis Series
by Robin Saxon & Alex Kidwell

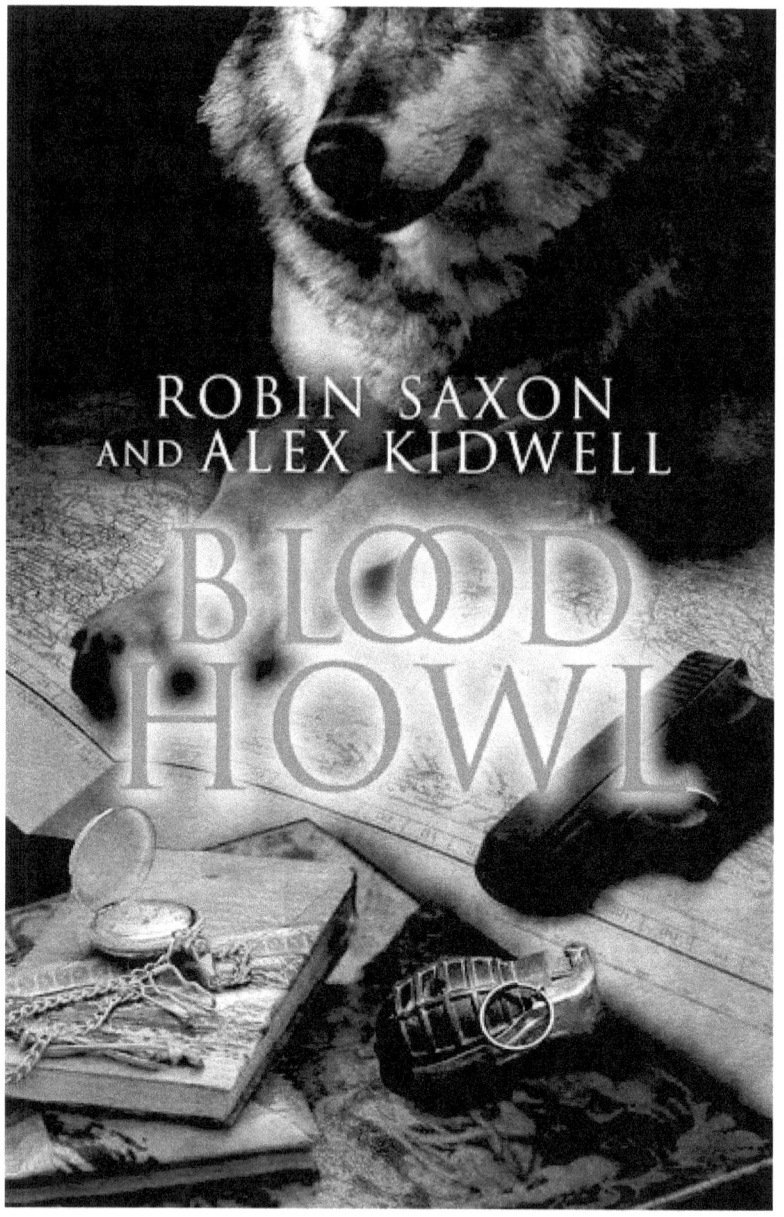

http://www.dreamspinnerpress.com

The Sanguis Noctis Series
by ROBIN SAXON & ALEX KIDWELL

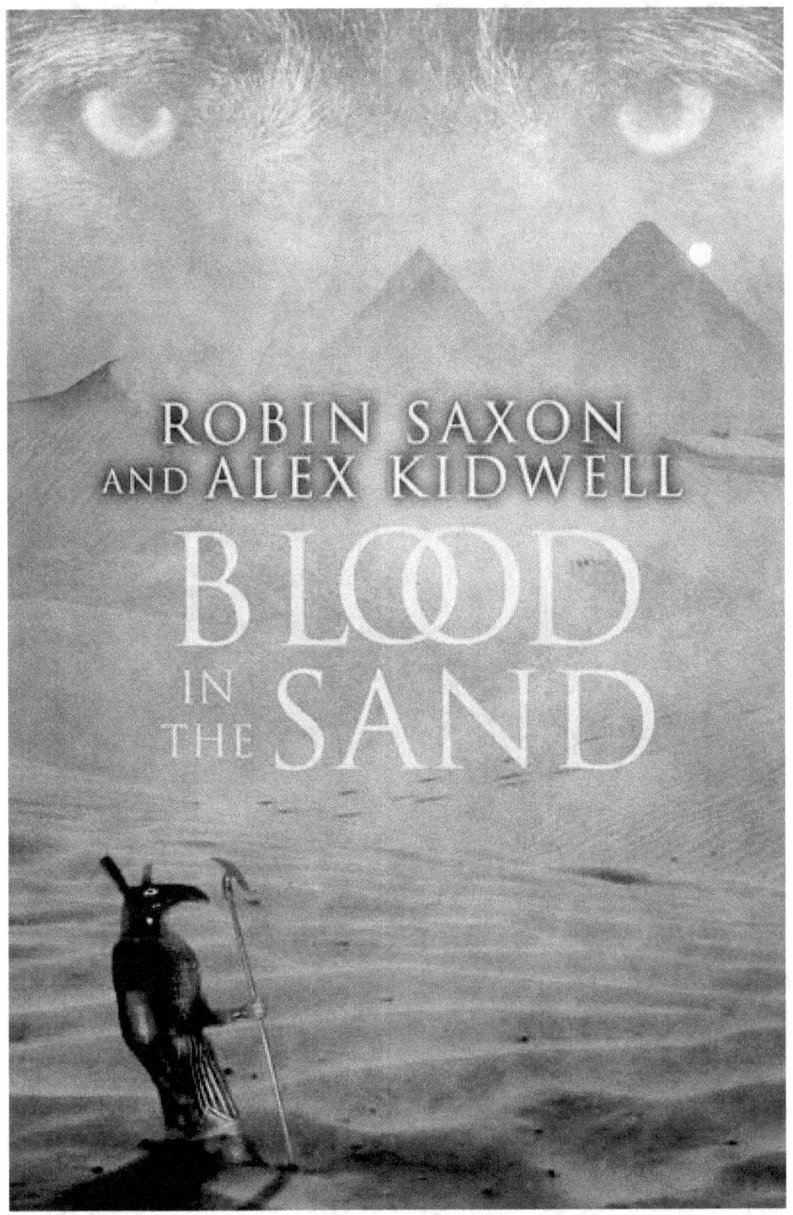

ROBIN SAXON
AND ALEX KIDWELL

BLOOD
IN THE SAND

http://www.dreamspinnerpress.com

Also from DREAMSPINNER PRESS

http://www.dreamspinnerpress.com

Also from DREAMSPINNER PRESS

http://www.dreamspinnerpress.com

Also from DREAMSPINNER PRESS

http://www.dreamspinnerpress.com

Also from DREAMSPINNER PRESS

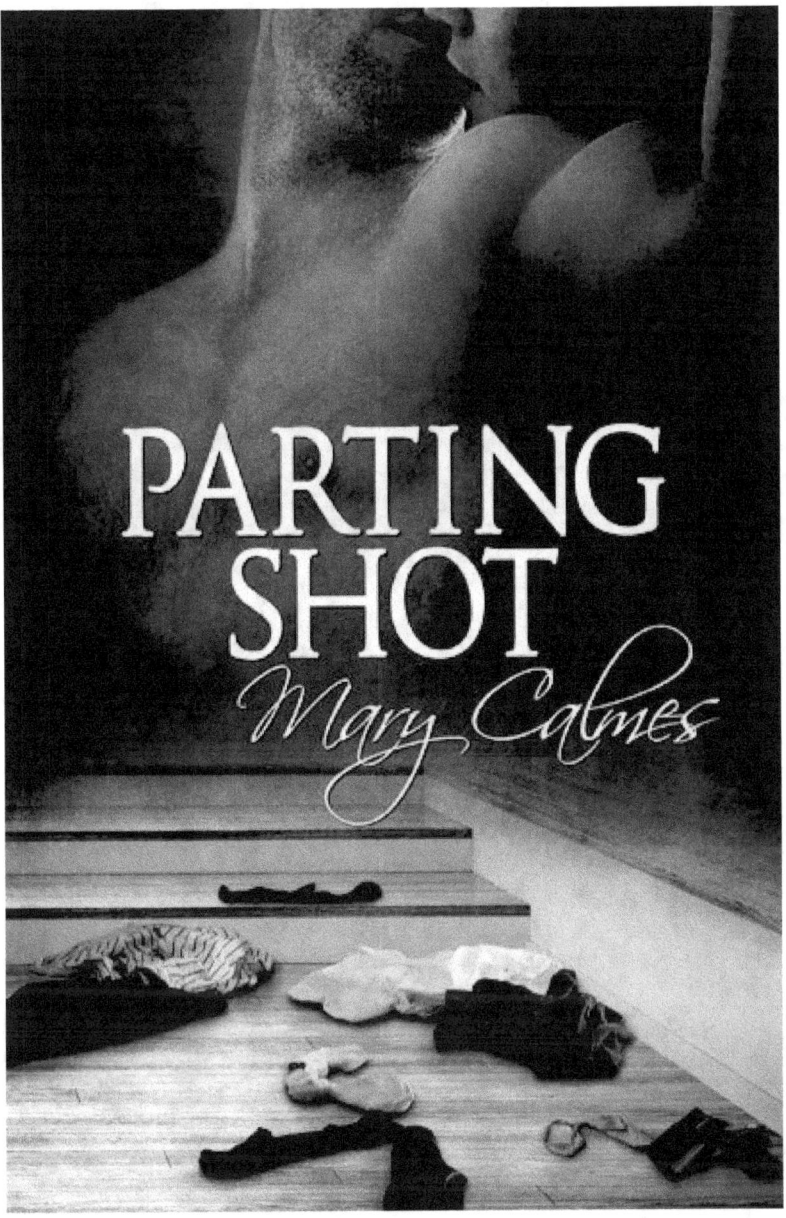

http://www.dreamspinnerpress.com

Also from DREAMSPINNER PRESS

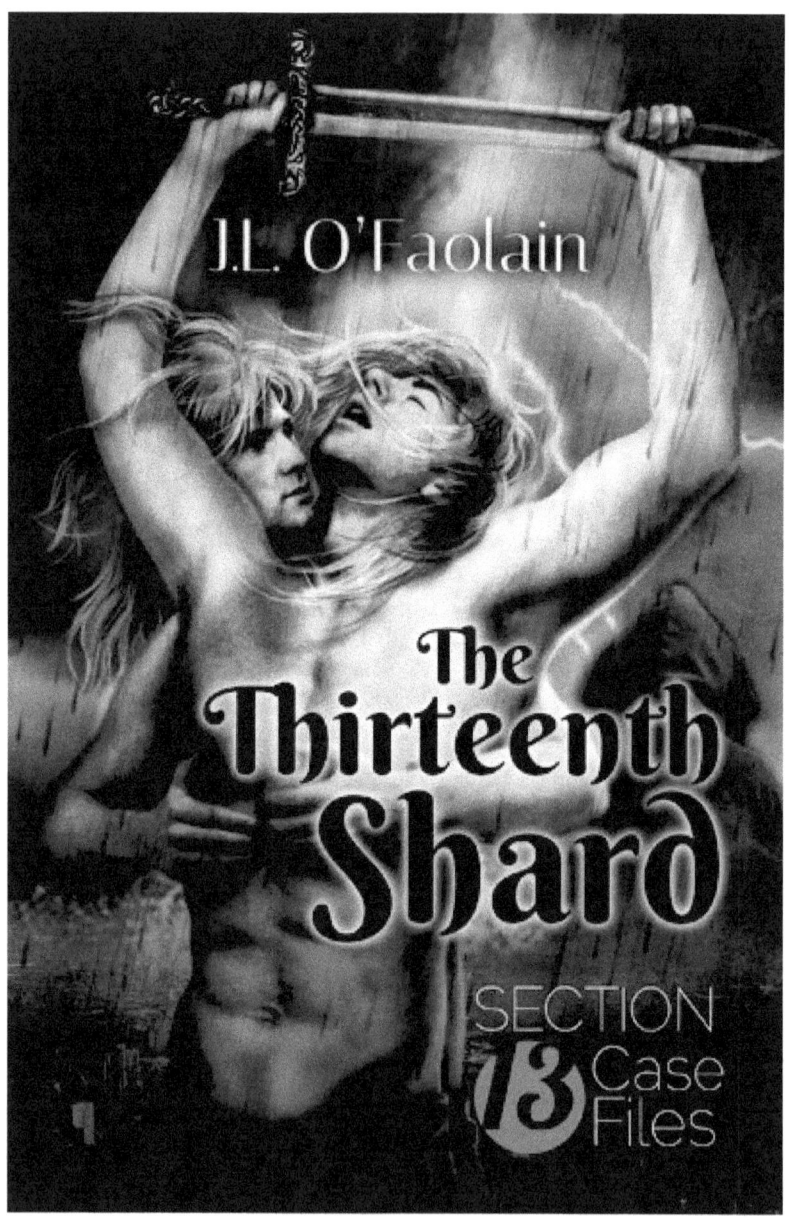

http://www.dreamspinnerpress.com

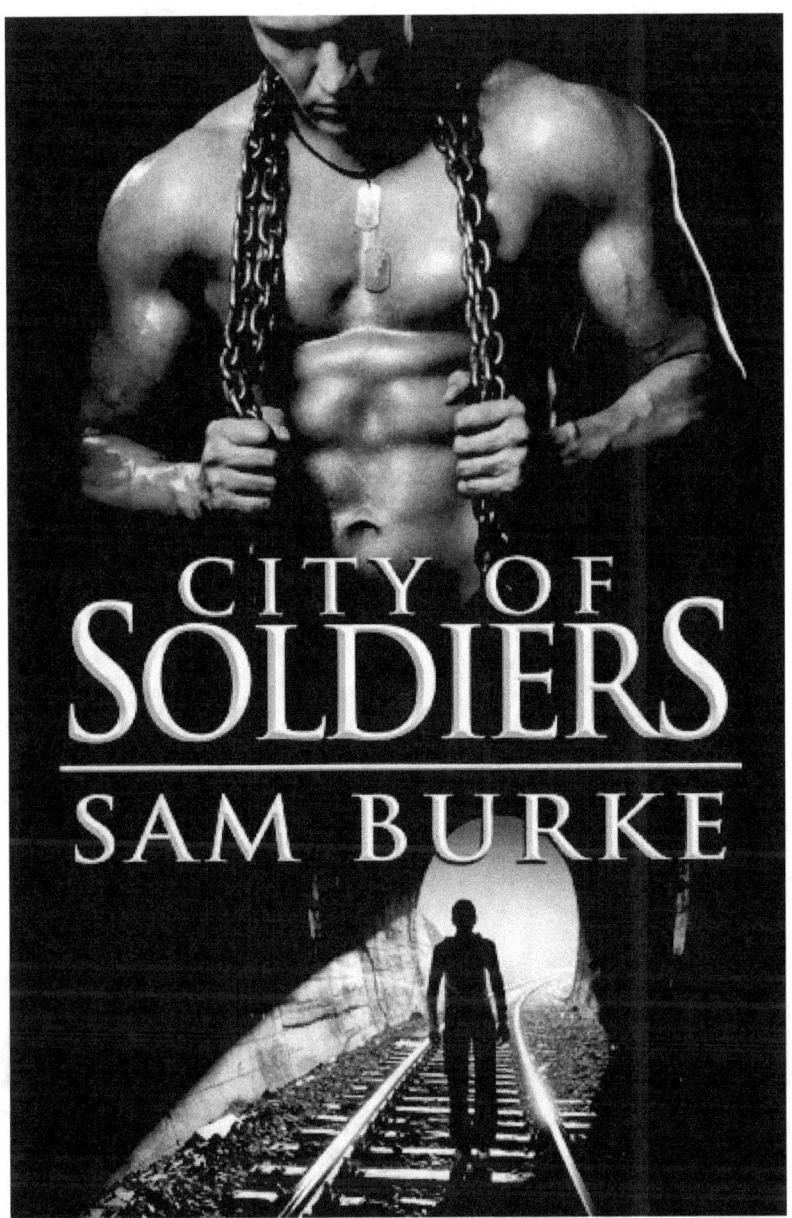

Also from DREAMSPINNER PRESS

ANDREW GREY

STRANDED

http://www.dreamspinnerpress.com